PRAISE FOR
My Diary from the Edge of the World

★ "Fans of J. K. Rowling's Harry Potter will enjoy
this heartfelt, bittersweet, and ever-so-clever
coming-of-age fantasy."
—*School Library Journal*, starred review

★ "Anderson leaves no stone unturned as she creates
characters with zest and heart, as well as settings that
encompass the best of all imaginary land."
—*Publishers Weekly*, starred review

★ "Anderson's charming novel is part road-trip adventure,
part maritime quest and part coming-of-age story."
—Shelf Awareness, starred review

"Gracie's sparkling narrative voice is funny, smart,
and convincingly ingenuous. . . . An endearing narrator,
a beguiling world that accommodates both mermaids and
Pixy Stix, and a genuinely moving family story."
—*Kirkus Reviews*

ALSO BY
Jodi Lynn Anderson

My Diary from the Edge of the World

JODI LYNN ANDERSON

Aladdin

NEW YORK   LONDON   TORONTO   SYDNEY   NEW DELHI

This book is a work of fiction. Any references to historical events, real people, or real places are used fictitiously. Other names, characters, places, and events are products of the author's imagination, and any resemblance to actual events or places or persons, living or dead, is entirely coincidental.

ALADDIN

An imprint of Simon & Schuster Children's Publishing Division

1230 Avenue of the Americas, New York, New York 10020

First Aladdin paperback edition January 2017

Text copyright © 2015 by Jodi Lynn Anderson

Cover illustration copyright © 2015 by Jennifer Bricking

Also available in an Aladdin hardcover edition.

For information about special discounts for bulk purchases, please contact Simon & Schuster Special Sales at 1-866-506-1949 or business@simonandschuster.com.

The Simon & Schuster Speakers Bureau can bring authors to your live event. For more information or to book an event contact the Simon & Schuster Speakers Bureau at 1-866-248-3049 or visit our website at www.simonspeakers.com.

Cover designed by Jessica Handelman

Interior designed by Mike Rosamilia

The text of this book was set in Adobe Caslon Pro.

Manufactured in the United States of America 1216 OFF

2 4 6 8 10 9 7 5 3 1

The Library of Congress has cataloged the hardcover edition as follows:

Anderson, Jodi Lynn.

My diary from the edge of the world / by Jodi Lynn Anderson.

pages cm

Summary: Spirited, restless Gracie Lockwood, twelve, of Cliffden, Maine, living in a world where sasquatches, dragons, giants, and mermaids are common, keeps a diary of her family's journey in a used Winnebago as they seek The Extraordinary World in hopes of keeping her little brother, Sam, safe against all odds.

[1. Family life—Fiction. 2. Automobile travel—Fiction. 3. Animals, Mythical—Fiction. 4. Supernatural—Fiction. 5. Death—Fiction. 6. Diaries—Fiction.] I. Title.

PZ7.A53675My 2015

[Fic]—dc23

2014039910

ISBN 978-1-4424-8387-3 (hc)

ISBN 978-1-4424-8388-0 (pbk)

ISBN 978-1-4424-8389-7 (eBook)

For Mark,
and our
baby star
soon to be born

Diary Number

⊰ One ⊱

"There are more things in heaven and earth, Horatio, than are dreamt of in your philosophy."
—*Hamlet* [from the tattered copy on our Winnebago shelf]

September 7th

I'm on top of the hill, looking down on the town of Cliffden, Maine. It's an early fall day, and so far no one's noticed that I'm where I'm not supposed to be. It's one of those days where the clouds and the sun chase each other. A pretty breeze plays with my hair as I sit here with my back against the crumbled stone pillar that makes my seat. I can almost imagine I'm Joan of Arc surveying the siege of Orleans.

It's been almost two months since I got this journal (for my twelfth birthday—from Mom), but I haven't felt the urge to write until now. I've seen two bad omens since breakfast: a crow sitting on the fence at the edge of our yard, and a deathwatch beetle on my windowsill. These are both signs that someone is going to die, so I thought I'd better write them down in case someone *does* die and no one believes me later. I want to be able to prove that I knew it first. Though now that I'm here nestled in my favorite spot, I have to admit it's hard on such a perfect day to imagine anyone ever dying.

Mom says that to tell a story you have to set the scene, so I'll try that here, even though this isn't really a story but just a diary. From here the town is drenched in light and shadows. To my right is Route 1 with all the fast food places: McDonald's, Taco Bell, Wendy's. To my left is downtown, a cluster of old colonial brick buildings. I can see the green cast-iron steeple of Upper Maine Academy, which I attend, and the fairgrounds beyond.

The valley is bustling: People are scurrying along the crisscrossing streets, rushing to finish their errands and get back indoors. It's not exactly safe to be out: The dragons are on their way south again, from the northern reaches of Wales and Scotland and Ireland, to hibernate in South America. It's the time when everyone takes cover in their houses, and when we mostly use the tunnels under downtown to get from shop to shop.

The dragons have been especially destructive this year. People are blaming it on the weather: It's been colder than usual, so the migrations started early. (Dragons hate the cold I guess, and I do too. I wish *I* had wings to fly to South America every year.) Last week one burned down the T.J.Maxx in Valley Forge (all those bargains literally up in flames).

I'm not allowed to sit out here during dragon season, but today it's too hard to resist. My mom would say I'm just "looking for trouble," which I do manage to find surprisingly often. Sam's scooter is still sitting neglected in the garage from when I crashed it into a boulder over Christmas. Last year I had to get stitches after falling off the lunch table while I was trying to get my classmates to throw Cheerios into my mouth. I've broken my collarbone—which is supposed to be the hardest bone in your body to break—twice. Dad calls me the Tasmanian she-devil. Millie calls me Mrs. Bungles, but I never listen to what Millie says. At least I'm not like the guy who was featured last week in the *Cliffden Dispatch*, who was found putting hundreds of dollars worth of 7-Layer Burritos from Taco Bell in his front yard so that the dragons would come and eat them.

The sky is a cool crystal blue except for one very distant Dark Cloud. It's the same cloud my dad was looking at through his telescope first thing when I woke up this morning. He's a meteorologist for a local TV station.

"I don't like the looks of it," he said when he came down to breakfast, his forehead all wrinkled. That's about as much conversation as you'll ever get out of my dad unless he's going on and on about scientific theories of some sort. Millie says he's "not the communicative type" and a "misunderstood genius," but I know that he embarrasses her just as much as he does me.

I have to admit though, I agree with him about not liking the looks of the Cloud. He and I have both decided that it looks a bit like a misty galaxy with a black hole in the middle (the kind of black hole from Dad's amateur astronomy lessons that swallows up everything in its path).

Dark Clouds come for people when they die. Usually the person is sick beforehand, and most of the people Clouds come for are old, but sometimes Clouds arrive with no warning at all. They wait outside people's houses until it's time, then they scoop up their souls and carry them away. Just last week, a Cloud floated up our block and collected Mrs. Elton, who was ninety-six.

Millie thinks this particular Dark Cloud looks like the face of an evil circus clown—but I think that's just because she's never gotten over her fear of the circus from when she was little (she fell in a pile of elephant poo and it scarred her for life). Dark Clouds are like regular clouds in that everyone who looks at them sees something different. I wonder what Mrs. Elton's Cloud looked like to her.

Millie and I discussed it. "Maybe it looked like an old friend. At ninety-six," I suggested, "you're probably only half-alive anyway, so you don't mind dying as much."

Millie's long, perfect eyelashes fluttered in annoyance. "You're an emotional mutant," she said, then wiped away a tear, which I can only suppose she squeezed out in order to be dramatic about Mrs. Elton. Though secretly I do feel guilty now about saying Mrs. Elton probably wouldn't mind death. I guess Millie's right that no one is going to be happy to see that kind of thing arrive on their doorstep, even if they're ancient.

The truth is that, other than the occasional Dark Cloud, nothing terrible or exciting ever happens in Cliffden. Only baseball games and lying on the grass and chasing the ice-cream man in the summer, building igloos in the winter, sometimes collecting earthworms in the puddles after rain or hunting for dragon scales in the fall (Mom puts them in a big glass jar on the coffee table because, she says, "They add a splash of color,") and trick or treating. (Last year a real ghoul escaped from the Underworld and ran around scaring children and stealing candy on Halloween night, which *was* pretty exciting. But none of the kids from my neighborhood got to see him, and he was quickly caught and escorted back underground by the local police.) There are science lectures about botany, zoology, the aurora borealis, and all sorts of other discoveries in a lecture hall in the caverns downtown. There's the occasional parade or party at the firehouse (to thank the firemen for all their work with the dragon fires) or outdoor movies in the spring, and there's the carnizaar (part carnival, part bazaar) at the fairgrounds for Cliffden Day. But that's about it.

I just opened to the inscription Mom made on the inside cover of this book. It says, *To Gracie, May this diary be big enough to contain your restless heart.* She says I fling my loud personality at everyone and that one day it will poke somebody's eye out. I don't completely understand her—she's a little obscure and poetic. She used to be a professional violinist. She said she gave me this diary because I need something to pour my loudness into. She says it's better to sit and write my feelings than to spend all day dreaming up ways to irritate Millie. So far I've only filled six pages, and I've been here thinking for over an hour. I'm actually supposed to be doing my reading for school, but *Sasquatches, Sailors, and Uncle Sam: An American History* is, so far, unbearably boring.

So I've just been sitting here chewing my pen and trying to figure out how to write what's around me, but it's hard to capture. The sun is sinking and it's getting chilly out. The air smells like fall—that exciting dry smell that reminds you of all the falls of your life. Behind me our big ambling Victorian is winking at me. I've always thought of our house as a lady's face, with the two highest windows as the eyes—and one of the eyes closed because the curtain's always drawn in that room. My little brother, Sam—whom we call the Mouse because he's small for his age, and quiet, especially because he always has a cold—is silhouetted in one of the parlor windows practicing the flute (Mom made us each learn an instrument; we're all disasters). Millie is probably watching *Extreme Witches* at top volume as usual, where they put six witches together in a big house and film them arguing with each other. Mom tries to get her to watch more informative stuff, like this segment CNN does once a week on the gods called *The Immortals, Where Are They Now?* Each week they feature a different god: Last week it was Zeus, sitting on a lawn chair up on top of Mount Olympus, where only authorized camera crews are allowed to go. But Millie couldn't care less.

With two siblings it's the quiet that you want, trust me. Especially when you're not the oldest or the youngest or the beautiful, graceful one but just the one that happened to fall in the middle. I'll tell you in one sentence what it's like to be the middle child, in case you don't know: Everyone on either side of you squeezes you until you almost explode, and all the time that they're smushing you they're not really noticing you're there. So you have to find a place that's just yours, and that's how I found this old church stone at the corner of our yard.

Ugh. Mouse just called out the window to say Mom's looking for me and that it's time to take a shower. I hate bathing in general. When I was little, Mom used to threaten me into the bath by saying dirty children get sent to the Crow's Nest, where my grandma lives (speaking of witches), deep in the heart of the Smoky Mountains. Supposedly, in the seventies, Grandma caused three people to disappear forever just by cursing hairs she got from their hairbrushes. She—

Oops, Mom just spotted me—she's hanging out her bedroom window yelling. Her hair is all wet from the shower and flopping down the sides of her face like curtains. How's that for descriptive?

September 8th

I'm back on the hill—I think this will be my favorite spot to write and record my life. Mom's taken Sam the Mouse to a doctor's appointment and Dad is home working on a new invention to record something called "entropy" (I can't imagine a word that sounds more boring) so he won't notice where I am.

Dad was in the paper today, right between an article on a new mall in Waterville with a giant for a security guard, and a meeting announcement about the lady's quilting guild. There was a picture of my dad and then a headline underneath it that read METEOROLOGICAL SOCIETY OF UPPER MAINE OUSTS THEODORE LOCKWOOD DUE TO PHILOSOPHICAL DIFFERENCES.

I guess that explains what happened at Dairy Queen

yesterday: Dad was just about to buy us our Blizzards (Heath bar for me, Oreo for Millie, M&M's for Sam, and Mom always gets a cherry dip) when a man stepped up to the register and paid for us. My dad was looking at him in confusion, smiling to be polite, when the man said, "You'll need all the help you can get, since you'll be out of a job soon."

My dad just looked down at his wallet and shuffled his feet. He doesn't like confrontation. My mom, on the other hand, doesn't mind it at all, and she pushed her cherry dip against the man's shirt, pretending it was an accident. "Looks like you're out of a shirt," she said. Then she turned on her heel and led us out the door, making us leave our Blizzards on the counter. I glanced back at my large Heath Blizzard in agony as we made our way out, but when Rebecca Lockwood, a.k.a. my mom, makes up her mind on something, you follow along. She's just that kind of person.

Mom says Dad is a great scientist but an unlucky one. He invented a special sort of barometer only to find out someone else had patented the same exact design eight days before. He was invited to present a paper on the three major types of clouds, titled "Cumulus, Stratus,

Cirrus, Seriously," but got booed offstage by everyone, including the mayor, because he'd made one simple mistake on the math that threw the whole thing off. He actually wanted to go into physics in college instead of meteorology (he loves learning about the stars and planets more than anything else), but he didn't get good enough grades. This is the second time he's been kicked out of the Meteorological Society, which he helped to found. Sometimes it's like my mom's the only person who believes in him at all.

All the failures make him sad, I think, and sometimes he goes into a "swamp" (that's what Mom calls them) where he wears his pajamas for days. But it never stops him from being obsessed with science. Even last night after Dairy Queen, he watched the sun set in his usual way: First he stood at the living room window, then he walked upstairs to see how it looked from higher up, then he wandered out into the yard to view it from a few different places on the grass, all the while taking notes in a little notebook he carries everywhere. Meanwhile Sam was calling out for someone to reach the Teddy Grahams on the top shelf, and Millie and I had to stop fighting over the remote control and who would get up to adjust the antennae (the TV is *always* fuzzy) and help Sam, when we're not even the parents. Dad doesn't notice *life* kinds of things at all. He lives in his brain.

Millie says that when I was being born, Dad brought his notebooks to the hospital and worked on some calculations while he waited. I'd rather not believe that he wasn't more concerned about my arrival . . . but the sad thing is that I do. Mom calls him "science haunted." Instead of coming to our ball games or school plays like the other parents do, he climbs the hills around Cliffden with his instruments almost every weekend, long after dark, recording the positions of the stars and changes in temperature. Mom says, "He's got a great but unorganized mind."

Still, beyond all his failures, the one thing that makes my dad such a target for jokes in our town, and the thing that's gotten him kicked out of the Meteorological Society twice, is his stubborn insistence on the existence of the Extraordinary World.

The Extraordinary World is an old legend—a land rumored to exist at the Southern Edge of the earth. Dad's one of the few people who believes it's real. He's written three letters to the editor about it in the *Cliffden Tribune*. He belongs to the Club for the Discovery of the

Extraordinary World with a bunch of weirdos, including the guy who put the burritos out for the dragons, and a lady who says she's secretly married to Prince William.

In the Extraordinary World, the legend goes, there are no dragons or krakens or sea serpents or Dark Clouds or bad omens. There are no demons or nymphs hiding in the forests, no vicious mermaids or yetis. "It's clear," my dad wrote in his third editorial, "that the unexplored Southern Edge of the earth is the place we have to look for it, and we should pour our money and resources into doing so as soon as possible, for the benefit of mankind." They also ran his editorial in the *Enquirer* alongside headlines like I WAS KIDNAPPED BY AN ALIEN AND NOW I'M HAVING HIS CHILD! and THE EASTER BUNNY VISITED ME IN MY SLEEP WITH A MESSAGE FOR THE WORLD.

The Extraordinary World, people like my dad claim, is what our world would have been like too, if it had turned out—once the great explorers did their great exploring in the fifteenth and sixteenth centuries— that dragons and mermaids and things like that didn't exist. Without the beasts and monsters and wilderness that populate so much of our planet, they claim, life would be easier, more orderly . . . *safe*. Also it's supposedly full of all sorts of amazing technology: things floating around space called satellites, all sorts of flying machines, highways and travel networks all over the world, and cities without number.

My dad's outspokenness on the subject means we get heckled pretty often. People call him La La Land Lockwood. I've seen the way people look at us when we're out shopping or at one of Millie's piano recitals, and I can't say I blame them. Not that *Dad* ever notices.

His hero is an astronomer named Prospero, who lives somewhere out west. People are constantly quoting him and citing his studies in their scientific papers. His newest book, *An Atlas of the Cosmos*, is a bestseller, and sometimes (rarely, because he's a bit of a hermit) he gets interviewed on *60 Minutes*. My dad reads everything he publishes. Apparently they went to college together, and while Prospero soared to the top of their class and became wildly popular, Dad worked diligently and got okay grades and graduated unnoticed by anyone but my mom, who was studying music theory, whatever that is.

Mostly Dad just contents himself with studying the weather and appearing on the local weather station every morning. I don't think it's so great to study something that always changes and always disappears, and then to spend your free time studying something that doesn't exist. It's like he's spent his life concentrating on thin air. I wish he worked on something more permanent and interesting. Anything would be better: rocks, bugs, volcanoes . . . anything.

I'm watching a bird swoop in the distance over Bear Mountain. Then again it may be a dragon and farther away than I think. I just put this journal down and squinted to see, but I still couldn't tell.

Mom and Sam just got home, but I ducked behind the church stone so they wouldn't see me. I'm sure Mom's in the kitchen putting groceries away. Usually she sings at the top of her lungs while she does it, but today it's quiet in there. I hope everything went okay at Sam's appointment.

Now the bird across the valley is doing something weird. I'm going to stand at the edge of the lawn to look.

September 8th
(After Midnight)

We just got home from the hospital and my arm is in a cast. I've survived a near death experience!

Millie says I'm being dramatic, but I can tell she's dying of envy because I'm the center of attention for once. Apparently she and Mouse made potato candy for me (my favorite) while we were at the hospital, but it turns out they ate most of it while they were waiting for us to get back. I hate Millie more than ever. No one ever hates Sam the Mouse.

Anyway, I'll try to get down what happened, as realistically as I can.

I was up on my hill just finishing my last entry, when I saw the baby dragon flying across the valley. At first, like I wrote earlier, I thought he was a bird, but then when I stood to get a closer look I noticed the little puffs of smoke wafting behind him and the blue glint of his scales. I know that blue scales mean it's a male dragon and orange scales mean it's a female, but the strange thing was, he wasn't behaving like a bird *or* a dragon at all—he flew crookedly, as if he didn't quite know how to keep himself in the air. With every few strokes of his wings, he dipped farther and farther toward the valley and the busy streets below.

I figured he might be the smallest of his litter and maybe not strong enough to migrate so early; Mom says that happens sometimes. From this distance he looked to be the size of a miniature pony, but I couldn't be sure. Then, very faintly, I heard him let out a desperate howl, and then another. With each howl he sunk a little farther toward land and a little puff of smoke floated up and away from him.

Just as I was making sense of it all there was a horrible screech behind me. I must have been too distracted to hear him coming until he was too close. As it was, I barely had time to turn around before something eclipsed the sun above me, and in a rush of horrible stench and a thud of giant wings, the father dragon was overhead.

He was about the size of a large city bus, and his blue

reptilian wings stretched out twice as long in either direction. He looked down at me only once, craning his neck to glare at me, his eyes green, speckled, and bright as limes. For a moment we were gazing at each other, and it sent a chill right through me. He smelled horribly of caves and moss and rocks and dead, burned animals. If he'd so much as let out a heavy breath, he would have melted me. But he gave me only a momentary glance before he turned his attention back toward the valley, swooping over me with a sound like sails catching wind. He was so close I could see the pearly scales along the bottom of his tail as he glided past.

I don't know what came over me, but instead of rolling into a ball—which is one of the first things they teach you in kindergarten about surviving dragon attacks—I stretched my hand toward that pearly blue tail, mesmerized by his glistening scales. That was a bad idea.

The impact threw me back against the church stone. There was a horrible crunch, but at first I thought I'd broken the stone instead of myself. Then for some reason I had the thought (it makes no sense now) that my arm was a carrot wedged in the refrigerator door.

The dragon kept going—I could see him soaring into the wide open space over the valley like an enormous blue kite, casting a dark shadow over a line of cars on Route 1 and then hovering just above the baby, flapping his wings, his screeches echoing off the mountains. The baby called back to him with a weak screech, then seemed to gain courage. Soon he was flapping harder and straighter, and lifting instead of sinking. I think that's when I first suspected it was me that was broken instead of the church stone. I guess it was the scalding pain that suddenly shot out of my right elbow. Then the pain was everywhere.

Now my right arm will be in a cast for weeks. Well, at least I'm left-handed.

In the hour since I've been home, I've revoked my membership in the Orphan Dragon Rescue group online that Millie signed me up for, though I'm staying in the group that helps the endangered unicorns that live in the Sierra Madres. Arin Roland says her dad says that only "bleeding-heart crazies" sign up for dragon rescue groups anyway, though Arin Roland is the most annoying girl in my sixth-grade class.

PS: Mostly the rescue groups buy large rural pieces of land in England and Scotland so the dragons can have somewhere to live where they won't wreak too much havoc. It actually helps people, too, because in the sixties about half of London was occupied by dragons and nobody could do anything about it. Real estate prices for the safer side of the city skyrocketed. So take that, Arin's dad.

I just went down to the kitchen to see if maybe Millie lied and actually did hide some leftover potato candy somewhere, but instead I ran into Dad, sitting at the kitchen table and studying a big paper chart. Tilted the other way and lying half across the chart was a map.

"Hey, honey," he said, glancing up at me distractedly. "What are you up to?" Dad always forgets we have a bedtime, which isn't surprising since he sometimes forgets we exist at all (or at least it seems that way). Even at the hospital tonight he kept asking the doctor to give him the details of how they were resetting my bone, as if I wasn't sitting right there wincing and trying not to cry. ("Dragons breaking arms in Cliffden in September!" he kept saying. "And migrations didn't even used to start till mid-October. That's what the world is coming to!")

"Just hungry," I said.

But he'd already forgotten what he'd asked me—I

could tell. I shuffled up behind him, unnoticed. The chart was scrawled in his handwriting with markings of longitudes and latitudes and degrees, cloud appearances at various heights, and phases of the moon. The map showed the familiar rectangle of the earth: Alaska all the way to the upper left (a paradise for sasquatches ever since the Alaskans lured a lot of them up there to solve their rodent problem), Royal Russia to the right.

Clustered on each continent were the red dots marking the major cities: Moscow, Beijing, Paris, London, Istanbul (I've always liked to look at those dots and imagine what the cities are like) . . . surrounded by empty, barely marked space. It's the same in the US: The major cities—New York, Boston, Washington, DC—sprawl out toward towns like ours, and then mostly wilderness covers the rest of the continent. Dad calls the cities of the world "industrialized pockets" and the empty spaces "wild." Though I guess the spaces aren't really empty, at least not here—there are towns stretching as far west as Arkansas (a lot of them grown over by the woods) and then scattered frontier towns beyond that. But mostly, the farther you get from the cities, the farther you are into the territory of the beasts.

Now Dad was running his fingers out toward the

edges of the map, and down over the Hawaiian Islands (which have always sounded wonderful because they're ruled by someone called the Sugar Queen—Hawaii is the world's biggest exporter of sugar), muttering something unintelligible about something called superstrings.

Most of the world, according to my geography teacher, was connected because of spices. People got tired of eating food with just the spices that they could grow in their own backyards, so they sent explorers out into the world for pepper, salt, cinnamon, and whatever else they could find. But people found more than that: They also found sea monsters, tigers, horses, mermaids, dragons, and eventually the edges of the earth. (When I showed Mom my homework essay about this, she smirked in her wry way and said, "I guess there's something to be said for never being satisfied with what you have.")

Ferdinand Magellan reached the western edge in 1520, confirming for the first time that the earth was flat. There's a famous quote by him that goes, "I have seen the earth's shadow reflected on the stars. I've seen that, compared to what's beyond our edges, we are very small indeed."

*   *   *

Anyway, after planting a flag there and splitting off from his flotilla, Magellan set a course due south to see the remote continent known as the Southern Edge, but was never heard from again. It's widely assumed he accidentally sailed off the earth, but others think he was drowned by the Great Kraken at Cape Horn, who's still alive and drowning sailors to this day.

Dad has a different theory. He thinks Ferdinand Magellan went to look for the Extraordinary World. He also thinks that he found it. Dad thinks that once you cross over to the Extraordinary World, you can never come back.

"What are you doing with that map?" I asked now.

Dad snapped his head up, seeming to really notice again that I was there. My dad and I have the same eyes—hazelish-brown—and the same pointyish chin, even though I wish I looked more like my mom instead. My face is pretty much a girl version of his—though *he's* usually all stubbly.

"Just . . . daydreaming," he said, turning red and folding up the map abruptly. He adjusted his black glasses on his nose and smiled at me in the fake way adults do sometimes when they're hiding something from you.

Then he glanced up at the clock above the sink. "Hey, shouldn't you be in bed?"

So here I am back in my room. But now I can't sleep.

I can't stop thinking about the father dragon and his baby. I hope they're somewhere safe and warm, even if they did smell bad and even if they eat disgusting things. I guess I can admit this here: I can't help thinking that if I were flying over a valley and my wings were drooping and giving out, my dad wouldn't even notice, much less be able to save me.

One more thing about the Extraordinary World. Something that *is* real about it is that many of the ships that went in search of it in the old days never came back— not because they found what they were looking for, but because of the Great Kraken. And now the southern ocean is scattered with phantom ships sailed by ghosts. They can't be caught on film (no ghost can), but they are widely known to be real. That's one of many reasons no one goes sailing around the Southern Sea exploring anymore.

And with that cheerful thought, I'm going to bed.

September 10th

Boring.

September 11th

I'm so bored.

September 12th

I may be the only twelve-year-old on earth who's managed to break her arm and get grounded in the same week.

Tonight I'm a prisoner in my own room. I've renamed myself Andromeda and am trying to pretend that I've been trapped in a tower by a greedy centaur who wants to marry me, but my imagination doesn't always work as well as it used to.

Anyway, I may as well just write the embarrassing truth here: I hit a girl in my class on the head with a stick.

I'm sitting in my windowsill as I write this. Sam the Mouse is feeling better today, and he and his friend from down the street are roughhousing in a pile of leaves out front. This may be the last year I'll even jump in a pile of leaves—Millie says I won't want to do things like that much longer. Even though she usually doesn't know what she's talking about, I worry that she might be right, because last year I raked up a pile of leaves and didn't even have the patience to lie under it for more than a few seconds. I used to be able to do that for hours, looking up through the cracks in the leaves, but certain things don't excite me the way they used to.

The Dark Cloud has come closer in the last few days, and it does seem that it's headed for our neighborhood, since we're the only collection of houses on top of this hill. I've added up all the old people on our block and there are four—five if you count Michael Kowalski's grandma, who's sixty-eight, which is sort of in the middle between old and not so old. I hope it's not her, even though she's always yelling at me not to ride my bike so fast.

My mom says we're having ravioli for dinner and that I have to eat it in my room, even though I told her I'll barf if I eat it. I reminded her of the last time she made me eat ravioli three years ago, when I *did* throw it up . . . all over a pile of Barbies beside my bed.

"That was self-motivated vomiting," she said, closing her lips in a thin determined line and running a hand through her long dark hair, which is the exact brown (almost-black) color of Millie's, only straighter.

My mom is the opposite of my dad—she's admired everywhere she goes. Millie says it's something about the way she "holds herself." I think it's that she looks like a painting and is always thinking of other people (she's fascinated by our neighbor Mrs. Lipton's boring tips on planting flowers, and she never forgets my teachers' birthdays). How she and Dad ended up together, I'll never know. Once, I asked her about it, and she just said with a smirk, "Your dad was really, really lucky," and then looked at my dad to see his reaction. He didn't even look up from his book.

Anyway, she always seems to know when I'm being honest or when I'm just being dramatic, which is annoying.

Today was my first day back at school since the dragon incident. Millie, Sam, and I walked down the long green hill into town, then descended into the tunnels that we use during migration season. Sometimes students from other schools heckle us because of our dad, but not today; today I was on top of the world.

I held my cast up high as we passed people so that they'd be able to see it in all its arm-length glory. "It's not a trophy," Millie said. (She's refused to sign it because she says she can't bring herself to "celebrate stupidity.") Then she just waved a hand to billow her long, perfectly coifed hair, as if 90 percent of what goes through her head is, *My hair, ahh my hair.*

We crisscrossed through the tunnels, past the entrance to the bank that's guarded inside by one of the few vampires in Maine. (They prefer darker, rainier regions—though I guess if you're a vampire and you can get a job in a dim cave, you're pretty happy.) He always gives me the creeps, but Millie says she thinks he's kind of cute. I think she's just trying to shock me— he looks completely bloodless and his fangs are always sticking out, especially when he smiles and tries to be polite. Because of a law passed in 1965, vampires are only allowed to feed on animals (never people), but they give me the creeps all the same.

After the bank the tunnels widen into a series of connected, well-lit caverns, where most of the stores are. We walked past the 7-11, where I usually buy M&M's with money I'm supposed to spend on lunch, and past the little museum sponsored by the Ladies' Historical Society of Cliffden. It gives a miniature but ambitious history of the events leading up to our town: from a diorama of the ancient Romans taming the Pegasus, to the signing of the Declaration of Independence by fifty-six men and one well-respected ghost, to the founding of our town by a fur trapper on the run from a ding-ball, which is a kind of cougar.

In the aboveground foyer we parted ways: Millie sashaying off to her building and Sam coughing and trying to make himself invisible as he scurried toward the primary wing. I cut out through the door onto the grassy inner courtyard and made my way to my homeroom. I entered it bellowing, "WHO WANTS TO SIGN THE ARM THAT TOUCHED THE DRAGON?" There was a collective gasp, a room full of faces with mouths in the shapes of surprised and admiring Os, and then I was surrounded.

All through geography and Monsters of the Sea II, I played with a penny on my desk (tracing the giant on the back and Abe Lincoln on the front, and flipping it to see if it landed heads or giants over and over), and contemplated swallowing it to see how it would taste. My gaze kept drifting to the window, where the occasional dark silhouette of a dragon drifted across the horizon. Twice Mr. Morrigan, our teacher, scolded me for kicking my feet too loudly against Arin Roland's desk, once for not having done the homework, and then finally for swallowing the penny after all.

To tell you the truth, I don't know what came over me at recess. Arin and I were foraging along the edge of the school building for a stick to use as a vaulting pole for the Lunch Olympics (which I invented on the spot, even though I'm not supposed to participate with only one good arm). I found one that would work perfectly, only suddenly I didn't want to use it as a vaulting pole at all, I just wanted to keep it for myself and maybe use it as a curtain rod in my room. Even now I can't imagine why I wanted to keep it so badly. I guess it was because I knew everyone else wanted me to hand it over. And then when Arin stepped forward to grab it from me, it was as if I were possessed, because the stick rose so quickly and hit her across the head before I even thought about it. And then she was grabbing her ear, and Mrs. Corsiglia was standing in front of me, yelling at me so loudly I couldn't even make out the words.

I know I'm too old to hit people with sticks. Once I stop being annoyed, I'm 80 percent sure I'll feel truly sorry.

Anyway, now I'm grounded. It would be a lot more interesting being stuck in here if my imagination worked halfway as well as it used to.

Oh, something else interesting happened, between math and Flying Reptiles. Today we got Oliver. He's skinny and has a fish face and his whole body seems to want to disappear, as if he thinks that if he hunches his shoulders down far enough no one will see him. He's got bright green eyes and hair that looks like it's never met a hairbrush and a long scar down one side of his cheek.

We have such a small school that we only get a new student every couple of years. The last one was from Sweden and named Inez; she barely spoke English and smelled like bananas. This boy is no improvement. He's quiet and bizarre. I think if I were as quiet as him, I'd disappear.

At lunch he sat at the far empty end of the teachers' table by himself with a bag of Skittles, not eating them like a normal person but instead slipping them under the table. It took a scouting mission by Matthew Howard to figure out that he was slipping them one by one to some kind of creature he keeps in his pocket, but we don't know what. Arin thinks it's a frog, as if frogs eat Skittles.

Oliver looks like he's mentally very far away, and he has a habit of touching the scar on his cheek as if he keeps reminding himself it's there. I heard Arin Roland whisper to someone that he's from Connecticut and his family was killed by sasquatches, and now he's an orphan living with a foster family in town, so I guess maybe the scar is from the sasquatch attack.

The thing is, personal tragedy is the kind of thing that can get you a lot of attention at my school. If he'd tell people his story, they'd be flocking around him. But Oliver just sat through lunch quietly, barely looking at his surroundings. Everyone stared at him all through lunch, and some people looked at me to see what we should do. I just ignored him.

Walking to the front office to be sent home later, I noticed him sitting by the fountain, whispering to the thing in his pocket, and I decided he was even stranger than I thought.

PS: A note on sasquatches, from history class: The sasquatches were instrumental in helping the north win the American civil war. Sasquatches are generally brutal creatures with little or no conscience, but they abhor the enslavement of anyone, even their enemies (humans!). So in the 1860s hordes of them emerged from the deep woods of the Smokies to fight on the Union side. Thanks to them, the war was over three months after it started.

September 16th

ꟼ write this from under the covers with a flashlight. I'm too worried to sleep.

Sam has one of his endless colds, and I can hear him coughing in his room down the hall. He went to the doctor again today and they're doing some tests and I can tell that my parents are tense about it. Everyone has been quiet tonight. Dad is in one of his "swamps."

"Please stay out of trouble and don't worry your father," Mom keeps saying. But I don't think it's fair that Dad gets to hide in his swamp while the rest of us have to go on acting like normal people all the time.

The Dark Cloud was on our block tonight when we came home from school. We were coming up the hill and there it was, just hovering about twenty feet above the street where we usually play roller hockey, gray and still and puffy, with that black hole swirling in the middle. (Millie says it's the clown's leering mouth.) We skirted widely around it, walking behind our neighbors' houses and coming into our yard through the back, Millie pulling Sam along beside her.

When we got inside, I noticed that Sam's hand was a bright red from how hard Millie had been clutching it. She and I exchanged a glance, and I didn't like what I saw in her eyes.

There are only a few houses left on our street before the Cloud gets to ours. One of them is Michael Kowalski's, though. I hate to say that's where I'm hoping it'll stop, but, well, I'm just being honest, and besides probably no one will ever read this diary.

My parents, of course, already knew when we told them. Since my dad's a meteorologist, clouds are practically his middle name. I was hoping he'd reassure us and make everything seem fixable like always, but he looks even more tense than Millie.

The thing is, Dark Clouds are the most obscure branch of meteorology and—Dad explained to me once—few scientists choose to study them because they are an unsolvable mystery. Those scientists who *have* spent their lives studying them haven't figured anything out. We know that Dark Clouds, unlike other clouds, keep their shape in any kind of weather. They're always a dark gray, but they never give off rain. You can't see into them, and where they take people when they die is a complete mystery. My dad, more than anyone I know, can't stand unsolved mysteries.

Anyway, Sam, for the moment, is blissfully unaware of it all and has been running around the house despite his cold, stripped down to his underwear, with another pair of his underwear on his head, yelling that he's the Undie Bandit and to give him all our money.

Some yellow leaves are falling past the window, lit up by the floodlights, and I've been staring out at the dark silhouette of Bear Mountain, which I've said good night to every night before I go to bed ever since I can remember. I used to imagine it was a real giant bear, but a friendly one. Now telling it good night is just a habit.

A while ago I went downstairs and no one even told me to go back to my room—I guess everyone's forgotten I'm grounded. Millie and I flipped through *Jeopardy!* and *The Biggest Octopus* (a boring fishing show) and landed on the news. There were shots of the city of

Chicago, showing trees and roots growing up through the sides of buildings. The city, over the past ten years or so, has become a forest again. Most of the people have left, and wolves and bears live in Millennium Park. These things happen, especially the farther west you go. The wilderness is always pushing back.

Finally, unable to distract myself, I came upstairs and now here I am writing again. There's something about putting things down on paper that helps me feel a little less lost in my head.

Now I can hear Mom and Dad's muffled voices arguing in their room, and I think they must be arguing about the Dark Cloud. Dad has his swamps, and he's been kicked out of the society and people think he's slightly crazy, but he's also been voted Best Meteorologist by the *Cliffden Herald* three years in a row because he's always right about the weather. If anyone knows what to do, it should be him, shouldn't it? I keep telling myself not to worry, but it seems like when you do that you worry ten times more.

Years ago in the sky over LA there was an outbreak of guardian angels. The angels started pouring out of the clouds like rain, and then they just scattered to the four winds. Most of them stayed in LA, but some of them went into hiding in the national parks and some flew off to other continents.

I like to imagine that one of the angels who headed north flew over Cliffden, saw me sitting on the grass out front, and thought, *That girl is special. She's worth protecting.* I can just picture my angel somewhere up in the sky or hiding on the roof, secretly watching over me. Sometimes I even whisper to her at night in case she can hear me. Tonight before I go to sleep, I'll whisper to her to please protect Sam instead.

I just looked out the window, but it's too dark to see any clouds now, and the sky is filled with a million clusters of stars that hang low over the hills. The lights of Cliffden in the valley below are like stars in a sky of their own.

I just dozed off. I guess I'm too sleepy to keep writing.

September 18th

Oliver was absent from school today. Arin is talking to me again, and she said she's pretty sure he was taken by sasquatches. She said she heard the ones who killed his mom and dad had some kind of vendetta against his whole family (sasquatches are excellent trackers, so if she's right, it wouldn't be much trouble for them to find Oliver), and I can't tell whether she's just being dramatic or not.

Also, the doctor's office called, and I guess it must have been with Sam's test results, because after Mom hung up the phone she held her hand to her eyes and then disappeared into the bedroom with Dad.

I'm usually nosy, but not right now. I know this sounds weird, but I don't want to know what the doctor said.

And it works out, because apparently Mom and Dad don't want to tell any of us. At dinner tonight we all just ate quietly, and now there's more arguing coming from the bedroom. I have my pillow squished around my head to make sure I can't hear what they're saying. It's hard to write while trying to hold the pillow, so I'll stop.

September 19th

Just home from school. I now know what my parents have been arguing about, and it isn't what I thought. I saw it in the yard when I got home from school today. My dad has bought a Winnebago.

The Dark Cloud has passed the Kowalskis' house and is now in front of the Liptons'. They have an old basset hound named Dinky, and I've suddenly just had the thought that *that's* who the Cloud's coming for. Oh joy! Wouldn't that be the best news of all time! Dinky is the worst dog anyway—all she does is bark and fart. Please let it be Dinky. Please please please, Dinky, die die die.

I'm wondering if I should cross the last bit out, since it's so awful. But the truth is, I really do want it to be Dinky, and I'm superstitious that if I cross it out, it won't be.

LATER THE SAME NIGHT

I wish I could go back in time to this afternoon when I didn't know why Dad bought the Winnebago. My whole life has changed since then.

Dinner started out quietly enough—nobody was talking about the Dark Cloud *or* the Winnebago. Sam the Mouse was hiding under the table, pretending to be our pet cat and asking to be fed milk in a bowl on the floor. Dad was sitting in his usual spot but clearly far away in his mind (not unusual). I was seeing how many peas I could fit in my mouth, when Mom said, in a serious tone she hardly ever uses, "We have something to tell you, kids."

At the tone of her voice even Sam got up off the floor and sat on my lap to listen.

"We're putting the house up for sale."

If only there was one word you could write to capture the feeling of the world falling from beneath your feet. I think it would probably sound like *thkkkuddge*. A sudden heaviness landed on me, and I think Millie and even Sam felt it too.

Dad sat by her silently while Mom went on, saying stuff about "expanding our horizons" and "seeing new places" and "having new experiences."

"Not that the house will sell quickly. It's a down market," she went on jibberishly. I knew without her saying it that this had something to do with the Cloud. And that Dad was behind it all even though he wasn't the one talking. He always avoids talking to us when things are unpleasant, and it makes me want to scream.

We were all completely silent. Finally, Millie stood from her chair, whispered, "How can you do this to me?" and then, chin held high, walked out of the room. That made Sam crawl back under the table. I just stared at my plate with an enormous lump of unswallowed peas in my mouth.

Mom went on to tell me and Sam how we'll start packing up, when our last day of school will be, and so on. Toward the end, Dad—who still hadn't said a word—limped off upstairs, tapping his head as if he had a headache.

I stayed in my seat, festering. "I think it's coming for Dinky Lipton," I said, and Mom's eyes shot to Sam, then back to me.

"What's coming for Dinky?" Sam asked.

"The groomer," I lied ingeniously. "Haven't you noticed he's getting shaggy?"

*   *   *

My anger kept building until finally, as soon as we were excused, I followed Dad upstairs. He was up in the cupola, where he loves to hide from us, looking out the window with his telescope.

I was trying to think of what horrible things I wanted to say, when he turned and saw me, reached a hand toward me—careful not to bump my cast—and pulled me onto his lap, which he probably hasn't done since I was ten. He hugged me tight, which took me by surprise, and then pointed out the window.

A shudder ran through me once I saw what he wanted me to see.

There above the middle of our lawn, still about twenty feet off the ground, but waiting as if to be let in through the backdoor, was the Cloud. It seemed to be a deeper gray than it had been yesterday, a thick mist I couldn't see through, about three feet across.

A strange whimper came from somewhere, and then I realized it had come from me. All I could think was *Sam Sam Sam Sam Sam*.

"You have to make it go away," I said to Dad. "Please, just figure out how to make it go away. I know you can do it."

"I *can't*, Gracie."

Dad didn't say anything else for a while. Finally he held the telescope eye toward me.

Reluctantly, I leaned forward. Dad wasn't pointing the telescope into the Cloud, though, but upward, toward the dusk-darkening sky. A tiny wavering white light glowed in the middle of my vision, much brighter than the tiny bright lights around it.

"It's a new star, just born" Dad said.

I squinted. It looked like a dot to me, nothing special. I tried to imagine what it must actually look like if you got close—a giant burning ball in all that darkness—but I couldn't. I tried to imagine I was one of the neighboring stars who'd watched it get born, but I couldn't picture that, either. Like I said, my imagination is not as good as it used to be.

"Do you know the universe is getting bigger all the time?" Dad asked.

I swallowed the lump in my throat, annoyed, wondering why he was talking about this now.

"It's blowing up like a balloon," he went on, "but really slowly."

I pulled away from the telescope and looked at him. His glasses had slipped down his nose a little, and I noticed for the first time his hair was graying at the temples. He looked tired.

He pushed at his glasses and rubbed at his stubble. "You and Millie and Sam are my baby stars," he said. "You are my magnificent works. I can't make the Cloud go away, but I'll do what I need to do to protect you."

I felt the angry words I wanted to say dribbling away. "Where will we go?" I finally asked.

"First, we'll go to your grandmother's. To the Crow's Nest. We don't have much choice. Your grandma knows things. She'll help us figure out how to get there."

"How to get where?" I asked, getting chills at the thought of meeting Grandma, and something more.

Dad didn't answer. But I know where the *where* is that he means.

And I know that it doesn't exist.

It's almost midnight and I still can't sleep. My glow clock casts a light across my room, and the shadows make the old rocking chair against the wall look three times bigger than it actually is.

It feels like I'm coming down with strep throat, but my mom said it's "psychosomatic," which she explained means that I want to cry but I don't know it. She said hurting in weird places is my body's way of crying for me. She made me a bowl of chocolate pudding after dinner, but I couldn't eat it.

"Mom," I asked, glancing around to make sure Sam wasn't nearby, "what does the Cloud look like to you?"

Mom gazed at me for a moment as if she wasn't going to answer, then she went and stood at the window. "It looks like a snake . . . ," she said, ". . . trying to steal a robin's egg." She turned away from the window and picked up my bowl of pudding. "It looks like something I hate."

I've just tried looking, now that she's gone. But as hard as I stare at the Cloud, I can't make out a robin's egg at all.

I keep thinking of the Dairy Queen and the papery smell inside our post office, the bike store that smells like rubber and oil where I got my first bike, the cracked linoleum in Mr. Morrigan's classroom and the place on my flowery wallpaper that looks like a mother rose rocking her baby to sleep, our yard and the view from the church stone. I just can't believe that we're going to leave it all behind. It gives me the feeling of falling into a big empty hole.

I keep getting up and getting back in bed. When I press my face against the window, I can just see it. The Cloud is out there in the yard, lit slightly by the moon. I guess it's one of the ones that waits patiently for you to be ready to go. I guess we are lucky.

Still, no Cloud waits forever.

September 21st

Sitting on the front stoop, under shelter. It's a drizzly, gray afternoon.

This morning when I got up, my face was even crookeder than usual. I guess it's because I cried a little before falling asleep. My features always take a few minutes to settle into themselves in the morning anyway—at first my face looks pretty much uglyish, but then it smoothes itself out into being halfway presentable by the time I leave for school.

Mom kept Sam home today. I brushed my teeth and prepared myself to tell everyone in my class the news about moving, knowing there'd be crying and some squealing over me and generally everyone would be thinking about me the whole day, leading up to several presents this week, and of course going-away-party planning. Millie says I'm a "sociopath" for even caring about that stuff right now, but I can't help it.

I sat through history and Monsters of the Sea trying to think of the most dramatic moment to share the news. I was still working up to it when there was an announcement over the loudspeaker about Oliver.

"Attention please, students. As you may know, Oliver Wigley went missing from his home several days ago." Everyone murmured nervously. "We are confident Oliver will be found safe, but we ask that anyone who spoke with him before his disappearance or who might have any information leading to his whereabouts contact the school office immediately. Thank you."

So Oliver really *is* missing. We all whispered about it after class and basically the class broke down into two camps: the doom-and-gloomers who think he's definitely been eaten by the same sasquatches who killed his parents (that's the Arin Roland camp), and the more hopeful ones who think that he might have run away.

By the time I got around to telling everyone my news about moving, it got lost in the discussion about

Oliver, and only Arin pretended to cry a little.

It's actually a relief that people are distracted, because nobody's asked why we're moving, so I don't have to tell them about Sam . . . and where we're trying to go.

Anyway, I've started to feel guilty about ignoring Oliver so completely. I have to admit that when I think about that strange boy who is so quiet that he might disappear, out in this chilly, wet evening, it makes me feel glad that I have my family and a warm place to call home (at least for now).

I'd like to sit against my church stone in the backyard with binoculars to scan the town for him—a little lonesome speck on one of the streets below—but I don't want to go back there because of the Cloud. I'm sitting in the front instead. I have a thorn in my toe from walking barefoot around my mom's rosebushes, pretending to be Saint Francis and trying to talk to the butterflies. I was trying to talk them into saving us somehow, because it seems animals must have special powers we don't understand. But I guess you can't just make up a butterfly language and expect it to work.

So here I am, bundled up in my orange rain jacket in the shelter of the stoop, propping my cast against a railing, looking at the Winnebago in the driveway.

We haven't had a single person interested in the house yet. But Mom and Dad have started packing anyway. They say no matter what, whether we sell or not, we'll leave on Wednesday.

September 27th

Our life is in boxes. Most of it's going to Bernard's Self Storage on Witches' Pike. The rest will be squeezed into the Winnebago (which Dad has christened the Trinidad after Ferdinand Magellan's ship—so dorky), though how we're going to squeeze anything besides ourselves into that old banana on wheels is anyone's guess. So far Millie and I have refused to set foot inside the awful thing. Mom keeps telling us how nice and homey it is inside, but even *we* can see she's stretching the truth by the way her nose wrinkles whenever she looks at it parked out there in all its lumpy, yellowing glory. Only Sam scrambles in and out of it, because he's the peacemaker and he wants Dad to be happy. He's been hiding in there for hours at a time. Dad attached a small pod trailer to the back for extra luggage, with a tiny screened window on each of its four sides. Millie asked if that could be her room, because it's the farthest away from everyone else. Mom laughed, but I don't think she was joking.

Sam is blissfully ignorant that all of this is for him. He's convinced we're going on some kind of adventure, and he seems to be feeling a little better because of it. He even asked me last night why everyone keeps staring at the Cloud out back. I played dumb and said, "Cloud? I didn't notice."

His answer chilled me. He said, "You know, the one that looks like a face smiling at me? The smiling man."

Sam is too innocent to know what he's supposed to be afraid of.

My cast comes off Wednesday. That's all.

October 3rd

I found Oliver! It's a secret I can only write here . . .
when I have more time, after dinner.

LATER

Okay. So today I skipped school. I needed some time to
walk the streets of Cliffden and say good-bye to some
favorite things. I pretended to be on my way to class when
I parted with the others, but really I went down past the
angel statue and out the underground exit. When I got
aboveground again, I wandered in the direction of the zoo.

The Cliffden Zoo is tiny but impressive. I love to
watch the monkeys, and when something's on my mind
I can stay all day. You can tell how intelligent monkeys
are and that they have senses of humor. It's nice they

don't hold it against us that we've taken them out of the thrilling jungle and stuck them in what is pretty much a big glass box.

Well, to get to the monkeys you have to go past the banshees, who give me the willies, and also the aquarium, which I'm not fond of because of the giant sea snakes and cryptids. (They stare out through the glass like they want to devour you, because they *do* want to devour you.) As I was rushing along my way, I saw a boy who looked like Oliver on the other side of a big pane of glass, gazing into the beluga whale tank while slipping Skittles into his pocket. I skidded to a halt.

I followed him past the seahorses, which are even weirder looking than the cryptids, moving very stealthily until I was sure it was him. He walked so slowly it was hard to be patient. At the octopus exhibit I finally stepped out of the shadows in front of him triumphantly. Oliver didn't seem shocked in the least.

"Aren't you surprised I'm here?" I asked.

"You're too loud to be a good spy."

"I didn't say anything the whole time I was following you."

"You even look loud," he replied.

I decided not to dwell on this. Oliver stood with his hair even messier than usual; it tilted to one side so much that it looked like his whole skinny body would tip over. His scar had gotten a little less pink and was less noticeable than it had been the last time I'd seen him. He was looking at me with a mixture of suspicion and concentration, like he was measuring me in his head.

A little crunching sound was issuing from the pocket of his jeans. We both looked down: A pair of big black eyes were peering at me from a tiny crooked face that had just poked out. The creature—about the size of a dragonfly—was bald except for a red patch of hair right above its eyes, and its ears were twice the size of its little head.

"Is that a faerie?" I asked, surprised. It's illegal to own faeries as pets in the United States unless they go through a very expensive quarantine process. Usually only celebrities and really rich people own them—Meryl Streep has one that she always brings to the Oscars.

"My mom was from Ireland," Oliver said. "Everyone has faeries over there. So when she immigrated, she had a license for them. She made them little habitats in these big aquariums in our house. This one's called Tweep. I inherited her when . . ." He trailed off. He rubbed Tweep's head and the faerie purred and cooed. She was an ugly little thing, and I wondered how Oliver could care for her so tenderly. "None of the pet stores carry faerie food around here, but she eats flies and Skittles."

"I'm sorry . . . about your family," I muttered.

"Thanks," he said.

"I guess you ran away from your foster family." Oliver frowned, and nodded.

"Everyone's worried about you."

He thought on this, seemingly torn. "I don't want people to worry. But I also don't want new parents." There was an edge of anger in his voice, but I suppose if I'd been through what Oliver has been through, I'd be pretty angry too.

"Where are you staying now?" I asked, ignoring Tweep, who'd disappeared into Oliver's pocket and begun to chirp.

He looked at me forlornly. There were circles under his green eyes. "I've been living at the fairgrounds; I sleep in a Ferris wheel car that was taken down. I still have twenty dollars left from my allowance. I've been eating McDonald's."

I nodded, trying to look knowledgeable about what it's like to run away. "We're moving," I offered, thinking moving to escape a Dark Cloud might be almost as bad as losing your whole family to bloodthirsty monsters. I wanted him to know I was on his level.

"Where?"

"I'm not sure. We're going to my grandma's." I hesitated, then went on. "But I think my dad really wants to try to get to the Extraordinary World." I don't know why, but talking to Oliver made me feel like it was okay to be honest.

The silence stretched on and on. Most people don't like long silences, but Oliver seemed completely content to let the empty seconds stretch between us. "When are you leaving?" he finally asked politely.

"Wednesday afternoon, I guess." I was still hoping, counting on, a miracle that would let us stay.

"I'm sorry you have to go," he said.

"Thanks," I said, and looked at the ground.

"You can't tell anyone you saw me," Oliver went on. "They'll try to bring me back to my foster parents."

I promised, but I wasn't sure it was the right thing.

Before I left, Oliver looked at my cast, pulled out a marker from his backpack, and wrote on it, on the underside where I couldn't see.

My mom says that one of the reasons she loves paintings and poetry and things like that (which I mostly find extremely boring) is that they focus not only on what *is* but what *could be*. She says that it's very important to accept what is but also to never stop dreaming about what could be. Sometimes we play this imagination game where we come up with ideas of what life would be like if there were no sun but only a moon, or if we spoke in music instead of words. . . .

Anyway, walking home I tried to imagine the world without sasquatches and Dark Clouds—how Oliver's parents would still be alive, and how Sam would be safe and we'd get to stay in Cliffden. It cheered me up for a few minutes.

I debated whether to tell my parents about Oliver, and I couldn't decide. So far I'm only writing it down here. Now I'm on the couch, and Mom has lit a fire in the fireplace and closed all the curtains that look out on the backyard. Everything is cozy and warm, and seeing Oliver feels like something I only imagined. Except that, just before I started writing this entry, I remembered to look in the mirror to see what he'd written on my cast. It said *I was never here*.

October 7th

It's hard to write because my hands are shaking. We're all packed. The Winnebago is stuffed to the gills. The Cloud is hovering above the back deck this morning, just a couple of feet from the door, as if waiting to be let in. We're leaving and I'm writing as fast as I can.

Yesterday Arin Roland surprised me by showing up at my door with her mom to give me a big hug and also a present. It's a tiny silver suitcase with the words *Home Again* engraved on one side. It's sort of a dumb little knickknack, but I've decided to make it into a lucky object that'll bring us back here someday.

I want to record the curve of our driveway and the missing tiles of our gingerbread roof. I want to keep in my mind forever the paint smudges along the trim of my bedroom window and the tree stump I tripped over once while we were playing ghost in the graveyard, the church stone just peeking out over the top of the hill and the blinking eye of my house. I've picked up several rocks from the yard to take with me. I smelled each and every flower left in my mom's garden. I touched the grass in several spots and buried all my pennies, and then I took my favorite glass prism from my room and buried that, too. I've also resolved to bury this diary. It seems like I should leave it here as a reminder of me. Sam is curled on my mom's lap on the front stairs, crying into her chest, and Millie is already in the Winnebago waiting, but I just want these seconds to last forever. Good-bye to the—

I'm writing from my seat in the camper. Something big has happened.

A few minutes ago Mom got in the driver's seat and called us all to get in. There wasn't time to bury this diary in the yard after all. We were pulling out of the driveway when suddenly Dad looked in the rearview mirror and said, "What the heck is that?" Millie and Sam and I smushed our faces against the back window to see what he was talking about.

There was a tall wiggly blob running after us down the road, nearly falling over, carrying a big sack of stuff up near its head so that it looked not like a person but a giant hopping worm, like a sleeping bag come to life. My mom stopped the Winnebago and the side door whooshed open, and climbing up the stairs was . . . Oliver.

He dropped his stuff down at his feet, the scar down his cheek extra bright on his flushed face, looked around at us as he tried to catch his breath, and asked, "Can I come with you to the Extraordinary World?"

Millie helped him in with both hands and explained his story to my parents, as much as we know of it. There was a kerfuffle and arguing and pros and cons and Millie kept hugging him like she was this sweet mama bird, which was annoying because she's nothing like that in real life, and it only made Oliver look shy and uncomfortable. He pulled out of her arms as quickly as he could, rubbed his scar, and patted his pocket to calm his faerie, who'd begun to squeak and rumble.

I guess my dad is superstitious after all, because he said, "Maybe you'll be our good luck charm," and welcomed Oliver on board. Oliver turned to me, his green eyes flashing, and he gave the hint of a smile, relieved. "Is it okay with you, Gracie?" he asked.

It took me by surprise, because no one in this family *ever* asks me if anything is okay with me. I made a big show of nodding, knowing Millie had heard him. "Of course, Oliver," I said . . . rather nobly.

Oliver smiled in relief, then he pulled Tweep out of his pocket and cupped her in both palms, whispering to her. "I'll be back in just a second," he said to my mom. He stepped out of the Trinidad onto the grass and opened his hands, letting the faerie fly away. Then he climbed back in and sank onto one of the couches by the table, pulling his stuff close to him so that it'd be out of the way.

When he looked up, we were all staring at him, curious. "She gets car sick," he said. "She always wanted to go back to Connecticut anyway—she has friends there." I couldn't tell for sure, but it looked like he was about to cry.

There's really no room for Oliver, but I'm glad I don't have to worry about him now that he's with us. And I'm relieved I kept this diary with me, because there's too much happening not to be written down. I'm just trying to keep up.

Now we're out of downtown Cliffden on Route 1, and driving past the strip malls that sprawl at the very edge of town. We just rolled past the T.J.Maxx, still charred and half burned down. (Mom just said they haven't been able to rebuild because they didn't have dragonfire insurance, as if talking about insurance could distract us from what we're leaving behind so fast.)

Now I can see, not our dear hill anymore, but dear Bear Mountain in front of our hill, and the Dairy Queen, and the bike store.

Now only a vaguely familiar stretch of road. I just looked out the back window and there's no sign of the Cloud following us.

Now we've pulled onto Route 80 and left Cliffden behind forever.

Now we are gone.

October 15th

I've decided to go back and put an epigraph on the blank page at the front of this diary, though I haven't decided on what yet. Who knows, maybe I'll be a famous writer someday and this'll be my first work of literary genius.

I'm writing from my bed, hiding behind the curtain I've made from a blue flannel blanket. We've each claimed our own small piece of the Winnebago: Mom and Dad have the "master suite"—a small room nestled against the back window and next to the bathroom. Oliver is on the vinyl pullout couch, and Sam is sleeping with Mom and Dad, though he's also claimed the little cupboard right behind the front passenger seat, filling it with boxes full of goldfish crackers and his bear Jim who has one droopy glass eye. He sometimes crawls in there for hours at a time and won't come out even when I offer him my Oreos. (We each get two a day.) Millie has claimed the bigger of the two pull-down bunks, which come down from the ceiling on either side of the main cabin, and plastered her wall with pictures from *Vogue*. Not that she lets me come up there.

My pull-down bunk is small, practically a shelf, across from Millie's and just barely big enough to fit me. Still, I've decorated it as nicely as I can with some lucky items I've taped to the wall, including a perfect clamshell from the beach and the tiny *Home Again* suitcase Arin gave me.

Mom's added sophisticated touches everywhere. She's made a "library" of the shelves above the kitchen table with some classics she couldn't bear to leave behind: *To Kill a Mockingbird*, *The Giant's Lament*, *Little Women*, *Hamlet*. She says they're all required reading for us on this trip, because "Books are the way to stretch out people's souls, and I won't have children with small souls." Whenever it's open, she covers the fold-out table with a tablecloth, and she's laid some afghans along the back of the vinyl couch.

Her traveling outfit today consists of a maroon

floor-length dress. All the other moms in Cliffden wear pants and jackets and shirts they bought at the mall, but my mom wears dresses and always smells like sandalwood, because, she says, "I'm a hippie born at the wrong time." She doesn't wear a gold wedding ring, but instead a big turquoise one that she insisted my dad get for her when he proposed.

We've been on the road for seven days and about four hours, and so far there's been no sign of the Cloud. Still, Dad insists on driving long into the night to put some distance behind us.

How great would it be if it didn't follow us?! Maybe it'll just stay and wait on our back deck forever. We wouldn't ever be able to go home, but at least we wouldn't have to worry about Sam, *and* we wouldn't have to go searching for the Extraordinary World, which will never amount to anything anyway. We could find somewhere else to live, sad as that would be.

It may seem like I should have more faith in my dad, but to be honest, Millie doesn't either, and my mom is noticeably tight-lipped about the whole thing . . . which means she probably has her doubts too. It's not just that everyone back home thinks he's crazy. It's just hard to put your trust in someone who never really looks you in the eye and who's more interested in the weather than the people around him.

I also have a more immediate concern, which is that Grandma might tie us up and use our toenails for spells. That's what the witches in *Extreme Witches* do, though Mom says they're playing it up for the camera and that Millie and I shouldn't watch junk TV.

About an hour ago Sam climbed into my bunk wanting to be told the story of the night he was born. I've been telling it to him ever since he could talk, and he loves to hear it whenever he's feeling afraid or worried (or, in this case, homesick). I let him snuggle in next to me and began the way I always do.

"The night you were born, Dad called from the hospital to say you were a boy, and . . ."

"You cried your eyes out," Sam put in, rubbing his eyes sleepily and then nestling his chin against my shoulder. His breath smelled like goldfish crackers, and I could tell he hadn't brushed his teeth even though it was his bedtime.

"I cried my eyes out because I wanted a little sister to torment just like Millie torments me." I took a breath, then went on, feeling Sam's little heartbeat against my shoulder. "When Mom and Dad got home, I refused to hold you. But then Dad tricked me and slipped you into my arms, saying . . ."

"Can you hold these potato chips!" Sam shouted.

"Shhh. Yeah, he said, 'Can you hold these potato chips?' and then put you in my arms. And when I looked at you . . . and you looked at me . . . I felt . . ."

This is the part I can never describe quite right, and it's the only part of the story that ever changes. I tried to remember that exact feeling of looking into Sam's eyes, so new to the world.

"I think I felt so happy that it made me scared, too. Like that I might drop you or lose you, and never recover."

Sam seemed satisfied. He squeezed me tight around my middle.

"I'm amazing." He sighed.

"Don't get a big head."

I didn't even have to tell him to go to bed. Sam always behaves, almost too well. (Well, except he hates brushing his teeth.) He slithered out of my arms and slipped silently off my bed.

I poked my head out to see him off, and watched him give everyone a kiss good night. He even walked on tiptoes (he loves walking on his toes) over to the pull-out couch where Oliver was reading (*Little Women*, of all things—he's so peculiar) and laid a big sweet kiss on Oliver's cheek. "Night, Oliver," he said, and then disappeared. Oliver looked over at me from his book, and a rare smile climbed onto his face. "I never had siblings," he said. Then his smile kind of melted and disappeared. Maybe he was thinking that he doesn't have a mom and dad either now. I didn't know what to say, so I pretended to get really interested in something on the ceiling, and then ducked back into my bunk.

We just passed a mall that looks like it's been closed for years, with stores like Pottery Barn and Toys "R" Us all grown over with weeds. I've been sitting here writing, on and off, and playing with my *Home Again* suitcase: opening and closing it.

Now I can hear Sam in Mom and Dad's bed talking to Jim the bear. I can't hear what he's saying, but it's clearly a very lively conversation in which Sam is convincing Jim that, actually, Grandma is not going to be awful at all. I suppose he's just convincing himself. I wish I could convince myself too. Dad says that once we get to Smoky Mountain State Park, it's just a short hike through the mountains to the Crow's Nest. I have to say that part doesn't sound so appealing either.

I wonder about the Crow's Nest. Is it really a nest? Does Grandma have a flock of crows that will peck our eyes out? Recently, in New Hampshire, a witch made a boulder fall on a couple who cut her off in the parking lot at Safeway. I'm not sure Grandma is that violent, but Mom and Dad never told us why they stopped speaking to her. Millie has always said it's because she put a curse on Sam, and that's why Sam is always sick and why he's so small. She met her once when she was little, before the big rift, and she says she has pointy teeth and that she's one of the most infamous witches in the Smokies, which are full of infamous witches.

I guess now I have a habit of thinking of pleasant things before I try to go to sleep.

October 16th

Eighty or so years ago, according to Dad, people tried to build highways across America, but the forest monsters—mostly sasquatches, ghosts, and wood demons—harassed and kidnapped the workers. The dream of the highways was soon abandoned, and that's why, in order to get to Grandma's, we have to take this winding, crumbling road that makes Millie carsick. Even now, sitting on the bench near the back windows, she looks a shade of green, which I find pretty satisfying.

No sign of the Cloud again today, though I suppose if it were following us we wouldn't see it anyway, since the road is so curvy. I've decided I'm going to tap three times on my silver suitcase for luck every morning, to keep it away.

In the past hour I've been noticing that lots of the bill-boards along our way have been ripped down or torn to shreds. I've seen some lying on the side of the road, crisscrossed with gashes that could only come from large and vicious animals. I keep looking at Oliver to see if this worries him. He *looks* calm, but I've also noticed he has a habit of rubbing his ears when he's nervous, and that's what he's doing now.

Sam has found his new idol, and he likes to wait beside Oliver's bunk in the morning for him to get up. He's even started squeezing his hair to try to get it to stand straight up like Oliver's. He then walks around raising his eyebrows at us. It seems he thinks raising the eyebrows heightens the effect. Little kids are so indecipherable.

October 17th

Dusk is falling and we've crossed the border into West Virginia. ("Welcome to Wild, Witchy West Virginia"— I learned from the sign posted at the border—is the state motto.) I just had the most surprising conversation, which I'll try to record faithfully here.

Oliver and I were sitting together at the kitchen table. He's been teaching me bridge, which he says his mom taught him. Every time I think I have the hang of it, I miss some big rule and he has to patiently explain things to me again.

"No, spades are ranked higher than hearts," he said apologetically.

"That's stupid." I sighed and laid my cards, mostly hearts, face down on the table.

"I'm sorry, Gracie. We don't have to play."

His politeness made me feel embarrassed about my bad temper. He's very good at bridge, which annoys me. Actually, he's good at everything, because he's patient—patiently going through the rules with me, patiently helping Sam tie his shoes, patiently cleaning around the camper even when it's not him who's made the mess. He's managed to keep his little area of the Trinidad neat and inviting, while my bunk is permanently disheveled. I've noticed he also has a great attention span for reading. *I* get bored so quickly and end up flinging books over the side of my bed, while Oliver lies perfectly still and can read for hours. He's already finished *Little Women* and moved on to *The Giant's Lament*. He says he read *To Kill a Mockingbird* last year, while I've only gotten to the part where Scout dresses up as a ham for Halloween.

Also, he's been trying to find things for me to do to pass the time. Yesterday he showed me how to make paper boxes out of loose-leaf. He puts little gifts in them—like a single goldfish cracker or a penny—and leaves them on my bed. Millie just raises her eyebrows at me like she can't believe someone would like me enough to give me presents. I don't think it's that Oliver likes me especially, but just that he's extremely thoughtful (almost too thoughtful) and maybe extremely lonely.

Anyway, back to our card game. When I'd had enough, Oliver began collecting all the cards and shuffling them. "Don't worry, Gracie, you'll get it next time." I sat back and stared at the table, feeling grumpy.

He opened the cabinet above the couch to put the cards away, and I noticed a photo lying on top of his things. He saw me looking at it and pulled it down to show me.

"It's my parents," he said. I stared at the photo: In it was a younger Oliver, scarless, looking happy and bright. His dad looked sporty, like he might be just about to go for a jog, and his mom was wearing a net over her face.

"My dad worked at McCormick spices—they import cinnamon and nutmeg and things like that. My mom was an accountant, but really she thought of herself as an amateur naturalist. That's why she's wearing the net over her face. She loved to take us into the woods behind our house and collect butter-flies and bugs."

"Sounds risky," I said. "All that time in the woods."

"Mom said if you want to enjoy the wilderness, you have to take risks." There was an awkward silence while I wondered if it was her belief in risks that had gotten her tangled up with the sasquatches.

"Oliver . . . ," I said, wishing there was more privacy on the Winnebago, "why did you decide to come with us? I told you where my dad wants to go. Surely you could have picked some people less . . ." I glanced toward my dad in the driver's seat and then lowered my voice. ". . . um . . . destined for failure?"

Oliver smoothed down his hair, thinking. He was quiet for several moments. I was just about to give up, when he finally spoke. "I want to get as far away as possible . . . from them." He looked up at me, his green eyes extra bright in the dim afternoon light.

"From those sasquatches?" I asked. He shook his head.

"No. I know it sounds bad, but I mean . . . from my parents, and where we had our life, in Connecticut. I just want to be far away from that. The Extraordinary World sounds like it's about as far away as you can go." He ran his fingers along the edges of his photo, looking sheepish. "I shouldn't want to forget them, but I do. I wish I could forget I ever knew them and that they ever loved me." His hair sprang up again from where he'd smoothed it down. "Though, so far being with you guys actually makes me think about them more. My mom loved road trips—she had all these Irish traveling songs she liked to sing. The weird thing is," he went on, looking out the window, "she loved animals—all kinds. Even the beasts and monsters. She always said you can't blame animals for doing what's in their natures. She would have said not to blame the sasquatches." I could tell by the angry way he said it that he didn't share the sentiment.

We were silent for a while. I was thinking to myself how we're going to the Extraordinary World to protect someone, and Oliver is going to forget the people he couldn't protect. I thought of how I'd looked at him when he'd first arrived at school, how I thought he'd looked like a fish. But really he just looked sad, I guess.

Mom is driving today, and instead of spending time with us, Dad has his nose stuck in a book (of course) called something ridiculous like *Einstein's Cat* or *Einstein's Cricket* or something like that. Sometimes I'm tempted to pull down the lucky penny on my wall that's dedicated specifically to keeping him safe and throw it out the window.

Millie just poked her head up into my bunk, her brown curls sticking to the flannel of the blue sheet I've hung around it for privacy.

"Do you know we're broke?" she whispered. "Nobody's made an offer on the house, and Mom and Dad are almost out of money."

"But they have savings."

Millie shook her head, ducked out for a moment to make sure we weren't being listened to, then appeared again. "Not as much as you think. We may have to sell our hair like in *Little Women*." She then gazed at me appraisingly, taking in my messy dishwater-blond mop. "Well, *mine* at least." She looked almost sorry for me, and then she disappeared again.

Millie can be dramatic, but I think she must be telling the truth, because yesterday Mom was adding length to my jeans with some scrap fabric and a needle and thread instead of just promising to get me a new pair. Also, when we stopped at a rest area for lunch earlier today, we were only allowed to order one thing each off the McDonald's dollar menu.

I've just poked my head out of the cubby to see if our

surroundings are shabbier than I've had the chance to notice, but it all looks pretty much how I thought—pretty shabby generally, but not *destitute*. Dad's still reading, and Millie's looking out the window and stroking her hair, as if she's thinking it may be one of the last times she has the pleasure of doing so.

Outside, the landscape has changed a lot over the past few hours, but there is still no sign of the Cloud. We're surrounded by dipping valleys full of mist, like bowls of milk—fog rising off creeks and riverbeds and leaking up into the hills to hide the mountaintops. It's witch country, for sure.

Witches tend to like their privacy, and the hills give them lots of places to keep their lives and their secrets hidden. That's what Millie says. I guess the only bad thing is that they have to share the hills with all manner of beast—not only sasquatches, but also ghosts.

The thing with ghosts is that they pop up wherever there are caves, and the Smokies are just *riddled* with caves. Ghosts use them to come and go from the Underworld, even though that's not technically legal. They have a tendency to try to snatch people into the Underworld. That's one main reason why they aren't allowed up here aboveground, and why—if your house does end up being haunted—you have to "disclose" that before you sell it. (I overheard Barbara the real estate agent mentioning that to Mom.) They're only supposed to officially interact with humans at the Mausoleum Headquarters in Florida, where there are psychic mediums on call twenty-four-seven to handle their concerns, but they're sometimes seen floating into towns to visit relatives. It's hard for the police to keep them completely contained—especially in hills like these or out on the open sea, where they're hard to catch. I suppose the witches tolerate them somehow.

I guess, knowing all that, it's no surprise these hills give me an eerie feeling—I can barely see through the thickness of the trees, and the houses are all surrounded by tall wooden fences, as if to keep creatures out. The deeper we get into the Smokies, the more wild the woods become.

PS: The most disturbing thing about ghosts is that they're the souls of people who were never taken by a Cloud at all. Either they died too suddenly and unexpectedly, or somewhere too remote to be reached. So they drift around in Limbo. As terrible as it is to be taken by a Cloud, it's supposed to be even worse to die *without* being taken by one.

Luckily, neither is going to happen to Sam, because he's going to get better. Just to prove it, I looked out the window a second ago, and the sky behind us is perfectly clear.

October 21st

I can't believe where I'm writing this from. My fingers
are freezing, and Millie says I'm crazy for working on
this diary so obsessively. She may have a point. Right
now there's barely enough firelight to see the words.
Because here I am in a sleeping bag in the woods, in
the ghost-infested, witch-infested, sasquatch-infested
Smoky Mountains.

This morning we parked the Trinidad in a dusty lot,
climbed out, and saw the sign marking the trailhead that
Dad said led toward Grandma's: WELCOME TO THE SMOKY
MOUNTAIN STATE FOREST! WARNING: HIKING AND CAMPING MAY
RESULT IN DISMEMBERMENT BY SASQUATCH, WITCH, OR BEAR,
AND POSSIBLE KIDNAPPING BY SPECTRAL INHABITANTS. PLEASE
RESPECT DESIGNATED WILDLIFE AND WITCHCRAFT AREAS.

It was far from encouraging.

"I hiked these woods a million times as a boy," Dad said brightly. "I wouldn't take you if I wasn't sure I could protect you." I just blinked at him, my heart sinking with trepidation. My dad is pretty spindly, and since he's always muttering and nudging at his glasses, and always looking disheveled because of his stubble, he is pretty much the last person you'd expect could protect anyone from any of the things we saw listed on that sign.

Millie and I exchanged a doubtful glance, then I popped into the Winnebago to search for weapons. All I found was a corkscrew, a skewer, and a spatula, all of which Mom confiscated from me as soon as I emerged with them.

Still, she too seemed to hesitate on the verge of boycotting the whole thing. She looked in the direction we'd driven, as if searching for the Cloud. Then she sighed, turned to the trailer at the back of the camper, and began unpacking: sleeping bags, a gas stove, pots and pans, and her portable violin case that attaches to her back. (She's always prepared for anything, even remote musical interludes.) "I've read there are lots of witch villages up in the hills," she said, putting on a brave face. She stuffed sleeping bags into knapsacks and attached pots to straps. "That'll be interesting. I'm sure they're charming."

Once Mom and Dad are united on something, there's no amount of protesting that will change their minds. So I hefted a knapsack onto my back, and Millie and Oliver did the same. Sam only grabbed Jim the bear while Mom gathered his things.

We left the Winnebago locked up and abandoned at the foot of the trail. It looked a little forlorn there with no other cars in the lot to keep it company. And then we were off . . . Dad at the front, then me and Oliver, then Millie, and Mom and Sam bringing up the rear.

Luckily, our first day's hike was pretty uneventful. We saw a few openmouthed caves to the Underworld—but no ghosts—and possibly the shadows of a few tree demons slipping through the woods. (Tree demons are timid and especially scared of humans—supposedly they only pick fights with angels, and there are barely any angels in the east.) We did see our first witch village, though we didn't really get to see much of it. It was positioned off to the right of the trail and had a big unmarked wooden gate at the front with an elaborate silver lock. It was surrounded by a spiky wooden fence too high to see over. But from one spot farther up the trail, we could make out the tip-tops of pointy black hats bustling back and forth beyond the gates, and we could smell the cookfires, and hear the occasional cackly laughter and the sound of someone playing a fiddle.

All day, taking advantage of his captive audience (we were too out of breath not to be), Dad went on and on about physics. "There's no reason we should think time *only* moves forward, just because it looks that way to *us*," he expounded over his shoulder. "The only thing that really tells us time has a direction at all is entropy. Entropy is when things move from order to disorder. The universe gets more disorderly all the time."

I looked helplessly back at Millie, who caught my glance and pantomimed fainting from boredom, and then over at Oliver, who was listening with his head to one side as he walked. When he noticed me watching him, he smiled. "Your dad's really interesting," he said.

I suppose one person's most-boring-lecture-of-all-time can be another person's "interesting." I guess stranger things have happened than somebody finding my dad worth listening to.

*   *   *

Now we're camped beside the trail not far above the village. Mom's pulled out her violin and is playing something soothing to distract us from the eerie sounds of the forest all around us, her fingers moving on the strings like elegant spiders. Sometimes I nearly forget she's a classically trained musician and that she ever had a life before being our mom.

I can still hear the creaks and distant howls (possibly ghosts, hopefully not sasquatches) and nearby croaks, but she says the fire will keep them all away. Dad is smoking a pipe and staring at the sky. He probably prefers being here in the woods rather than being boxed into the house with all of us, where he has to have table manners and talk to us at dinner. I'd like to ask him if he thinks we've lost the Cloud for good, but Sam is curled up against me in my sleeping bag like a hot water bottle, and I don't want to wake him or risk him overhearing me.

Millie is reading by flashlight. Oliver has been working on something mysterious across the fire. He always has to be doing something, and everything he does, he does *just so*.

Oh, he just came over and gave me what he was working on. It's a wooden whistle. He said it's a safety whistle.

"Just blow on it if you ever get lost or in trouble, and I'll hear you," he said. I don't know what good a whistle would do me if something really bad happened . . . like, say, if my legs were in the process of being gnawed off by a tree demon. But I thanked him politely. Sometimes I think Oliver's weirdness is just weird, and other times it's sort of touching. I can't figure out which way I feel about the whistle.

In other news, I found some dry raccoon poo earlier, which I picked up with a tissue and put in a pocket of my knapsack. I'm planning to put it in one of Millie's hiking boots once she falls asleep.

I've decided that next time I write, I'll just continue right where I've left off so this feels more like an actual book and I seem more like a real author.

October 22nd

We knew we must be getting close to a witch's house yesterday when, around dusk, we started seeing the charms hung along the path: wooden chimes and star-shaped bells and twirly mobiles made of fine little bird bones hanging from branches. There were whistles lodged in the crevices of trees that made low moaning noises as we passed, and all sorts of dangling symbols made of twigs. I couldn't decide whether it was all enchanting or eerie, and decided it was both. "Not much farther," Dad said, getting visibly more tense. We stumbled along under a thick shelter of trees until, all of a sudden, we emerged into a clearing, and the Crow's Nest came into view.

It was an astonishing sight—resting on enormous boulders at the peak of the mountain, made of dark logs and planks of wood, and lit up brightly from inside by firelight. It looked half wild and half civilized, sort of crooked to one side, old and breathtaking, with attachments and additions veering off this way and that and poking over the sides of the boulders and low cliffs. There was one high room built up to the left side and one low porch to the right that *did* make the whole thing resemble the shape of a crow—with the highest point being the head and the lowest being the tail. It was surrounded at the bottom by a large, wide fence made of spiky pine trunks carved to points and facing upward, which had a nestlike appearance but was clearly built to keep the wild beasts out. Beyond the fence, high enough so we could see, THE CROWS' NEST was burned into a cedar sign, and a set of stairs curled up, up, and up past it, lit with candles at each small landing. My dad fiddled with the elaborate latch on a tall wooden gate for a few minutes and then let us inside, one by one.

At the top of the stairs we came to a wide wooden porch covered in old rockers, with cobwebs in the high corners and little wooden statues and straw dolls hung everywhere. Wind chimes and deer hides and all sorts of dried flowers and herbs hung from the rafters. ("For curses," Millie whispered to me.)

A long, thick deer skull took the place of a door knocker.

Dad hesitated, looked at my mom uncertainly, and then rapped it against the wood. "Out of the frying pan, into the fryer," I whispered back to Millie, which made her snort. She says I always get my sayings wrong.

Standing there in front of Grandma's front door waiting, I had a sudden mental picture of us in my head: the Lockwood family plus one orphan, all quiet and exhausted and dirty. What would we look like to someone who wasn't expecting us? We huddled together as we listened to the shuffle of feet approaching, the *click* and *squeak* and *scrape* of several latches being unlatched, and then the *creak* of the door giving way. And then there she stood, in a halo of warm orange firelight. She was dressed in overalls with a big tag on the front pocket that said GAP, and wore a crown made out of leaves in her hair, which was wild, curly, white, and circled her head like caterpillars. Her cheeks were saggy, and her hands were clawlike and veiny. She looked old, but her eyes were bright and wide-awake, and she smelled like nutmeg.

My mom took a hesitant step forward. "Mrs. Lockwood," she said. "It's us."

"Mom . . . we didn't know where else to go," Dad added. "We need your help."

Grandma eyed us up and down. She had one glass eye that trailed along behind the other one. A smile spread itself across her face. She grabbed my dad and pulled him in tight, pincering his arms against his sides.

"Well, you are welcome here!" Tears welled up in her one real eye, and she clasped and wrung her hands as she pulled back again to take us all in. A crow flew from somewhere inside the house and alighted on her shoulder, but she didn't seem to notice. "My son is home!" she cried, and then turned to hug my mom, who tried to pull away but failed. Another crow flew up and perched on Grandma's other shoulder, ignoring the chaos and pecking gently at my mom's hair.

I glanced at the others. Sam was squeezing behind my legs to hide. Millie had her arms crossed defensively in front of her. Dad looked rigid and uncertain, and Oliver had stiffened into his shy wanting-to-disappear posture. I was wondering what they were all thinking, because from the very first moment I had made my own mind up about Grandma Lockwood.

I thought she was magnificent.

* * *

Inside, the house was bigger than it had looked from outside. But really it was hard to tell what was indoors and what wasn't: There were mostly screens instead of windows, jutting screened-in rooms surrounded completely by woods, and long hallways that led into elaborate, colorful cloth tents.

Grandma ushered us into the family room, which had a huge stone fireplace and walls hung with all sorts of fiddles and banjos and guitars, mobiles of hand-carved birds hanging from the ceilings, and plants growing from tiny pots lodged in every spare nook. Pages of poetry were taped above the doorways, there was a giant telescope pointed out into the backyard, and the high ceilings were covered in glinting copper. The only thing that kept running through my head was *My dad grew up here*. Never have two things fit together less than this magical place and my distracted, boring, mathematical father.

"Mom, you've done a lot to the house," Dad said.

Grandma grinned. "Wait till you see what I've got in the grove."

She opened a big wooden door at the back and nodded us forward onto a deck. It looked down onto a wide, grassy glade, wedged between two enormous boulders that seemed to come together in a dark, deep opening at the middle. But when we saw what the glade contained, Millie screamed.

Sorry, I had to stop for a minute because of a hand cramp.

The glade was full of ghosts.

There was no mistaking them, of course, though I'd never seen one in real life. They were filmy, wearing morbid expressions and old-timey clothes and floating a foot or so above the ground. These particular ghosts seemed to be from about the 1800s, but I've never paid much attention in history, so I'm not sure. Millie took it as proof that Grandma meant to murder us and keep us as ghosts forever and ran for the front door. Sam asked if we had any food, wanting to throw it to them like he likes to do with geese at the petting zoo.

"Is that . . . ," Oliver asked, pointing to the dark gaping hole that peeped out from between the two boulders, "a cave? Like, to the Underworld?" He'd gone so pale his scar stood out extra bright.

Grandma nodded. "Of course. Where else do you think they came from?"

Dad eyed her critically. "Mom, that was plugged up for years. What happened?"

"The poor things couldn't come out. So I unplugged it. I rented a jackhammer. Had somebody hike it up here from Lowe's for an extra fifty dollars."

"This is very dangerous, Mom, " Dad stuttered. "Not to mention illegal. You know it needs to be refilled. Do you know any licensed contractors?" He shook his head, readjusting his glasses and rubbing nervously at his pointy chin that I wish wasn't pointy, just like mine. "What if they dragged you underground with them?"

Grandma put her hands on his cheeks and squeezed them. "You always liked rules," she said, then kissed him on the forehead, making him blush. "They'd never hurt me," Grandma went on. "They're mopey, not dangerous. There's a difference. This one's a bit of a pyromaniac. . . . " She thumbed downward in the direction of a dour-looking spirit who was playing with a book of matches and appeared to be singed on one side. He kept looking at us distrustfully—as if he didn't like the presence of strangers—a frown pulling at the corners of his pale face. "But with the nasty ones, I have my spells." She winked at me.

"That's very reassuring," Dad said dryly, trying to regain his composure.

Even standing this far above it, the cool air from the cave blew at my messy hair, and I could hear faint laughter, singing, and then a moan, coming from somewhere deep down in the darkness.

"Anyway, I'll get you all some tea while I whip up dinner," she said, turning to Millie. "You guys look *awful*." Millie crossed her arms tighter.

I think there was some kind of lizard eye in my tea, and Oliver pulled a feather out of his, and none of us could bring ourselves to take a sip from our mugs even though Grandma kept saying it would make us feel "like a million dollars."

An enormous dinner was on the dining room table when we walked in, laid out in huge wooden bowls: fried chicken and steamed collard greens and mashed potatoes and iced tea (without eyes and feathers, thankfully). Grandma had cooked it all so quickly, and even though it seemed crazy, I eyed the crows with suspicion, wondering if they'd helped. Some perched on the shelves and a couple sat on the back of Grandma's chair, but they groomed themselves and stared back at me dumbly. Was I just imagining it, or was there a little flour on one's cheek? (Then again, wouldn't crows boycott making fried chicken even if they knew how?)

"These are your cousins," Grandma said to the two on her chair, dotingly. Millie looked at me and mouthed, *Crazy*, and then Mom, noticing, said under her breath that she really just loves her pets.

When Millie asked for the salt, it floated out from the kitchen and gently landed in front of her. She tried to act nonchalant about it, even though we only ever see people do magic on reality shows.

"Mom, can you just act like a normal person for once?" Dad said. (He's one to talk.) He didn't seem amused by any of Grandma's tricks, like the way she was making her glass eyeball roll around in its socket, or how she lit the fire in the family room fireplace just by doing something flourishy with her hand. As we ate, he kept glancing out the kitchen window in the direction we'd come.

Grandma watched him intently. "I don't think *you're* such a normal person," she finally said. "A normal person would have at least thought to bring me some Taco Bell. Or a newspaper. Or would have written me a letter every once in a while in the past few years." Dad dug into his food, looking sullen and angry, more like a kid than an adult.

"Dad's in trouble with his mom," Sam said giddily to the table-at-large.

Finally, Grandma put down her fork. "Okay, let's have it. You know I'm not a mind reader. What's after you?" She looked first at Dad, then gazed around at the rest of us. "Tell me what we're dealing with here."

Everyone turned serious and waited for Dad to speak, while Mom lifted Sam from his seat and brought him into the family room, out of earshot. And then, softening a little, Dad sank back in his chair, pushed his glasses up on his nose, and told Grandma about first noticing the Dark Cloud, and seeing it drifting closer and closer to the house until it came to rest in the backyard.

The color was gone from Grandma's cheeks by the time he finished speaking. Her eyes drifted to the window, then toward the family room.

"Oh, Theodore."

"We didn't know what else to do but come here," he said. "We think we may have left it behind. But if not, we need your help."

A silence stretched across the table, then Grandma leaned back in her chair thoughtfully.

"You're bringing death here. The ghosts won't be happy."

"But they're dead already," I blurted out. "What do they have to be scared of?"

Grandma's eyes darted to mine; they were the color of amber and it felt as if they could see right into my soul. "Not scared. Jealous," she said. Then she turned back to my dad. "We're well hidden. Anything can get lost in these hills, even the weather. And I've put a hiding spell on the house for eyes to pass over it, even the eyes of storms. You're all welcome here as long as you like. But"—she looked around the table—"I can't make a Cloud go away. There's no spell that can stop it, not once it's chosen what it wants. A Cloud picks one person, and one person alone. And eventually, it'll find its mark. It's coming, you can be sure of that." I think we all must have felt the heaviness that came with her words.

"Well, I was thinking, actually," Dad said tentatively after a few moments of silence, "of a different kind of help."

Grandma gave him a sharp, appraising look. *Here it goes,* I thought. Dad would tell her his plan, and she'd look sorry for us—like people do sometimes when we get recognized walking through Cliffden. I braced myself.

"I was hoping you could tell us how to get to the Extraordinary World," he said, so quietly it was barely above a whisper.

Grandma stared at him in shock for a long moment. She sank back in her chair as if she'd suddenly turned to Jell-O. And then she did something that shocked me. She smiled.

"That . . . ," she said. "Now, that I can do."

I can barely keep my eyes open and have fallen asleep twice while making this entry. More tomorrow.

October 23rd

Late into the night, Grandma was telling us about the Extraordinary World. Not only did she agree that it exists . . . she told us she could prove it.

After dinner she brought us into the library, which juts out so that you're just looking out into thin air and treetops, and which is lined from floor to ceiling with shelves bursting with dusty old books, some of them so old their spines are crumbling: books on spells, on the special powers of various trees, on gemstones, some romance novels . . .

She went straight to a shelf at the far side of the room and extracted a book with a disintegrating yellow spine, then sank down cross-legged on the thick Oriental rug. We all gathered on the floor around her, Sam curled up in my lap. As she opened the book, she blew on it, and a tiny puff of dust rose up from its pages.

"I haven't looked at this in years," Grandma said. She spread it open on the floor so that we all could see, then turned page after page for us. It was full of illustrations depicting a beautiful round blue planet. There were orderly streets and clean, gleaming skyscrapers and shiny aeroplanes.

"There used to be aeroplanes *here*," Grandma said. "When I was a girl. They were like beautiful metal birds." I nodded. I'd seen old black-and-white photos of them; I'd always thought they were beautiful too.

"What happened to them?" Sam asked.

Grandma leaned toward him, and her caterpillar curls flopped. "The angels got jealous and broke them in half. Same thing with blimps, hot-air balloons, helicopters . . . People invented them and the angels knocked them down."

"Did anyone take them to the edge of the world?"

Grandma shook her head. "Only the oldest, strongest angels have been to the edges of the earth, and *they're* not telling what they've seen there."

Further into the book, there were drawings of rockets sent to the moon, people happily swimming in the ocean (apparently unconcerned that a mermaid might drag them under), gleaming cities and highways that gave no sign of being devoured by forests. The skies were full of white puffy clouds—not one drawing of a Dark Cloud or a dragon. No sasquatches or ghosts. Grandma pointed to one picture of several round planets with arrows drawn to indicate they were moving in circles. "The Extraordinary World moves around the sun," she said. "It's not at the center of the universe like we are." (I can't imagine not being at the center of the universe. I can't imagine the sun not moving over the middle of our planet from west to east like it's on a belt.)

"It's just drawings and paintings," Millie said. "It doesn't prove anything." Which was exactly what I'd been thinking. Sometimes I hate how Millie and I can have the same exact thoughts at the same time. "It's not real."

Grandma got a twinkle in her eye, stood up, and went into a closet in the corner of the room. She came back with three objects in her hands and laid them down on the rug.

One was a page from an encyclopedia, showing a photograph of a jellyfish called the *Turritopis nutricula* (and showing on a map of the round earth where such a creature could generally be found). One was a little unopened foil packet labeled SNACK BAG from Delta Airlines. ("In the Extraordinary World aeroplanes are so commonplace, just about everyone rides on them!" Grandma explained.)

But the most convincing thing of all was a simple postcard. It was a photo, taken from the air, of a city full of real, gleaming hotels, helicopters hovering overhead, lights pulsing along the tops of soaring glass buildings. *Viva Las Vegas, Nevada!* it read at the top.

There are no cities in Nevada. There are no helicopters. The reality of what she was showing us settled around me. I felt my pulse pounding in my wrists. Somewhere, I realized, there was another Nevada. How could that be?

"They're yours to keep," Grandma said with an easy smile, as if she hadn't just turned our world upside down. "I want you to take them with you when you go. To remind you of where you're headed."

"Where'd you get these things?" Millie asked. She sounded breathless and as shocked as I felt.

Grandma and Dad looked at each other. "I used to be something of a treasure hunter," Grandma said. "Always looking for rare items—antiques, artifacts . . . I found these at an estate sale. The guy was some kind of explorer, himself."

"Why didn't you ever tell us, Teddy?" Mom breathed. "That you had proof?" She looked so astounded that I realized, suddenly and with certainty, that she had never really believed in my dad's theories at all.

"You're my family. I didn't think I needed to," Dad said earnestly. He ran a hand down the side of his face thoughtfully, scraping his stubble.

My mom took his hand in hers and kissed his knuckles.

It's evening again and I'm sitting on the edge of my bed, looking down on a dim field full of glowing ghosts shining in the dark. My room is in the crow's head and my window is one of his eyes.

We spent the day soaking in a hot spring Grandma took us to in the woods (it felt so good after all the hiking), learning how to call the crows to our fingers, and watching Grandma bake a cake for us by flurrying her hands around to one side while also playing Monopoly with us.

Millie was much nicer to Oliver the whole day than she ever is to me. She led him and Sam on a walk around outside, while I was helping Grandma in the kitchen. (If the crows are helpers too, they didn't do it in front of me.) I watched the three of them out the window, a lump in my throat: Millie likes to steal my friends. It used to annoy me so much that I started an I Hate Millie Club when I was nine and forced all my friends to join. The thing is, she is so charming when she wants to be that people can't resist her. I, on the other hand, fall a little short in the charm department.

After we were done in the kitchen, Grandma went down to the glade muttering that she had to do something for the ghosts, and I was so curious about what it might be that I went after her. As I stepped outside, she turned and gestured me forward. She was standing beside a big cardboard box, and as I cautiously walked up beside her, I glanced into it at a pile of knickknacks. The ghosts retreated at my approach and hovered a few feet away from us.

"What are you doing?" I asked.

"Giving them some presents I found at a garage sale last time I was in town," Grandma said, bending over and pulling things out of the box, then laying them on the grass: brass candlesticks, a roll of tinfoil, a package of silver barrettes. "Ghosts love anything that shines. To them it's as good as gold and jewels."

The ghosts eyed me warily. Finally, the singed one with the book of matches I'd noticed earlier floated closer. He tried to smile at me, but only managed to grimace, and held out his hands as if to offer me the matches.

"That's okay." I shook my head. "I don't need any."

He frowned, nodded, then turned his attention to the shiny things on the ground. He leaned over and took two candlesticks in his hands.

"Only *one*, Samson my pet. You know that. There needs to be enough to go around." Grandma turned to me, grinning. "They can't talk," she explained, "but they can understand well enough." Samson laid one of the candlesticks down and then floated backward toward the cave. He clutched his treasure to his chest with pride as he disappeared into the darkness.

"Poor Samson," Grandma said, shaking her head. "Sad story. He was burned in a big fire. I read about it in the archives at the library in town—I like to know about my ghosts." She handed a roll of tinfoil to a woman in a filmy bridal gown, who darted away quickly. "He set the fire himself, couldn't resist playing with matches. Clouds came for the others who died, but no Cloud ever found Samson." She sighed. "I just feel so sorry for the poor creatures. It must be so hard to be stuck forever in one place. To never move on."

The ghosts went on taking their shiny objects from her, one after the other, and then retreated into the cave, no doubt to stash their treasures somewhere in the Underworld far below. I breathed a little easier once they were all gone. Grandma smiled with satisfaction and closed up the top of the empty box.

"Grandma," I asked, "if the Extraordinary World is real, why did *we* get stuck with all the monsters and the ghosts and the Underworld? Why are *they* so lucky instead of us?"

"Ohhh." Grandma pursed her lips and shook her head. "We get what we get. You can't really compare. I bet they have their own troubles."

"But they don't have Clouds."

Grandma turned her eyes to me, the glass one trailing the real one. "That's true. They don't have Clouds."

"Do you really think it's still coming for Sam?" I asked, barely above a whisper. "Do you really think Dad's right and we can save him if we go far enough?"

Grandma placed a hand on my shoulder. "I'll tell you something about your Dad, Gracie. Ever since he was a kid, he holds on to everything like *this*." She squeezed her hands into tight little fists at her chest and scrunched up her face, shutting her eyes tight. "He thinks everything has to be just the way he wants it to be, or else . . . disaster! He can't be happy when things are messy, and trust me, things are *always* messy." Grandma opened her eyes again; they twinkled with good humor. "But letting go . . . it isn't always as horrible as it seems. Just look at these poor ghosts." She nodded toward the cave. "They're stuck forever. And that's much worse."

I can't imagine ever letting go of Sam. Without him, I wouldn't be me. We, the whole Lockwood family, wouldn't be us.

"But to answer your question, yes," Grandma went on, "I believe you can make it where you want to go. It just takes a little trust." She looked up at the sky, as if searching for answers, then back at me. "Easier said then done, I know."

Tonight I've just been sitting here thinking about Grandma's words and watching the sky deepen and darken. Supposedly there is a man on the moon who watches over us, but nobody's ever been there to discover whether it's true or not. It's the same with the constellations, People say they battle it out every night, ruling our lives on earth. But if that's true, we can't say for sure.

Oliver came in a few minutes ago and has just left.

"Hey, Gracie," he said, standing in the door a little shyly, "just wondering if you needed anything."

"Like what?" I asked.

He rubbed his ears, looking shy. "Well, I guess I was really thinking about me. I don't like sitting alone in my room. I shouldn't admit this, but I keep thinking about ghosts looking in my window."

I motioned that he was welcome to come in, and he sat down beside me on the bed. I'd never sat alone next to a boy who wasn't Sam in any room, anywhere, and it made me feel sophisticated. Sometimes I wish that there was an audience around to watch my most interesting moments.

Since I was positive Millie had been charming all afternoon, I wanted to make stimulating conversation, maybe even a joke, but I couldn't think of anything good. . . . And anyway, Oliver has this effect on me like I can't pretend to be something I'm not when

I'm around him. I guess deep down, at that moment, I wasn't a jokey someone.

"I've just been sitting here thinking about how far away we are from the stars," I finally said, even though I knew it was a peculiar thing to be thinking about. "It makes me feel really tiny. And that makes me feel scared."

"I like it," Oliver said. "I like feeling small."

I can't imagine why anyone would like feeling small. But I didn't say that. I just sat next to him and tried to be as okay with the silence as he was. After a while it started to feel kind of nice, actually. Maybe I should try being quiet around people more often.

"I feel better now," Oliver finally said, standing and moving toward the door. "Thanks, Gracie."

"Okay. Good night, Oliver." I gave him a little wave as he walked out.

And now I'm back to staring out at the sky, which every moment is more and more speckled with stars. I just wished on a shooting one. (I cheated and made two wishes—for Sam to be okay and for us all to go home to Cliffden.)

What I haven't mentioned that's been on my mind a lot today—while soaking in the hot springs and eating cake with Grandma and even standing in the glade of ghosts—is that for the first time in my life, I've realized I may have been completely wrong about my dad. All his letters to the editor, all the times I've felt so embarrassed of him, all his crazy certainty about something I thought was impossible. And it looks like he was really right all along.

I do also want to say that I think Oliver's face isn't fish-like at all, the longer I look at it.

October 27th

We've been here for six glorious days. We've soaked in the hot springs until our fingers turned to prunes. We've gone butterfly hunting with Grandma. (She says she can understand the language of insects, which—she also says—have a thousand different words for green. Dad says not to believe her.) We've had our auras read. (Mine is fuchsia, Millie's is a soft lavender, Sam's is a pale green, Oliver's is brown. Dad refused to have his read, but Mom was pleased to find out hers is a rainbow and always changing.)

Grandma hasn't tried even once to put spells on us, and I've realized that it's not some huge terrible thing that made her and Dad stop talking—it's just that they're so different, and don't seem to agree on anything except the Extraordinary World (even though you can tell they love each other). Try as I might, I can't picture my dad growing up here and feeling anything but out of place.

The biggest thing that's happened is that we've planned a route to the edge of the earth. A few nights ago after dinner, Grandma cleared the plates and then leaned her elbows on the table. I knew just by the look on her face that the conversation was about to turn serious.

"The world is more dangerous than it used to be," she said, once we'd all resettled ourselves.

"Kids," Mom said, "why don't you head outside and find something to do? Just don't go near the glade."

Grandma put her hand in mine as I reluctantly stood up. "The older ones should hear this."

We all stood looking at Mom expectantly, halfway between leaving and staying. Finally, Mom only sent Sam off to his room to play, and the rest of us settled back into our chairs. Sam dragged his feet across the room, casting disgruntled glances at us before trudging upstairs.

"The world is more dangerous than it used to be," Grandma repeated, laying her palms firmly on the table for emphasis. "The northern and southern sheets of ice are growing, pushing all the beasts closer toward us. Our cities get swallowed by trees, the Great Kraken rules the Southern Sea, mermaids are building underwater villages even in the inlets now, and sasquatches outnumber people here in West Virginia three to one." Grandma slid her hands together and folded them tightly. "I don't know what else; I'd be more up to date on these things if someone would bring me a newspaper every once in a while."

She sighed, touching her curls to smooth them out. "I'm just saying it's wild out there . . . and getting wilder all the time."

A cupboard opened in a corner of the room, and a crinkly, yellowing scroll floated toward the table. Grandma reached up, grasped it in her left hand, then spread it out on the table in front of us. It was a map of the United States.

"Now, let's just see here what your choices are. You have Chicago." She jabbed a finger near the top of the map. "Home of architects and journalists. Lots of freshwater mermaids, because of the Great Lakes. It'd be nice to gather more information there from one of the great archives, but Chicago's been taken back by the woods, ivy growing to the top of even the tallest buildings. . . ." She sighed. "There's nothing there for you." She scanned the map thoughtfully. "There's New York, the Magic City." (We learned in fourth-grade bio that it's been scientifically proven that magical ability is caused by a special gene in our DNA. New York has more magical families than any other place in the US. Incidentally, the city is home to the only TV stations and movie studios in the country, and it's where most of the manufacturing happens, which is why the farther you get from the northeast, the harder it is to buy anything nice and new.)

"But you don't want to go back the way you've come," Grandma went on. "And if you were to set off on the Atlantic, the sea serpents wouldn't let you get past Halifax." She shook her head and pointed west. "Now . . . LA, city of Lost Angels. So hard to get to with the roads being what they are, and the west being what it is . . . but it's the best port to launch from. . . ." She paused here for a moment, thinking, and then moved on.

"Washington, the Brain City." (Washington is home to the country's biggest, dustiest library, a white monolith which—I've heard from Millie who went on a school field trip there in sixth grade—is covered in cobwebs.) "You could find some good old maps there, but I don't think you'll need them. Florida," she went on, sliding her hand south, "has too many alligators."

I sighed, disappointed. I've always wanted to see Disney World, which was built in the seventies but quickly grew over with strangler vines and swamp grass. Now most of what's left of the state of Florida is swamps littered with gators and old cemeteries and, in the Everglades, a monster named Guyascatus who snatches lumberjacks. And of course, Mausoleum Headquarters . . . but only foreign dignitaries, elected officials, and certain celebrities get to go there.

"There's really no place in the country where a Cloud won't be able to follow you, of course. . . ." Grandma leaned her elbows on the table, lost in thought. Then she let out a short, decisive breath. "The long and short of it is, you're gonna have to sail south, and you're gonna need to hire a guardian angel to have any chance of making it." She looked around at us, discouraged. "And all the angels for hire are in LA."

She jabbed her finger at the west coast again.

"But the roads," Dad said, adjusting his glasses to see better. "The west is uncrossable."

Grandma shrugged. "People do it. But it's not easy. With any luck, the Great Western Road is open. If not . . ." Her voice trailed off. "You'll figure out a way."

Mom and Dad looked more tense by the second, but I was still back at *guardian angel*.

"And we can't afford to hire an angel," Dad said.

Grandma waved a hand, and suddenly Dad's lips shut tight. He gave Grandma an exasperated look. "Don't talk back to your mother," she said. "You can't afford *not* to hire one. There are creatures in the ocean that no human stands a chance against . . . and the ocean is the only way to get where you're going. Of course, an angel is only under contract until he or she has saved your life *once*, which is pretty paltry under the circumstances, but I guess that's up to the lawyers and not me. It's better than nothing. Anyway, I've got some savings I'll give you, and you'll use that to pay for it all—the ship, the angel, everything." I expected Mom and Dad to protest, but they were silent, and I wondered again if we really *are* broke.

Finally, Mom leaned closer over the map, her cheeks flushing with sudden excitement. "It looks like," she said as she tucked her dark hair back behind her ear, "if we make it through Arizona, we'll go right by Luck City. Why not try our luck with the genie? Genies can change anything they want to, even Clouds, can't they?" She looked at Dad, who also looked suddenly hopeful.

My heart fluttered with excitement. Luck City is the only city in the country (maybe even the world) run by beasts and supernatural creatures. It's a place where people bet all sorts of things in hopes of winning big: A game of poker can get you the services of a giant (who'll build you your own mansion, or anything else you desire). Slot machines and roulette wheels are run by wish-granting creatures like leprechauns. You can win rides on mystical creatures or a kiss from a mermaid . . . The city is said to be both dangerous and wonderful; the kind of place where all your dreams can come true or where you can lose everything in the blink of an eye. And it's almost impossible to get to. (The ads only come on during day-time TV, between soap operas and court shows, and Mom says that's because they're targeting people who don't have much to lose.) I don't know much about genies, but I know they're vaguely related to angels—kind of the way tigers are vaguely related to pet cats. And there are only a handful of them in the world.

But Grandma's eyes darkened. Her mouth drooped into a severe frown, and her hands moved and tapped with agitation on the table. For the first time I could picture the powerful witch I'd always heard about.

"Promise me," she said, "that you'll never go through

with such an idea. Luck City is for monsters and fools. And people who try their luck with the genie are the biggest fools of all."

Mom was speechless. She fingered her turquoise engagement ring, seeming unsure whether to argue back or not. I'd never seen her so uncertain—my mom could out-argue a lion if she wanted. Dad covered her hand with his own, protectively. "Okay, Mom, okay. We promise."

Grandma studied the both of them, her mouth pressed together in a thin, worried line. And then she jabbed at California again with her index finger. "That's where you launch from. That's where you find your angel and a captain who might be brave enough to take you. It's your one good shot."

Dad's brow was wrinkled as he stared down at the map. "It would take us a year to do everything you're telling us to do. And the Cloud would be after us the whole time."

"Not a year," Grandma said. "But maybe half a year, yes." She frowned, softening. "I didn't say it would be easy. But it's your only chance."

Slowly, the map scrolled itself up and floated back across the room and into the cupboard.

Grandma looked at each of us—Mom, Dad, Millie,

me, and Oliver. "You'll all need to stick together. That's the most important thing. You're going to need each other." Then she reached a hand out and rested it on my dad's arm. "I believe in you, Theodore." She turned to my mom. "I believe in all of you. You'll make it through."

I tried to feel encouraged by her words, but I have to admit that the edge of the world seems so beyond our reach that I can barely believe we could ever get there at all.

TWO HOURS LATER

Something has just happened that I hate to put on paper. It means that, whether the edge of the world is reachable or not, we have no choice but to try.

About an hour ago I walked out onto the side porch. Dad was standing at the railing, staring into the trees. I stood beside him and rested my hand near his, breathing in the smell of the piney air. Since we were alone, I was thinking that maybe I should make some kind of big apology to him for doubting the Extraordinary World all these years—I've been trying to think of a way to say it for days. But before I could get it out, he took my wrist gently and pulled me close to his side. He pointed up into the sliver of washed-out blue sky peeking through the tops of the trees.

A dark shape was floating a few miles away, just above the treetops, gray and thick and unmistakable, with its familiar black hole in the middle. It was drifting back and forth slightly, as if searching the trees for something. Of course, I knew what it was searching for.

I suppose if we had any hope of the Cloud giving up, it's gone now.

Dad says we'll leave tomorrow night after dark.

October 28th

I woke this morning to the sound of Millie crying. My first thought, which took my breath away, was that the Cloud had arrived. But ducking to the window, I could see it still in the distance, drifting slowly. Down in the glade below me, the ghosts were gathered around a pair of Grandma's binoculars and fighting over who would get the next look at it over the treetops.

Hurrying downstairs, I found Millie in the kitchen, leaning on my mom, her hair all askew and her face puffy. I thought that maybe she was on her period, because every time she is, she gets so upset her eyes become like the eyes of this killer in a horror movie I watched one night after Mom and Dad had gone to bed. Here's a list of the top three most angry moments I ever remember her having:

1. The time I put the Poochie the dog (may she rest in peace), on the counter to eat the honey-glazed ham she'd baked for Christmas dinner
2. The time I took a photo of her barfing during the flu
3. The time Dad showed her homecoming date his collection of taxidermied ducks, especially pointing out the tail feathers (his favorite part)— basically putting all the duck butts in his face

"I can't spend another day in the Winnebago," she said as my mom hugged her and tried to comfort her. Across the room Oliver and Sam had just walked in holding—of all things—Ping-Pong paddles. They looked bewildered, turning and hurrying away before Millie could spot them.

"I know you guys have to go," Millie sniffed, sucking in deep breaths. "I know the Cloud's coming. But I don't see why we *all* have to go. If Dad would just let me stay . . ." She sniffed again. "It's not normal to be sixteen and living in an RV with your whole family. It's psychologically . . . traumatic."

"You know you don't mean that, honey," Mom said, looking at me as if urging me to add something sympathetic. "You wouldn't be happy if we left you behind. We know how hard it is for you without your privacy. Right, Gracie?"

I was about to say life in the Winnebago isn't quite *un*-psychologically-traumatizing for me, either, but I heroically kept my mouth shut and nodded. I turned so Mom couldn't see me rolling my eyes, and then went and got this diary from upstairs and came here to the living room to reflect on how selfish Millie is. I just looked out the window, but have lost sight of the Cloud. There's a strange breeze rattling the screens.

Millie—oh—something's happening. Going to find out what's going on. I'll be back.

October 30th

There's so much to say. Where do I begin?

We're back in the Winnebago, driving on a curvy road headed southwest through Tennessee. Our departure from the Crow's Nest, two days ago now, did not go as planned. I'll try to get down as much as I can, even though the curves of the road are making me woozy. I guess I'll start exactly where I last left off.

Millie was still crying, and I'd gone to the back deck to see what all the rattling and windiness was about. Below, in the ghost's grove, the trees were swaying like crazy. Two ghosts (both sullen-looking Victorian ladies) were standing on top of the tallest boulder, one holding the end of a rope while the other tossed the far end, looped like a lasso, up into the sky. She was aiming for the Cloud. Other ghosts were swirling around the grass or disappearing into the Underworld cave in alarm, moaning and flipping through the air. Samson was especially agitated, glaring up at the Cloud, then poking into the cave, then floating out again.

I turned at the sound of Grandma, who was just coming in through the kitchen door with a butterfly net and a fresh crown of ivy nestled in her hair.

"Hush that crying," she called to Millie. "You're agitating the ghosts, honey, and they're already stirred up." She came outside to stand beside me and looked down at the scene below. "Oh dear, they're trying to catch it. Pitiful."

Just then a blinding orange light flared up at us from the deck. Flames crawled along a railing below us.

Grandma leaned over to get a closer look, jumped back in surprise, and thrust her fists against her hips. "Well, now he's done it," she said. "He's set the house on fire." We all rushed to her side and looked down. "Stupid old thing!"

Samson was watching the flames as they rose, looking sheepish and a little uncertain of himself, glancing up at us, then at the flames, then at us again. He moved back toward the cave, but kept swiveling again to stare, as if he wasn't sure whether he should feel guilty or not. He still clasped the matches in both translucent hands.

"Y'all better get your things and go," Grandma said, running into the kitchen and grabbing a bucket, then nodding toward a hall closet that spilled suddenly open to spit out two big pots. The crows flapped around the house wildly. We all stood, stunned, until Grandma darted past again. "Things are gonna get ugly for a while. Go!"

The Crow's Nest—all wood, of course—was going up fast. Fire was soon licking toward the roofline, and the crows began a chorus of ungodly squawks.

We scattered to our rooms, grabbing our backpacks, with Mom yelling at us to forget them and get out of the house. As we banged into each other in the hall, Oliver took mine out of my arms and hoisted it onto his shoulder, but I pulled it back from him. (Side note: I'm not the kind of girl who likes boys to carry things for me, and I've decided I never will be.) There was no time to think if there was anything we were leaving behind. Mom stood in the doorway, waving me out wildly, stuffing the artifacts Grandma had given us (the postcard, the encyclopedia page, and the Delta snack bag) into the bag in her left hand.

Dad was on the front deck with Sam clinging to his legs.

Grandma, running back and forth inside and waving her arms in the air as buckets and pots full of water swirled around her, came to an abrupt stop at the door. She wiped her hair out of her face and hesitated in the doorway. "Don't worry about me." She pushed outside and thrust a sock, knotted at the top and bulging, into my Mom's hands. "My savings. For your angel and your ship, nothing else," she said. "Keep it safe and put away. You'll need every penny when you get to LA." She gave us each a fierce kiss. "I'll be fine. I promise. Stick under the trees as much as you can." She leaned out the open doorway and whispered something toward the woods. The uppermost branches of the trees bent toward each other ever so slightly, creating a shielding canopy over the trail. "You can't fool a Cloud forever, but you can get a head start, and that's better than nothing."

We ran down the front stairs just as the first drops began to spatter the ground. "Rain," my mom said in relief. "It'll help put the fire out." The trees swayed above us, blotting out the sky and keeping us mostly dry.

We hurried down the mountainside, half slipping,

half running. We were down around the first bend when two trees swayed apart and revealed, very low and close, the Cloud, directly above us.

A long tendril of gray mist floated down toward us like an arm and reached slowly toward Sam, who was in Millie's arms. She screamed and held him tight to her chest, covering his eyes. The mist retracted. Mom wrapped her arms around both of them and pulled them to the left, and the Cloud lifted again. From up on the mountain, we heard Grandma's voice yelling some kind of charm, and the trees closed together again.

We slipped and slid onward.

We didn't stop for what must have been an hour or more. Finally halfway down the mountain, we slowed for a few minutes. Dad carefully stepped out onto a rocky outcropping to take the lay of the land, and then signaled for us to do the same. We could see the Cloud, hovering peacefully up the mountain a ways, and beyond it the last of the flames flickering at the top of the Crow's Nest, dying out. The whole house was blackened on one side and giving off a long thin thread of smoke into the sky. But it was clear that Grandma was out of danger. We thought, for the moment, that we were too.

* * *

Close to the bottom of the mountain, the incline grew more gradual, and walking was easier. Millie sloughed along behind me, her legs and face splattered with mud, and I was thinking how she actually looked prettier when she wasn't so perfectly put together. I also couldn't shake the image of the Cloud: how it had reached for Sam almost gently, the way it had retracted so easily when Millie had screamed . . . like it didn't want to intrude if it wasn't wanted. I was wondering how such a terrible thing could be so gentle, when we emerged into the parking lot and the sight before us pushed the thought right out of my mind.

The Trinidad stood where we'd left it, but not *how* we'd left it.

"We've had visitors," Dad said, holding out his arms to keep us from taking another step closer.

We all stood there, our hearts in our throats. Oliver reached up and touched his scar nervously. The Trinidad's windshield was scraped right across the middle. The tires were all flat. The fender had been pulled off and bent in half. It smelled like maybe some animals had pooped on the roof.

"Sasquatches," Mom said.

She held us back under the cover of the tree line as

Dad stepped farther into the parking lot to investigate. "It looks like they've been gone for days," he said over his shoulder, though I don't know how he would have known that. He walked cautiously up to the Winnebago, circled it once, then knelt and peered underneath it. Meanwhile we eyed the woods surrounding the lot. After a few minutes Dad gave us the all clear to come closer.

He kicked one of the tires as Mom squatted to take a good look at it. "They let the air out. At least they didn't slash them."

"This was deliberate," Dad said. "They don't like us being in their woods." I glanced at Oliver, who stood beside Millie with his shoulders hunched toward his ears, looking like he wanted to disappear. Millie took his arm—either to make him feel safe, or to feel safer herself.

Mom swept the parking lot with her eyes and turned to us. "Don't worry about loading the trailer, just climb in. We can sort out your stuff later."

Our nerves frayed, we piled into the Trinidad with our wet things and landed wherever we landed, retreating to our bunks to change into dry clothes. Mom and Dad quickly filled the tires using some cans of Fix-A-Flat that Mom had stowed in the compartment behind the driver's seat. I breathed a sigh of relief when Dad started the ignition and the Trinidad lurched into motion.

One thing did catch my attention as we pulled out of the lot: a fragile, plaintive howl emanating from the woods at the edge of the pavement, and a rustling of bushes low to the ground. Whatever it was, it wasn't human. Safe inside the Winnebago, I thought it had nothing to do with us at all.

The rest of the afternoon was uneventful. The Smoky Mountains slowly softened into rolling hills. Occasionally I noticed a strange, vague tapping sound coming from behind the camper, but Mom said it was something loose and banging around the trailer and that we'd fix it when we stopped.

Occasionally I crawled into my parents' bunk to press my face to the back window. Far behind, the Cloud floated down the western edge of the mountains behind us, distant but steady. I tried to use ESP to thank it for not taking Sam when we were in the woods, and then in my mind I asked it to please forget about Sam completely and go find some other Clouds and take a Cloud vacation, or whatever it is Clouds do when they're not after people's little brothers. But as usual, my psychic skills turned out to be nonexistent, and the Cloud stuck with us for the rest of the day.

It was only after we'd parked for the night that we found out what danger had attached itself to us in the Smokies. It happened in the Burger King parking lot.

We'd parked almost directly under an old, peeling billboard that read: ANIMAL LOVERS! ONCE IN A LIFETIME OPPORTUNITY. TAKE A RIDE ON THE GLORIOUS PEGASUS. WIN A WISH FROM THE GENIE: BECOME A BILLIONAIRE OR BE MIRACU-LOUSLY HEALED! LUCK CITY, ARIZONA. In the center was a painting of a pegasus, glowing with sunlight behind him, dancing on his hind legs with wings outstretched. I couldn't help staring at the billboard and wishing Grandma hadn't forbidden us from going. I'd love to see a pegasus.

We were just turning in for the night after splurging on large fries for everyone, to go with our peanut but-ter sandwiches. Mom and Dad were settling into their room with Sam, Oliver was reading, I was *trying* to read but really daydreaming, and Millie was sitting at the table playing solitaire by lantern light, when we heard a shaking at the back of the Trinidad so loud and violent that the floor beneath us vibrated.

"What was that?" Mom said, darting out into the common area in her floral pajamas, eyes wide. Dad emerged behind her, and they exchanged one of their looks where they seem to say things to each other without speaking. And then Mom hurried to the front and grabbed the flashlight from the glove box.

"Stay inside," she warned us as they both climbed out.

Everyone obeyed except for me. I couldn't help it. I don't know if everybody feels this way, but when I'm curious about something it's like being grabbed by a fishhook and yanked along.

Oliver—who looked petrified—reached for my wrist just as I slipped out the side door, but he wasn't quick enough.

Up ahead, Mom and Dad were huddled together, training the flashlight on the trailer. Its door was rattling on its hinges, being shaken back and forth from the inside.

"Whatever's in there is trapped," Mom said. Dad slowly moved his face toward the tiny screen window on the side, and then just as quickly jumped back. Mom did the same thing a moment later.

"How did it get in?" she said nervously, biting her lip. "I thought you locked up before we left the parking lot!"

"I guess I forgot the trailer," Dad replied sheepishly. He soft-footed around to the back and peered at the trailer door, one foot back behind him as if ready to run. But then his posture relaxed. "The latch is closed. He's locked in *now*. Door must have shut behind him."

Mom gave him a desperate look.

"He must have been rummaging for food," he went on. That's when Mom turned and noticed me for the first time. She frowned.

"What is it?" I asked. She shook her head sharply and pointed for me to get back inside the camper. Dad was already closing the padlock that hung off the door latch, his hands trembling.

"Get back inside," Mom hissed. But then they turned to each other to confer about what to do, and I took advantage of the moment to step forward on one foot and peer quickly into the dim trailer. *Don't flinch*, I thought.

A huge hulking shape crouched in the darkness, breathing heavily. It was clutching a box of crackers to its chest. It was impossible to mistake for any other sort of creature. Looking like a human crossed with a giant monkey, it had fur sprouting in all directions around big dark eyes, enormous flaring nostrils, and an open mouth full of pointy, sharp white teeth that gleamed in the dark.

The sasquatch heard me breathing, and turned. His eyes met mine. Then, in a flash, he slammed an arm up and out, ripping a hole right in the screen and clawing toward me.

A hand on my collar yanked me backward just in time. At the same moment the creature started howling—such earth-shatteringly loud howls, the trailer shook as Dad guided me forcefully back in through the side door of the Trinidad.

Inside, Oliver sat at the dining table with his hands clasped in front of him, pale, his eyes big. Millie was on the couch behind him, with Sam pressing himself face-first against her belly like a koala.

"It's a—" I began, but Oliver shook his head to stop me.

"We know what it is," he said.

A few minutes later Mom and Dad climbed back into the front seats.

"What are we going to do?" Millie asked, stroking Sam's hair with her fingers.

I was wondering the same thing. This was the kind of creature who could kill parents. It was the terror of the world locked up in our back trailer. I kept looking at Oliver; I couldn't help it.

"Well, the trailer's secure," Mom said. "He can't get

out. We just have to decide what comes next. We can't set him free—too dangerous; he could attack us. Our choice is whether to kill him, or sell him to a zoo or a circus. Surely we could find one along the way."

"How would we kill him?" Millie asked.

Mom frowned, tense. "I'm not sure. I guess we could detach the trailer and leave it somewhere; eventually he'd starve. We could get some sasquatch poison from Walmart and put it in some food . . . slip it through the window?"

We were all silent, contemplating the possibility of death by poisoning or starvation. Only the sasquatch howled and howled. The sound was chilling.

"Oliver, sweetie, would you like to decide what we do?" Mom asked gently. (Her frown softened into something tender and tentative as she looked at him.) "You're the one who has the most reason to hate sasquatches. But I know it's a big responsibility, so you don't have to decide if you don't want to."

We all looked at Oliver, who unfolded his hands and rubbed at his scar. In the movies, I thought, this would be the big revenge scene. A sasquatch life was in his hands!

Oliver seemed to be arguing with himself. I thought

he wasn't going to say anything at all, but then he finally looked up at us.

"I think we should wait," he said. "And sell him when we can."

I couldn't believe my ears. "But your parents!" I blurted out before I could stop myself. Not to mention the danger we all felt.

Oliver looked down at his hands, embarrassed and uncomfortable under the glare of our attention. "It's not what my mom would want," he said. "Anyway, Gracie, I don't think I have the heart to kill him. Do you?"

I was searching for an answer, wondering whether I *did* have the heart and thinking that I probably did, when Sam interrupted. "I think we should call him Daisy," he said.

"But he's a *he*, Sam," Millie said, fighting a sudden nervous smile.

"Actually," Dad said, stepping in through the side door, "he's a she. A nursing mother by the looks of it."

Suddenly the fragile howl from the bushes of the parking lot, the search for food in the trailer, made sense. She must have been trying to feed her babies. (What will her babies do without her, I wonder. Also, do I feel sorry for her? Also, how am I supposed to feel sorry for a creature who'd probably like to eat my face off?)

"I think she's cute," Sam said, swiveling on Millie's lap and looking like he'd made up his mind not to be afraid.

"You haven't even seen her," Millie said.

"I still think we should consider leaving her locked in the trailer somewhere," I suggested.

Mom opened her arms, and Sam crawled from Millie's lap into hers. "You have a big heart, my little Mouse," Mom said.

"So does Oliver," Millie said, which made Oliver blush.

Nobody said *I* have a big heart.

So here we are, driving through Tennessee. We seem to be collecting misfits—first Oliver, and now a bloodthirsty monster called Daisy who could potentially escape and eat us all (even though Dad says that's not going to happen). Out of the frying pan, into the fryer, hardy-har.

Sam just climbed into my bunk and let out a huge fart and then disappeared. Boys are a species all to themselves. Closing this journal and going to make a bomb shelter out of my covers. Good night.

October 31st

I think Cliffden is an October town, though I said this to Millie last night and she looked at me like I might infect her with a rare and deadly form of insanity. Still, our town was at its best when the leaves turned colors and the orange glow of jack-o'-lanterns made beacons along the porches so that you could find your way home by candlelight on Halloween. All those nights I spent trick-or-treating, I always thought that it would go on once a year, every year, forever. Isn't it weird how things seem endless until they suddenly end?

We're on day twenty-four of our journey (it feels so much longer than that!), somewhere in Arkansas, according to Sam the Mouse. Or, in his words, "We're close to the squiggly line." The smiling man, a.k.a. the evil clown, a.k.a. the black hole, is following steadily behind us, up among the other clouds but always distinct—not getting too close, but also never far.

Sam's not feeling well and wants to be on Mom's lap all the time. He's decided in the meanwhile to be our navigator. He'll take a look at the map on Mom's lap and say to Dad, "Turn left at the mountain," or "Turn south at the red dot." He'll then look out the window for the red dot that he sees on the map, knitting his eyebrows in confusion because its not there. He looks so small and frail and cute that sometimes I could devour him more easily than any black hole ever could.

It's not easy to sleep knowing the Cloud's behind us, but now it's especially hard with a sasquatch attached to our camper. I think the first few nights we had Daisy, we all lay awake most of the night, ears pricked, envisioning her escaping and tearing off the doors and bursting in on us in our beds. But Mom and Dad assure us she's safely contained. And ever since the first couple of days, when she howled and thrashed and screamed every time we stopped and started the RV, she's quieted down. I wonder if maybe she's given up hope.

For some reason Oliver's insisted on being the one who gives her food and water. He's been buying her bags of beef jerky and taquitos and bottles of water at 7-Eleven (he must have had some money saved up), stuffing them through the slatted window of the trailer gingerly and then jerking away quickly. Every time I think I know him a little better, he becomes a mystery to me again—like how he's the most afraid of Daisy but also the bravest about taking care of her.

There are other things to worry about now too, the farther west we get. We've been driving through old rail tunnels that Dad says are haunted by the ghosts of miners: "Men who died blowing through rock to make room for the trains that never came," he says. The tunnels are poorly lit by a few flickering electric lights (the farther west we go, the spottier electrical service is), and I hold my breath through each one, because I've decided it's a lucky thing to do. So far we've only seen one lonely soul holding up a lamp and waving to us sadly as we passed.

Mom says challenges bring families together, but so far it's been exactly the opposite. Millie has been mostly in her bunk with her blanket-curtain drawn. (Sam is her "assistant," and whenever he sees a boy her age in another car, he gives her the signal—a triple knock on her bunk frame—at which point she refreshes her makeup and emerges to flirt out the window.) Dad is as far away as ever, barely talking during the day. (He's been in a medium-level swamp ever since we left West Virginia.) Even Sam, since he's not feeling well, has been in a bad mood, and sometimes takes it out on Jim the bear by stuffing him in the cupboard and telling him he's grounded. I can't say I'm in the best mood myself, and I've already made several trips up to the front today to complain to Mom about various things that annoy me, such as the new freckle on my right hand and my hair getting in my eyes.

Oliver and Mom are the real peacekeepers, and neither of them ever seems to be cranky. Mom goes out of her way to check on all of us, especially Oliver (she's always asking him if he needs anything) and Oliver tries to get me out of my moods by making decorations for my bunk: paper chains made from newspaper, spinning mobiles made of paper clips he found in the glove box. He never makes anything for Millie, and that makes me happy.

Yesterday morning Sam found a daisy in a patch of grass while we were stopped at a gas station. He asked Oliver if he could climb on his back, and then asked him to piggy-back him close to the trailer. He waved it in front of the window, though Oliver kept him at a safe distance. "This is a daisy and so are you," Sam said loudly into the trailer, then sniffled and coughed. Inside, Daisy was silent. I was sure at any moment she'd lunge at the window and scare Sam out of his wits.

"She can't understand you, buddy," Oliver said.

"Yes she can," Sam insisted. He waved the daisy back and forth, then nodded and smiled at the trailer, raising his eyebrows for extra effect. "Gracie says you look like Chewbacca, but that's not so bad." He turned to me. "We should get her a mirror so she knows what she looks like." (Oliver gave me a crooked smile—I think he adores Sam almost as much as the rest of us do.)

If Daisy was angered by Sam's loud, insistent presence, she didn't do anything about it; she was silent and still, which was frightening in its own way. Looking through a bunch of travel guides he bought at 7-Eleven, Dad has located a circus up ahead in eastern Arizona, right on our zigzaggy route to LA. We're all relieved to know she'll be out of our hands then.

I've been sneaking Mouse some Pixy Stix that Dad let me buy at our last stop. (With Dad, you wait until he's distracted to ask for things, which is pretty easy.) So right now Sam's not on Mom's lap as usual . . . he's actually jumping up and down on the couch. A few minutes ago he shouted, "There are fireworks behind my eyeballs!" If it were me acting so hyper, I'd get in trouble, but everyone is so happy when Sam is happy that no one wants to rain on his parade.

The rest of us have been talking about our soon-to-be guardian angel.

"I hope he's cute," Millie said.

"I bet he's, like, a commando type," I said.

"Angels aren't into war, dummy," Millie said dismissively.

"Yes they are," I argued. "They got into that war with heaven that made them all leave and come to earth." Everyone knows, from school, that the angels are naturally rebellious. They even rebelled against the gods— that was how they ended up in LA instead of heaven in the first place.

"I bet he loves raisins," said Sam, jumping down from the couch for a moment to weigh in and wipe his sniffly nose with his sleeve before resuming his sugar-fueled rampage.

Personally, I picture our angel as glowing like the sun, magnificently strong, bright, and wise. I also picture him (or her) paying special attention to me—recognizing how different I am from everyone else in my family, how generally misunderstood I am, and how much patience I must have to put up with them as much as I do.

"No one knows geography better than angels," Dad piped up from the front. We hadn't even known he was listening. Looking up at us in the rearview mirror, noticing his suddenly rapt audience, he touched the side of his glasses and went on.

"Though they won't share the secrets of the edges of the earth—it's against their code. Of course, coming from another dimension, they may know something about superstrings, too."

"What are superstrings?" Oliver asked. Millie groaned, then mouthed, *Please, no,* at him. But it was too late.

"Superstrings are the things that tell us that it's possible there are other dimensions out there. Basically, we've discovered that tiny invisible superstrings exist everywhere, woven throughout the fabric of space and the universe, but that they wiggle and disappear, and we don't know where they go. They have to go somewhere, so scientists think they go to other dimensions. They've worked out the math and they think there are eleven dimensions total. It's called quantum physics."

"Don't get him started talking about count 'em physics." Sam sighed sadly, crashing from his sugar high and laying himself down on the couch, staring up at the ceiling.

"Quantum physics means that in this world," Dad went on, "this is a Winnebago, but in another it could be an elephant. It means the universe is full of endless possibilities."

"In another dimension, maybe there's another Mouse," I said to Mouse to cheer him up, "and that version of Mouse doesn't like Pixy Stix."

"Maybe in that world there's a you who never gets grounded," Millie said to me.

"Maybe there's a world where you're not stuck up," I replied.

Oliver was leaning toward my dad with interest, but Dad just started muttering to himself about "M theory" and something called "angelic torque," looking up at the sky. La La Land Lockwood in action.

Other than the haunted railroad tunnels, Arkansas is a green, friendly-looking place. We've been passing scattered small towns, gentle creeks, pretty white houses with porches, small farms, and small fields of corn. Of course, the towns have become fewer and farther between as the miles have stretched on, and it's clear that we're headed into more rugged territory. Mom says we can only hope the roads stay drivable. (They've started to get bumpy and potholed.) The people here, exposed as they are to the open sky, have erected tall metal deflectors, like second roofs over their houses, to deflect dragonfire, though you can see that dragon crossings have burned some of the cornfields badly.

We've seen something else: other families, in old Volkswagen buses and Winnebagos like ours, heading west just like us.

Yesterday I went into a Circle K to buy a postcard for Arin Roland. My mom gathered some bananas and jars of peanut butter and jelly while I picked out a card bearing a photo of a wampus cat, which is apparently the state animal. I was just leaning on the counter, composing a short note that would make it sound like I was having the time of my life and that I felt sorry for Arin having to stay in Cliffden, when I noticed a family in a station wagon out in the parking lot giving odd looks to our trailer. (Daisy has been whining softly all day today, and I'm sure they're wondering what wild beast we've got in there.) I turned to my mom.

"Do you think their families are being chased by Clouds too?" I asked.

Mom shook her head. "Lots of families are just moving farther inland, even farther west, despite the dangers. Too many mermaids along the shores of the coastal towns, too many dragons burning down houses. They're adjusting to the wilder world."

"Do you think any of them are looking for the Extraordinary World?"

Mom laid her items on the counter. "Probably not. Not everyone's as brave as your dad."

"Dad's scared of spiders," I said. But then I wished I could take it back. Ever since Grandma's, I've been trying to be nicer in my mind when I think about him. Maybe he really is as brave and smart as Mom has always said.

Millie has just made a rare appearance in my bunk to borrow one of my pens. I told her I've been thinking about how we should be nicer to Dad, but she rolled her eyes.

"He barely even talks to us. Especially when he's in one of his moods. It's like he can always find a way to make everything feel worse." Her beautiful brown eyes (I can't deny, Millie's about ten times more beautiful than I'll ever be) were all big and solemn.

She has a point. Sometimes I'll be in a perfectly good and hopeful mood, and then I'll look at my dad bent over the steering wheel, wearing what Millie calls his classic Theodore Lockwood Look of Doom: jaw set tight, fingers scratching at his stubble, mouth in a distracted frown—and it's like letting the air out of a balloon inside me. Millie says I'm a moody person just like him, but I think that's different because I'm not a dad and dads should be better than that.

Since we were having this heart to heart, I decided to ask Millie something I'd been wondering ever since Oliver and I talked about his family and how he wants to forget them.

"Millie, what do you want most in the world? I mean, besides Sam being okay?"

Millie thought for a moment. She actually seemed happy I'd asked.

"I really want to meet my first love," she said, "and have a first kiss."

I was sorry I'd asked.

"Bubble head," I muttered.

Millie shoved me out of my bunk, and the peace was broken.

In the back Daisy roared from her trailer.

November 7th

I'm sitting on a railroad track beside the Great Western Road, or what's left of it, in my purple plaid jacket that Mom got me last year at Macy's. (It's a bit tight on me, but I guess a new coat isn't on the horizon any time soon.) The wind is blowing the chilly fall air through my hair, and Mom is changing a tire. The Cloud is sitting serenely in the clear, darkening sky about a mile back. Millie's gone for a walk and Oliver is standing at Daisy's trailer with an armful of doughnuts. Dad is working out some equations in the dirt with a stick. The road is torn up for miles from here forward.

Our route—at least the paved part of it—has come to an end.

It's just dusk, and lights are coming on across the

plains . . . but not many. We've been driving on a disintegrating road for days—the potholes getting so numer-
ous that for the past several miles the pavement has
been more holes than road, and now it's finally turned
into a dirt track. This is our second flat tire in three
days, though Dad says it's not just the potholes to blame
but the poltergeists that haunt the Goodyear factories
and put tiny holes in the rubber.

We're still not the only people trying to get across the
Western Road, and at least it's been drivable. There are
even a few renegade gas stations along the way, usually
just people setting up shop under tarps and selling big
drums of fuel, though every once in a while we still come
across a proper building. Sometimes we even see a car
headed in the other direction—and we'll stop to make
conversation with each other—but so far we haven't
talked to anyone who's come all the way from California.

"Dad?" I asked a few minutes ago, surveying the
warped, curled track on which I'm perched, and making
him look up from his math. "Why are there so many
railroad tracks when there are no trains?"

Dad laid his stick on his lap and looked across the
plains.

"Back in the late 1800s," he said, "there was a big push

to 'conquer' the west by spreading the railroad from New York to California."

I tried to picture it—a "tamed" west, a railroad that stretches from New York all the way to the Pacific Ocean. Of course, they'd talked about it in school, but I'd barely paid attention.

"Several big barons—men like Cornelius Vanderbilt, men who wore top hats and had lots of money—invested in the project. Laborers worked day and night to build the tracks." He paused as my mom dropped her wrench; he went over and picked it up for her, then walked back and sat down.

"They made it, pretty much uninterrupted, all the way to the Rockies, but that's when the yeti arrived." The yeti—a bigger version of the sasquatch—live in caves in the snowy, remote tips of the Rocky Mountains, and also up in Canada and the Himalayas, but I guess sometimes they come to the lowlands, too. "They began to tear up the tracks as fast as men could lay them down. You'd go to sleep with ten miles of new track laid behind you. When you woke up, it had been ripped up, thrown into the woods, or just taken away altogether. There were also trolls, who lurked under the bridges and pulled down passing trains when people did manage to run them."

He put his hand on the mangled track beneath us. The metal was twisted like taffy. It made me think of Daisy and how easily she could do that to any of us, but for now her trailer was quiet. "People hunted the yeti, even sent the army after them. But they were too many and too powerful and there was too much wilderness for them to hide in. The wild won out. Some people made it to LA, and some brave families settled there, but most had to turn around and come home. And the west . . . ," my dad said, "stayed unreachable for most people."

"Too bad," I breathed. My mind was full of trains racing across great expanses under the sky, how exciting that would be compared to meandering and doubling back along this slow road west.

Dad rolled his pencil around in his fingers in silence, but Mom suddenly chimed in, turning to us with the wrench in her hands. "I wouldn't say that. You never know which way things turn out is for the best." She sounded a little like Grandma. "Maybe it's nicer that the world moves at a slower pace than it would have with all those fast trains. Maybe it's nicer that the west stayed the way it was."

Dad raised his eyebrows, pleased. "Your mom is an optimist."

"There's nothing foolish about optimism," Mom said,

tucking her ponytail into the back of her sweater to get it out of the way, then turning back to her work.

It made me think of something Mr. Morrigan back at Upper Maine Academy said about the industrial revolution. He said that if it weren't for the monsters tearing everything apart and slowing down the rise of all the machinery, we'd live in a totally different world. He said that the industrial revolution, which promised so much change and order in the world, got sort of cut in half—in the cities it thrived, but in most places it didn't. "Take Mitsubishi for example," he said.

Mitsubishi is a Japanese company, founded in the late 1800s to build ships. As the company grew, they started making steel and glass, too. Factories cropped up in Tokyo and London and New York, but it wasn't long before these were invaded by poltergeists, and most of the plants had to be shut down in the end. Now there's only the factory in Tokyo, and it takes forever for them to ship their products all over the world.

Actually I'm surprised I even remember Mr. Morrigan talking about it since I spent most of that class nibbling on paper to see what it would do to me, and making a list of people who annoy me. (Teachers always write on my report card that I'm very verbal and smart, but lazy, and that I spend too much time goofing off. Maybe I *am* a bit smart, but since I can't see into anyone else's brain for a comparison, I really can't say for sure.)

Anyway, back to sitting on the tracks, watching my mom work. My dad was smiling at her back—one of his rare smiles, which are so nice because they look like glaciers melting.

When I asked my mom why she fell in love with my dad (when she joked that he just got really lucky), she also said something I didn't understand at the time: "His smiles were so rare. He reminded me of Mr. Darcy." Apparently Mr. Darcy is a book character who's rich but always in a bad mood, which Millie says is appealing to adult women.

Finally, Dad brushed the road dust from his jeans and stood up, heading over to help Mom finish up.

Oliver was still standing beside the trailer, and I walked up to him. I realized now why he was holding the box of doughnuts: He was gingerly, carefully feeding them to Daisy through the window, and also humming to her. She had her face pressed up against the opening, tilting her head this way and that as he hummed. Her sharp teeth flashed as she chewed, and her black eyes still gave me the creeps, but for the moment she was surprisingly calm and docile.

Oliver looked up at me as I approached, his hair sticking straight up. I wonder in what alternative universe Oliver's hair ever lies down flat. "I've been teaching her 'Hotel California,'" he said. "It was my dad's favorite. She can almost hum it, but it sounds pretty bad."

We've noticed a few things about Daisy over the past few days. She likes music, sugar, and meat. She is especially curious about Oliver and always gets quiet and watchful when he's near, staring at him through the window. Most of the time she's either completely silent, or whimpering forlornly, but every once in a while we'll just be sitting calmly, almost forgetting about her, and she'll let out an ear shattering roar that almost knocks us out of our seats and reminds us of what she really is, and how she'd eat any one of us if she ever got out. The other day at a gas station a dog wandered past, and she nearly knocked the trailer over trying to get out and grab it, thrusting her arm out the window and ripping off what was left of the screen.

"I feel bad for taking her away from her babies," Oliver said as I stood next to him and took one of the doughnuts for myself. I didn't point out the obvious, that sasquatches had taken his parents away from *him*.

But Oliver seemed to read my mind. "I'm not trying to pretend Daisy isn't a vicious creature. It's not that I'm not angry. It's just . . ." He touched the faded scar on his cheek gently. "I don't want everything my mom taught me to disappear. Remember I told you what she said about blaming animals for their natures? She used to say there's no place in the wilderness for holding a grudge. She said you have to make peace with the danger in the world . . . that it's the circle of life and all that."

I glanced up at the Cloud, pretty far behind us today, the most vicious creature I could think of (even though it isn't really a creature at all), and then said, "I couldn't do that. I'm not very peaceful."

Oliver laughed, his green eyes getting all squinty. "No. You're kind of fiery." He pushed the last doughnut into the window, and then backed up and looked at me, turning serious again. "I just want to be able to accept the bad things, and see the good things too. Daisy isn't all bad."

We both looked up at the window. Daisy gazed out at us with her head tilted sideways and a doughnut sticking halfway out of her mouth, making little grunts of pleasure. Her eyes were penetratingly dark, like big black marbles.

"Anyway," Oliver went on, "I think we're all doing our best. Even the monsters."

I don't think, upon further reflection, that Oliver wants to forget his parents as much as he thinks he does.

Once all the doughnuts were gone, Daisy ducked back out of sight and started whimpering softly. It's as if even when she's content, she's sad, too. I know this is a weird thing to write, but I can't help thinking that in a way, she and Oliver are a little alike—both sad, both missing their families, both a little wild inside, and faraway even though they're right here. I think Daisy is like Oliver's heart in animal form.

The Trinidad has roared to life and we've all climbed in. I'm at the table by the window, and we want to make it another twenty miles on this dirt road before we stop for the night, even though it's already dark.

It's helpful that the land has gotten flat. I wish there were a McDonald's or shops along the way, but instead the night's growing inky around us and you can go hours without seeing any lights. So many stars are popping out above us it seems you could almost dip your fingers up there and come out with a handful of diamonds.

November 11th

Mom says we're in "the heart of the plains."

The miles seem endless these days. The crickets are so loud—even during the day—and the grasshoppers twirl up and down out of the fields and all over the place as we pass. The smell of dry grass has filled the Winnebago. We've all been reading from Mom's library, and I've been keeping myself occupied by expanding my good-luck-charm wall from my bunk to all over the camper: taping up feathers and stones (and even one tiny bird's nest) I've found at stops along the side of the road.

We're a happy group this afternoon, believe it or not. Even Millie has abandoned her fortress for our company. I think we've all discovered that it's actually kind of nice to just be quiet and watch the scenery go by.

Every hour it seems there are more rocks littering our path. It's getting harder and harder to determine which way is the actual road and which is just flat land or dry riverbeds, and yesterday we had to swerve around a tree growing right in the middle of our path. The Trinidad is covered in a thick layer of dust, and we're missing three hubcaps because at night when we sleep, animals come out of the fields and sparse woods and steal whatever's not tightly bolted down.

Still, it's hard to ignore the beauty outside our windows. It feels like the landscape in my brain has grown, like I am bigger inside. There used to be only blank space in my mind beyond Cliffden . . . some ideas of other places I'd heard of . . . but now there's the Crow's Nest and the Smokies and Arkansas and the fields around us right now that seem to go on forever.

It helps that I've been trusting my dad more than I used to. I've started to feel like he's really looking out for us. Maybe he's even like that father dragon who broke my arm, who was looking after his baby.

Other than that there isn't much to say these days. I think I'm running out of material, and I don't think that's supposed to happen with writers. So I wonder if I'll ever be a real writer at all.

November 16th

BIG TEX'S CIRCUS AND MONSTER BAZAAR.

We sat parked in a dusty lot, looking at the ram-shackle, torn circus tent that stood at the side of the dirt road. We'd been seeing signs for Big Tex's for the past several miles, but now that we were here it wasn't at all what I'd expected. The billboards had shown a gleaming red-and-white big top surrounded by crowds and full of smiling animals peeking out through the front flaps. This place looked more like a flea market on its last legs.

"I have some business advice for Big Tex," Mom said. "He needs to go where there's some actual business."

"This place is a dump," Millie put in.

Sam pressed his hands against the window and peered

out for a moment, then crawled back into Millie's bunk, and Oliver—sitting at the dining table and looking up from one of my dad's books on meteorology—somehow managed to get *quieter*, if that's possible.

A sign at the entrance of the tent said CLOSED, but Mom and Dad unhooked their seat belts and got out of the RV. Curiosity overcoming our disappointment, Oliver, Millie, and I followed (Sam went back to sleep). We crossed the parking lot in a scraggly line, and Mom lifted one dirty, frayed corner of the tent entrance and walked inside. Before he went in behind her, Oliver threw a look back in the direction of Daisy's trailer, which was silent. I don't know if it was because she was sleeping, or because she sensed what we had in store for her.

The first thing that struck me was the stench: It smelled as if hundreds of animals had all been pooping in one place—and then I realized, that was exactly what it was. A man in a cowboy hat was shoveling manure at the far side of the tent and raking it over with dirt. We all covered our noses except Mom and Dad. I guess they were trying to be polite.

"Hello?" Mom called. "We're looking for Big . . . Tex?" The cowboy didn't even look in our direction, he just laid his shovel against a post and disappeared under a flap of the tent.

Peering around, we walked along a row of cages that lined the outer ring. There were lions, monkeys, a gorilla, several sasquatches crouched in low metal pens staring at us with dull black eyes, a tiny aquarium of goldfish, and one small, very sad-looking pygmy unicorn lying with her legs curled underneath her on some dirty hay. I'd never seen a unicorn in person, and I'd always wanted to, but this one only made me feel heavy and sad: Her white fur was matted and covered in dirt, and she only glanced at us listlessly for a second before going back to sleep.

"Is she sick?" I asked. But no one answered me. Oliver held to the edge of the cage for a moment as if he didn't want to let it go.

"This isn't right," he said.

There was a collection of dinosaur bones lying on a table near the center of the tent. A sign said you could pay two extra dollars to touch them, then went on to say that dinosaurs lived sixty-five million years ago and that they were distant cousins of dragons, and that the pterodactyl was basically a half-dinosaur, half-dragon hybrid. Millie reached out to touch a pterodactyl femur, and I reached forward too, but Mom pulled us back—scared, no doubt, of having to shell out four dollars.

"Big Tex?" she called out.

We'd made the complete circle and come to a standstill next to one of the pillars that held up the tent. "Hello?" Millie called from behind the shirt hem she was holding up to her nose to block the smell.

Suddenly, the pillar moved. We all leaped at the same moment. The whole tent fluttered and deflated slightly as the pillar bent and lowered, and we realized that it wasn't a pillar at all, but a leg wearing brown pants.

An enormous figure was, in less than a moment, kneeling beside us, staring at us with eyes as big as our TV set back home.

"Giant," I whispered.

"Thanks, that's helpful," Millie replied.

A note on giants from fifth-grade social studies: The first giant was confirmed to exist by a gold dynamiter in California in 1853, who captured it with one of the early cameras. (People had been spotting them for hundreds of years, but there'd never been any proof until then.) They live mostly in the west, and aren't particularly fond of regular-size people, though occasionally they come to towns and cities looking for work (usually in construc-tion, for obvious reasons). Several giants have gotten rich by owning the rights to some gold mines in California and Nevada, and the really rich ones live in gigantic and remote mansions they've built for themselves.

As you can imagine, we were surprised to see a giant running a circus in Arizona.

"Excuse me, sir?" Mom said. "Big Tex?"

The giant glared at us, frowning. Blond scraggly hair fell to either side of its ears, though it was bald on top. Its lips were like two big pink rafts. Its breath smelled like the rest of the circus.

"Or, um, I mean," Mom fumbled, "miss? We have a . . . sasquatch . . . we'd like to sell."

Suddenly there was a shuffling noise behind us, and loud, hearty laughter.

"I'm over here."

A man emerged through a slit in the tent walls, smil-ing as he approached us. He had a brown beard and a red-and-white vest stained with dirt. "I'm Big Tex. This is just one of my exhibits. Did she scare you?"

We all nodded. We hadn't noticed until then that the giant was chained to a post in the ground.

"We have a sasquatch to sell. . . ." My mom faltered. "We saw you were closed but . . ."

Big Tex looked as if he were sizing us up, his big friendly smile not reaching his eyes. "We travel a fair amount. But this is our home base. We're just making some repairs at the moment." He glanced over at his collection of sasquatches—still staring out of their cages at us. "Well, I'm pretty full up, but let's see him."

We all walked outside into the sun and to the trailer. Big Tex peered in at Daisy, then pulled back and squinted at us, still wearing the same broad, fake smile.

"I don't really need another sasquatch, and I can't pay much. But it looks like he's in good condition. People like to be a little frightened, and so many of mine have lost their spark. I'll take him off your hands for, say . . . two hundred dollars."

Millie let out a small whimper of delight. And I have to admit, the idea of two hundred dollars sounded like enough money to save us from having to sell our hair (since we're not allowed to touch Grandma's money), which excited me more than I would have thought. But it also made me feel a little sick, like someone had dropped pebbles down my throat. I was consciously avoiding glancing at Oliver, but suddenly he spoke and we all turned to look at him.

"It's a she," he said. He was clutching his fists together and staring at his feet.

Big Tex shrugged carelessly. "Makes no difference to me. People will pay to see either."

We all stood quietly in awkward silence.

"Make it two twenty-five," my mom finally said. She was tugging at her ponytail, which she only does when she's agitated.

Big Tex made a slight bow, and he and Mom shook on it. "I'll be right back with cash."

We watched his figure retreat into the tent. Behind us, as if she knew what was happening—even though that was impossible—Daisy began to whimper.

"She's a dangerous beast," my dad said to no one in particular. "We can't keep her with us. And we need the money." But his eyes, behind his glasses, were guilty.

Meanwhile Mom clasped and unclasped her hands, tugging at her turquoise earrings.

"*Big Tex* is the beast," Oliver said.

"I couldn't have said it better myself," Mom said.

We all stood looking at each other—or rather, barely looking at each other. The silence stretched around us and changed into something embarrassing.

"Let's go before he comes back," Dad suddenly said.

"Yes!" Mom gasped in relief.

We must have all been thinking it, because without another word we were all hurrying toward the Trinidad as if our lives depended on it, and Mom threw open the side door for us to pile inside.

Big Tex was just emerging from the tent as Dad climbed into the driver's seat and turned the key in the ignition. The Trinidad rattled to life. He slammed on the gas and we launched forward.

I don't know why it felt like such an escape—Big Tex didn't chase us; he just stood there waving a wad of bills in the air behind us. Maybe it was something inside ourselves we were escaping. All I know is that I felt giddy as we picked up speed on the craggy, bumpy road, the circus tent shrinking in the distance behind us. Everyone was beaming in relief, even Millie. And in the passenger seat, Dad let out a triumphant laugh.

"Did you see his face?" Mom said happily.

"Dad," Millie said, punching Dad on the shoulder and making him wince, "I didn't know you had it in you." She raised her eyebrows at me, as if to say some things could still surprise her. It was like, for a moment, we were all a team.

Oliver sat on the couch, looking out the window. I knew without a doubt he was thinking of all the animals we'd left behind.

"If I ever make it back this way, I'm setting them all free," he said.

"But we'll never be here again, Oliver," I replied. "We're going to the Extraordinary World, and we're never coming back."

Oliver kept his gaze behind us.

As relieved as I was, I couldn't help thinking of what he'd said about Big Tex. I wondered about the word "beast." I wondered if sometimes, the way everything looks—who's the beast and who isn't—depends on where you're standing.

Well, now I'm sitting on the fold-out table for a change of perspective, and we're not sure where we are. It seems that, apparently, when Dad pulled triumphantly out of the circus parking lot, he pulled triumphantly onto something that was not really the road.

The land is flat and dry, and tumbleweeds occasionally blow by us when there's a strong wind. Every once in a while it looks like *maybe* we're on the right track—but then the path seems to disappear, and we have to veer to avoid missing a boulder or a shrub, or we drive right over a little gulch with a thud.

Night is falling, and Mom's insisting Dad will have to stop soon so we can look at the map and figure things out and try again in the morning.

I wonder what we'll do if we end up stranded out here in the desert. I have to disagree with my mom that the west might be better without the railroads. What I wouldn't give for a fast train headed in the right direction.

Daisy, at least, seems to be the only one who's happy. She's been humming "Hotel California" loudly from the trailer all afternoon.

November 18th
Morning

Something happened last night that was so strange I almost think I imagined it.

Late in the night, probably around two or three, I got up to go to the bathroom. Climbing down from my bunk, I noticed that the side door was slightly open, even though Mom and Dad are always very careful about locking up. I was just leaning forward to pull it shut when I saw a figure outside in the dark about fifty yards away. I could tell by her silhouette that it was Millie.

The moon was shining down on her, her dark hair was glinting in the dim light, and she was shivering in her thin white pajamas. But the thing that shocked me—and sent chills down to the soles of my feet—was that beside her, very close to the ground, was the Cloud.

She seemed to be whispering to it, her arms across her chest like she was nervous. A moment later the Cloud began to drift back up into the sky, slowly, like a feather falling in the wrong direction, and Millie turned back toward the Trinidad.

Something told me that I wasn't supposed to see what I'd just seen, so I quickly backed out of sight, climbed into my bunk, and pulled the sheet curtain closed just as I heard her silently slip in through the door and pull it shut with a soft click.

She stood still for a moment, as if listening for something, and then tiptoed to her own bunk and crawled inside.

For a few minutes I lay with my heart thudding against my ribs, listening to see if she stayed in bed. I was sure I wouldn't be able to go back to sleep, but it seemed like the moment I closed my eyes I was out. The next time I opened them it was morning and I could smell that Mom was making coffee at the little kitchenette.

When I poked my head out, Millie was sitting at the table drinking orange juice and talking to Oliver about their favorite movies, as if nothing had happened at all.

I ducked back in here because I wanted to write it down right away, in case the further away I get from it, the more it starts to seem I really dreamed it after all.

November 20th

It's strange—I've never felt quiet in my life, but ever since Big Tex's Circus I've started to feel still inside. Mom once said, back in Cliffden, that I've got a "circus soul"— she says I'm full of elephants standing on their back feet, clowns doing flips, girls on high wires, and an extremely loud circus caller. But right now it feels like there's maybe only one pensive clown counting tickets by the front door.

I can't stop thinking about Millie and the Cloud. For one thing, I can't figure out what she was doing, and for another, I'm shocked by her courage in getting so close. I've always been braver than her. For instance, one time we found some poison ivy in the yard and got into an argument about who was the least allergic to it. To prove that I was barely allergic at all, I rubbed some all over my hands—but Millie looked horrified and stayed as far away from me as possible for the rest of the day. I did end up in misery when the rash spread all over my palms and between my fingers (apparently I *am* just as allergic as anyone else) but the point is that I was brave and Millie wasn't, and it's like that with everything.

At school when she was younger, boys liked to chase Millie with frogs, and she would always scream and run away (as if there's anything scary about frogs). She flushes toilets with her foot. She's always worried that something she owns is out of style, and keeps an eye on other girls in her class to make sure she's got her clothes and her hair just right. Mom says I was "born with an inner compass" while Millie will have to "work a little harder to find hers." She says instead of tormenting Millie, I should try to be compassionate. As if Millie's ever been compassionate toward *me*.

Anyway, I guess that's all just a long way of saying that I can't understand *how* Millie was brave enough to talk to the Cloud, much less why. I'd guess that maybe she was offering to trade her own life for Sam's, but first of all, that wouldn't be very Millie-like, and second, I know that's not how Clouds work. Just like

Grandma said, they pick *one* person, and that's it.

The way I see it, there are three possibilities:

1. She was offering the Cloud her beautiful hair in return for Sam's life, as inspired by *Little Women*.

2. She was trying to use all her charm to talk it into leaving us alone. (I doubt her skills are effective against death, but Millie's just conceited enough to think it could work.)

3. She was trying to trick it and set it off course somehow. Millie can be very wily when she wants to be. She's not half as much of a bubble head as she likes to pretend.

Oliver just interrupted my thoughts. He knocked on the frame of my bunk, and when I opened the curtain, he was smiling at me and looking a little mischievous (which makes me wonder how mischievous he was before I met him and before he got sad).

"I did something I shouldn't have," he admitted. "Back at the circus."

"What?"

He slid something into my hand, and I studied it. It was a small bone.

"It's from Big Tex's. It's a tiny bone from a pterodactyl's left wing. I thought it could be for your good luck wall."

"You just . . . *took* it?" I asked. He flushed bright red, but held my gaze and nodded.

"I wouldn't have if Big Tex wasn't so horrible."

I nodded. "I know." Still, I worry I've been a bad influence on him. Oliver is so good and I . . . well . . . I try to be good. "Thanks, Oliver. I love it."

I took the bone and taped it to my wall, and now I'm sitting here admiring it and trying to imagine dinosaurs being real. Sixty-five million years ago feels so far away that it seems almost impossible for that time to have existed at all. I've been trying to make the number squeeze into my brain like an accordion, but so far I haven't been able to do it.

Mom has been reading to us from a history book called *Trivia of the Twentieth Century* (which she found on a paperback rack at a gas station miles and miles back), about how there was almost a World War in 1914, but thanks to poltergeists in the factories (like the Mitsubishi factory, for example) nobody could make enough ships. I think she's trying to keep us distracted, because Sam still isn't feeling well and it's got us all a little down today. He's been tucked away in Mom and Dad's room all day, and Mom has been giving him more of his pills, but when I ask what they are, she changes the subject or says something like, "Just something to help him feel better."

Sam's like our sunshine—when he's down, the rest of us wilt. It's always been that way, but now with the Cloud always somewhere in sight behind us (today it's drifting low, as if it's tired or thirsty or bored), it's much worse. It doesn't help that we're still lost and that the Trinidad is only barely limping along. All morning we've been picking our way west*ish*, along what might or might not be a road, and there's been no one to ask for directions.

Deeper and deeper we've gone into the center of nowhere, and we've all grown more silent, as if the world's swallowed us. Everything is old here. Mom says it looks like "the dry heart of the earth." These are sun lands we've crossed into—there are no clouds except the one that pursues us, though occasionally we can see tiny storms form and disappear far off in the distance, across vast expanses of dry grass. At midday the sun's so bright I can feel it leaking into the camper, and the air has gotten warmer. Mom's flipped the map over and over in her hands for hours to try to find our way back to the main road, but at this point it's useless.

We've been seeing the fires of settlements in the far-off trees. Dad says they belong to people who've been all over the country since long before my great-great-great-grandma emigrated from Poland, and who prefer living a traditional life out here to being near the cities.

"We're only passing through because they let us," Dad says. I can understand how a junky old Winnebago might break the quiet and beauty of this place, so I think it's pretty nice of them.

Here's one funny thing: Mom is following Oliver around the Trinidad with her comb right now. If he isn't careful, she'll be trying to dress him next.

ABOUT SIX HOURS LATER:

Something unforgettable has happened to us!

It was getting dark, almost night. Millie and I were sitting side by side after I wrote that last entry, being civil for once. (She's been unusually gentle lately, and kind of thoughtful—looking out the windows a lot. She must be as mesmerized by the views as I am.) Sam had poked his head out from the back, wrapped in his blanket, which I knitted for him in arts and crafts last year (and which is full of holes), and we were all listening to Oliver. He was telling us about this time his mom was in charge of the Go Fish booth at their local carnival. Apparently, she thought fishing was a cruel sport, so she changed Go Fish to Catch the Clover.

"She spent all night," Oliver said, fighting back his laughter, "making paper four-leaf clovers with little paper clips attached at the end. Everyone was so confused when they had to catch four-leaf clovers with fishing poles."

I was laughing so hard (even Mom, squeezed in beside me at the table, was chuckling) and Oliver seemed so happy (talking about the mom he said he wants to forget), when the Winnebago suddenly screeched to a halt and we all went thumping forward, falling out of our seats.

"Kids!" my Dad hissed, and looked back at us with a hand to his lips to silence us.

My first thought was the Cloud. I looked up through the windows into the falling dusk, immediately sickened, my heart pounding. But the sky—a darkening purple—was empty for the moment. Then a movement drew my eye downward. The space surrounding our RV was moving like a wave, full of thousands of enormous shadows. They were all around us, moving in unison, engulfing us so that nothing—the road, the desert beyond—was visible but them. I couldn't speak. I couldn't even breathe.

"Buffalo," my dad whispered.

There had to be thousands of them, parting like a river as they moved slowly around the Trinidad. They walked smoothly and rapidly, but they moved like one creature. Their breath puffed out in the cold air.

We could hear the thud of their hoofbeats, muffled by the glass windows. "Just be still," my mom whispered. "Don't startle them." She didn't have to say it; we were frozen in place. Even Daisy was completely silent behind us.

At school I've heard about the great buffalo herds of the west. But I never imagined I'd see them for myself. I wondered how many hooves it would take to flatten a Winnebago and the people inside it. Hundreds?

"They're beautiful," Millie breathed.

It took almost an hour for them all to pass by us, all of us sitting silently, left breathless by the sight.

When the last few had straggled past, and we could see the back of the herd trailing off—shaggy tails and enormous rumps getting smaller and smaller in the distance, and dust rising behind them above the grass—Dad started the ignition. But none of us has spoken since.

November? 24th?

What day of the week is it? My mind is in a haze.

I want to tell you where I'm sitting, but I've decided that first I'll need to tell you how I got here. I'll start with when we first knew for sure we'd veered too far off course to recover.

"We're still on the right track," Dad said over his shoulder that morning. "We're just a little sideways." My mom glanced back at us from the driver's seat, her amber hoop earrings jangling, and I could tell just by her eyes that things were worse than she wanted us to know. Plus we can always tell when Dad's lying; he sounds extra cheerful.

I was sitting in my bunk, facing front with the curtain drawn open and looking out the opposite window. Tiny, scraggly trees occasionally lined our path, their limbs struggling up out of the red dirt, and a low, thin fog was drifting in patches across the ground.

"This feels very wrong," Mom said as we veered around a rocky outcropping, and the road rose upward, getting bumpier. "Where's that fog coming from? Teddy, we need to turn back, retrace our steps. It's foolish to keep pushing on in this direction."

"We'll never make it back to a gas station," Dad said, still trying to sound cheerful, but less so.

Everyone grew silent and tense as we drove on. The road was dust. It was not a road at all.

"I think . . . ," Dad began, turning to his left to address my mom, when three things happened at once. The camper shuddered like a train jumping its track, the brakes screeched as Mom jarred forward and slammed down on the pedal, and we all went flying out of our seats.

We were very still for a moment. And then Mom said quietly, "Everyone stand very slowly." She swallowed deeply and looked out through the windshield at something we couldn't see. There was something strange about the feeling of the RV, and then I realized what it was. We were *tilting*.

"We're going to move out the back, one at a time," she said. "We need to do it very gently but very quickly."

Dad, who'd been completely silent and still beside her, looked over at her. "After you," he said.

As Mom turned toward us, I could see the blood had drained from her cheeks, and her eyes were terrified. She put one foot in front of the other carefully until she reached Millie, and then gestured for her to go on in front. Sam followed, Mom grabbing his hand. I tucked this diary under my arm before I went slowly, gingerly behind them, so frightened my legs felt tingly and numb—though I didn't know exactly what I was frightened *of*. I knew that if we didn't move carefully, something terrible was going to happen—something that had to do with the tilting, tilting into *somewhere*. . . .

Oliver, who'd been sitting at the table, reached a hand out to make sure I was steady, biting his lip, and then fell in behind me. I looked over my shoulder to make sure Dad was behind him. Mom led us, not through the side door, but through her and Dad's room. She gingerly unlatched the big back window and raised it, and then one by one, Sam first with Mom lowering him down, we squeezed through the opening into the narrow gap between the back bumper and the trailer. Mom grabbed her knapsack from the overhead bin as she slid out behind us and turned to help the rest of us out. As I emerged, Millie and Sam were standing to the left, gawking, and I moved to join them, Oliver right behind me. As I followed their gaze, my heart flip-flopped in shock.

The front end of the Trinidad was hanging into . . . empty space. It was halfway over the edge of a gaping chasm . . . *more* than a gaping chasm, which was spilling fog at our feet. And it looked like there was nothing holding it back from falling straight in.

Now I turned to look in the other direction. And if the sight of our camper dangling into an abyss had been unbelievable to behold, what I saw next nearly knocked me to the ground.

There was Daisy's trailer, two of the four wheels tilted up in the air. A long, thick, hairy arm stretched through the tiny window at the back, taut, having ripped through the one remaining screen. A huge furry paw gripped a small scrubby tree growing out of the desert dust. From inside the trailer came a low, desperate howl. Daisy's claws slipped a little farther up the tree—it was the only thing, apparently, keeping our Winnebago, and her, from dropping over the edge.

Oliver was leaping forward before my dad's reaching arms could pull him back. He threw himself at the trailer and worked desperately at the pin that attached it to the Trinidad, and then, suddenly Millie (of all people!) was beside him, working feverishly to yank the pin out of its hole. Daisy's paw slipped again, the tree bent so far I could hear it crackle as it began to break, and she let out a high squeal of terror.

And then there was a clank and a thud, and both Oliver and Millie fell backward as the pin came out in their hands. Mom let out a sound like a yip as the Trinidad slid. The sound of metal as it scraped rock was deafening as the back end tilted up into the air while gravity pulled the front end down, and then there was a metallic screech as the whole thing tumbled out of sight, dust flying in a cloud around us.

For a moment, there was silence. Then came the *CRASH CRASH CRASH* somewhere beyond the chasm lip and down.

The trailer stood alone, Daisy's claws still digging into the tiny tree and holding on for dear life, though the danger was over.

Dad put his hands on top of his head and walked gingerly in the direction of the chasm, not getting too close to the edge, but peering downward. We all walked up behind him and gathered in a cluster to follow his gaze, but the fog that pooled inside the chasm, while thin, was enough to obscure our view.

"What is it?" I asked, gazing at the emptiness that had almost swallowed us. I had the sense of the hole being enormous, but with the fog it was hard to know for sure.

My father sighed, then nodded, then took a deep breath.

"It's the Grand Canyon," he said.

That's when Mom let out an inhuman sound, part growl, part string of swear words. She let out a scream and started kicking the dirt, like she was trying to kick the earth right down into the canyon. Then she ran to the trailer and started kicking that, so hard Daisy yelped. She crouched (her long red skirt flapping around her ankles—I don't think I'll ever forget the sight of her like that, like a woman gone crazy), grabbed a handful of dirt, and threw it up into the air toward the Cloud—which was about a hundred yards behind us, hovering low. "Let us go!" she yelled. "Leave us alone! He doesn't deserve you! He's just a little boy! He's a *good* boy! Go find somebody who deserves you!" And then she sat down on the desert floor and lowered her head, as if she'd given up.

She looked over at Sam, who was clearly scared and bewildered, and then pulled him in close to her and murmured to him that it was all right.

"Don't be mad at the smiling man," Sam said.

Swiveling with him in her arms, Mom turned her back on the sky.

So here we sit. It's nighttime, dark as ink except for the firelight. In Mom's knapsack we've found a spare set of keys to the Winnebago, some used tissues, some gum, the sock full of Grandma's life savings, and the artifacts Grandma gave us: the Delta snack pack, the encyclopedia page, and the postcard. At least the snack pack has some peanuts in it. It's slowly dawning on us all the things we've just lost. (Sam's most depressed about Jim the bear.) We are foodless, Winnebagoless, shelterless, on the edge of the Grand Canyon, at the end of a road that's not really a road. We owe our lives to a sasquatch. And almost everything we had is gone.

November Something

This morning I woke up just before the sun. My eyes popped open and it felt like the world was about to come awake. I've never felt the moments before dawn *vibrate*.

My mom was the only other person up. I could see her, sitting cross-legged at the edge of what I knew even in the dark was the canyon, bundled in her coat, her breath puffing into the air.

She heard me tiptoeing up beside her, and I crouched and sat next to her carefully as she held her hand out to keep me back from the edge.

I snuggled into the crook of her arm, stretching my feet out over the emptiness. We waited.

I've seen sunrises in Cliffden, pink and blue above the

clouds. But here, the first ray of light cut the darkness like a sword.

Pure gold climbed up the sky, sliding along the low scattered clouds, and bit by bit the scene below us crept into the light. The fog had gone. My eyes were blinded by the brightness of the canyon bottom below and how far away it was. It took my breath away.

I'm trying to think of the words for it, but I don't think they exist. I think the planet is more dangerous and beautiful and wild and vast than I ever could have imagined.

I think there is more magic in the world than we know. If not, how could there be the Grand Canyon? If not, how could there be the thousands of buffalo?

The Next Morning
(I Still Don't Know What Day It Is!)

After a lot of blaming each other for getting lost in the first place and arguing about what our plan should be, we've done the thing we most needed to do: We've set Daisy free.

Yesterday afternoon Oliver insisted he be the one to unlock her trailer door. We all watched, with a little fear for our safety, but less than I ever could have imagined a few weeks ago.

I held my breath as I watched Daisy emerge—her trunklike hairy legs stepping down slowly out of the trailer, her claws clasping the sides of the doorway before she moved her paws to shield her eyes from the sun. None of us had ever seen her stand at her full height, but now she did, stretching her back and neck, breathing the air in deeply. She was at least seven feet tall, towering above Oliver, who backed up slowly, gaping. She blinked down at him, slightly dazed, and suddenly I knew we'd made a big mistake and that she was going to kill us after all. I felt ill with sudden fright. But she only looked around at us, and then at her surroundings, and let out a low, meek whimper.

After that she wouldn't leave. I guess she was too confused, and didn't know quite what to do. She just stood several yards away from us as the afternoon wore into evening, watching us with eerily intelligent eyes. It made us uneasy, but with evening coming on we had to set about finding branches for building a fire, so we went to work.

Daisy lingered on. We would have given her food if we'd had any. As the rest of us sat huddled together around our meager campfire, barely talking, Oliver bravely moved closer toward her, pointing into the distance to try to convince her she'd be better off leaving us. She stayed put.

When it had gotten pretty late, Dad insisted we all get some rest and that he would keep an eye on Daisy. Cuddled against Sam on the hard ground, cold and shivering, I thought I'd never be able to get to sleep for fear of her, but finally I drifted off. I woke this morning to an amazing sight: Oliver asleep on the edge of our circle, and Daisy watching over him, her paw stroking his back, protecting him like one of her own cubs.

Late this morning we all heard a distant call, the telltale sound of a group of sasquatches on the move—even in this remote place. Daisy turned toward the sound, then turned to look back at us with her keen, dark eyes. Finally she stood and slunk away, looking back at us every few steps, until she ultimately turned and jogged in the direction of the sound. Her enormous silhouette grew smaller and smaller in the distance, and now she's gone.

I've been thinking a lot about Oliver, and how he, of all of us, was the one to make peace with Daisy, and the one to let her go, and the one to fall asleep with her stroking his back in the end. I've been trying to figure out why that is, and I think—for him—it's all got something to do with facing the unbearable.

Animals are made to eat each other, and sometimes I wonder why. I wonder if that's part of why the angels rebelled—because they thought the gods were mean in the way they made the world, or that they were making mistakes, and I have to admit that if I were an angel I think I might rebel too . . . because of Clouds, and people like Big Tex, and because of the helpless way I feel when I hear Sam coughing. (The weird part is that the more of the wild I see, the more I think maybe we're inseparable—people and animals and even the woods.)

Anyway, I can't deny that *I* have a mean streak too. *I* can be cruel. I'm the one who wanted to leave Daisy for dead, and it makes me feel embarrassed now.

I wonder that if you keep growing and changing like you're supposed to, if you always end up embarrassed about how stupid you used to be. Every year I realize how dumb I was the year before. It makes me tempted to cross out pieces of this diary so no one will ever see some of the more embarrassing things I've thought about. (Probably no one will ever read this anyway, so I don't know why I worry.) Still, I suppose a true autobiographer has to be completely honest and not sugarcoat themselves.

Ugh, now I've gotten a teardrop on this page from thinking about Daisy! I have to admit that I worry about her.

Will she make it across the desert okay? Will she get along with the other sasquatches? Will she make it home to her children? It drives me crazy not to know. Mom says handling not knowing what the answers are is one of the hardest things in life, but also a really nice mystery. It doesn't feel nice to me.

"Daisy has a good nose, Gracie," Oliver just said to me, sitting down cross-legged beside me, with that habit he has of guessing my thoughts. "She's an animal, so she has good instincts. She'll find water and food and find her way home."

"I hope you're right," I said. Looking over at him, I fought the urge to reach for his hand. Sometimes I want to do weird things like that. I'm sure Millie, with her head for romance, would say I have a crush on Oliver, but that's not really the way it feels. It just feels like I want him to be happier, and he wants me to be happier. It feels like he's my first really good friend.

I can tell he's worried about Daisy too. I guess what we should really be worried about is ourselves: stranded in the desert with no food and no way to get anywhere. Mom and Dad say that when the sun gets lower we'll have to start walking. Dad says he has a plan and knows exactly where we're heading, that he can navigate by the stars, but I think he's just trying to keep our spirits up.

If in fifteen years someone finds this diary next to my bleached bones, just know that—

Ugh. My pen is dying. I'm running out of ink.

We

December 2nd

It's been almost a week since I last wrote. No, I'm not just a pile of bones in the desert, and yes, we are alive. I'll resist the urge to jump ahead into everything that's happened over the past few days and instead bring things up to date.

The first thing that saved us in the desert was that we found a couple of bottles of water and some bags of trail mix under a pile of blankets in Daisy's empty trailer. (I really don't know where we'd be if Mom hadn't made that discovery!) The second thing was a little more complicated, as it turned out to be both a blessing and a curse.

That first afternoon after Daisy had left, we hiked for a couple of hours due west, along the lip of the canyon.

Setting off into the uncharted and empty desert like that gave me the same breathless, unhinged feeling I used to get at Wet 'N' Wild Adventure Park in Maine, when I would stand at the top of their biggest waterslide before launching myself down. I kept picturing these old western movies Dad likes to watch—where vultures circle over creatures, waiting for them to die—and looking at the sky to see if any vultures were waiting for *us*. When Millie asked what I was thinking about and I told her, she laughed at me, but it was a tense laugh.

As night fell, we began to look for a place to sleep—somewhere we might find a little shelter against a rock or a cluster of trees. I'm not sure what we wanted to be sheltered *from*, and I guess we didn't know. Maybe just from the roaming eyes of animals that might come our way. In any case, we were all at a real low point, and Sam was running a fever and taking turns riding on each of our backs. Mom had stopped trying to cheer us up, which was maybe the most worrisome part of all. Usually she's the glue that holds the rest of us together.

We finally found a hill littered with giant boulders, which might have given us a view from the top, except it was too dark. We decided to climb it in the morning to get the lay of the land, and then we huddled together with our backs toward one of the big rocks at the bottom. We were all very quiet and lost in our own thoughts, and nobody said good night to each other.

I was too cold to sleep, and I don't know when I first heard the music, because it seemed to drift into my awareness slowly. When I did finally notice it for sure, I thought I must be imagining it. Then it kept being drowned out by Sam's coughing in his sleep, and then when I'd try to listen again the wind would have shifted direction so that I couldn't hear anything at all. I might never have realized it was real unless Millie, the only other one still awake (she was staring up at the stars thoughtfully, which isn't like her) leaned forward and whispered to me.

"Do you hear that?"

I nodded.

She glanced up at the sky again, then back at me. "Doesn't it seem like there's a weird light coming from up there?"

"Up where?" I asked. Millie's eyes glistened at me in the dark while she nodded upward.

I looked up—there was a dim white glow to the night sky above us, but I'd assumed it was the light of the half moon floating over the canyon and filtering down on us. I whispered this to Millie, but she didn't seem convinced.

She gazed up the hill behind us, wearing her determined face (which comes out every now and then and makes me think maybe she's found her "inner compass" like Mom says she will). "I'm gonna go up and see if I can see anything."

"I'll come with you," I said.

"I can do it alone," she said, but as if she really wanted me to come.

I stood up and followed her. I didn't like to think of her going off alone, anyway. What if she got lost? Or if some boulder-dwelling creature attacked her?

We tried to make it up the hill quietly, but it was no easy feat—stones slid underneath us and we had to hold on to each other a couple of times just to keep our balance as we navigated between boulders and over the pitted dirt. I wondered if this might be a good time to ask Millie about her secret conversation with the Cloud, but I just couldn't work up the courage to do it. I don't know why sometimes things are so hard to talk about, when in the movies they seem so easy.

The music that I thought I'd imagined could now be heard again, more clearly. It had an echoey quality—like it was drifting up to us from the bottom of a bowl. And there was no denying it, the sky was strangely lit up in a way that couldn't come from the moon.

Millie was just ahead of me, climbing with more and more speed, hitching herself up over the rocks with difficulty. Just as we reached the ridge, she turned, breathing hard, to pull me up by my sleeve. She swiveled to look out at the view, and gasped. I was a second behind her.

We gaped at a deep gorge that forked off from the main canyon about a hundred yards in front of us. Clinging to the sides and bottom of the plummeting, craggy slopes was a sprawl of twinkling lights coming from thousands of dark little houses made out of clay and stone, lining roads and promenades carved out of the cliffs.

Stone staircases climbed their way up the sides, and standing on landings nestled in rock were tents, conical towers, pyramids with glowing windows—all lit with yellow, flickering lights. We could just make out other strange figures drifting up and down the crooked climbing streets.

"What is that place?" I breathed.

Millie looked at me, her dark eyes twinkling with excitement, as if this had been the answer we'd been looking for all along.

"That," she breathed, "is Luck City." And then she turned down the hill, hurrying to tell the others.

December 3rd

Okay, I had to stop writing, but now I'm back. I'll keep trying to catch up, even though there's enough going on right now to fill twenty pages. I'm so tempted to tell you where I am, but I'm practicing self-denial.

We walked into Luck City before dawn that next morning. We hadn't forgotten Grandma's warning, but what choice did we have? Where else did we have to go? And I have to admit I think we were all a little excited. Mom herded us like geese in front of her as we approached the stairs that led down into the city. "Stay close to me," she said. "Don't talk to anyone. Don't look at anyone funny. Look away if anyone looks at *you* funny." She held Sam in her arms, pressed against her tightly, but she also had a twinkle in her eye. "I never thought I'd see this place," she said, gazing about her. "How do they have electricity?"

"It's hydropower," Dad said. He pointed to the other side of the gulch, where we could see a waterfall gushing over the side. "I suppose they've built a waterwheel of some sort at the bottom, though it appears they haven't done a very good job." Even as we watched, the lights all over town blinked out for a few moments and then came on again.

Despite the early hour, the city was already wide awake, loud, and chaotic. It wove through the gorge like a blinky electric garden, even more intricate and dazzling than it had looked from on top of the hill. We passed clay buildings of all shapes and sizes, some opening outward like giant flowers, some arched or spiraled, some with openings to dark holes tunneling into the canyon walls. Ghosts and a couple of vampires walked past us as if we were nothing new or special, and we saw plenty of people, too—shady looking characters, men in cowboy hats, and tattooed women who looked like they could beat up the cowboys. "How do they all get here?" I asked.

Dad shook his head. "Some probably trek from the main road. Probably a lot come by horse. These are mostly desperate people looking to win big. The only humans who'd come here," he explained, "are either hiding out, or seasoned gamblers, or desperate and looking for their last hope."

We walked past a building that was shaped like a dragon's head on one side, breathing out a fire-shaped building on the other that glowed with the words SHOPPING! ARCADE! at the top, lit by hundreds of round, flickering bulbs.

Shouts and music and laughter and yelling drifted from inside.

"What do they gamble with?" Oliver asked.

"All sorts of things. Land, cars, the deeds to their houses. Maps, rare ones, like to the Fountain of Youth. Blueprints of the Underworld. Things like that. They deal in all sorts of currency here," Dad went on. As if to underline his point, we came, just then, to a building called the Western Beastly Bank & Loan, Lowest Interest Rates in the Canyon, Tastiest Meats for Bartering with Sasquatches. In the window hung shanks of meat and shiny antiques. (I remembered Grandma's trunk of gifts and wondered if the shiny objects were for paying ghosts.) One teller inside was counting out gold coins apparently being deposited by a leprechaun.

We squeezed together as we walked down a narrow

stairway—there was only a thin stone railing between us and the plummeting depths below, and Mom made us keep against the rocky wall. "Okay," she said, "we're going to find a hotel, get cleaned up, and figure out what to do next."

Somewhere across the city, a circus barker was yelling for people to "step right up" for the morning's show—a satyr tightrope-walking across the canyon—in fifteen minutes. A group of leprechauns rode past us on old rusty bikes, wearing tiny clothes. "I swear I saw that outfit in the children's section at Walmart when I was shopping for Sam last year," Millie said, staring at one of them.

Walking deeper into the city, we passed street callers (human and ghostly), jugglers, and cowboys playing poker with ghosts in ten-gallon hats (which they'd probably won from the cowboys). A fight burst out of a saloon just ahead of us, and we had to wait for the saloon keeper—a translucent lady in pioneer clothes—to come out and usher the culprits away. We passed a shop window filled with notices headed with words like *STOLEN* or *WANTED* or *WARNING*. The only one I was able to read as we hurried past was asking for information leading to the capture of a gang of ghosts that had been running loose in town and dragging people into the Underworld.

We walked past caves that stretched back into the darkness of the rocky walls, and crooked houses with ghosts circling the turrets. I gaped at the blinking, flickering signs encrusted into the canyon walls around the city:

- FRESHWATER MERMAIDS AQUARIUM SPECTACULAR!
- THE WESTERN GEM CASINO: BEST SLOTS! BEST DRINKS! BIGGEST GIANTS! WE TAKE GOLD AND CASH! WIN A RIDE ON THE BREATHTAKING PEGASUS!
- HAS GAMBLING WORKED UP YOUR APPETITE? TREAT YOURSELF TO A CHEESECAKE ZINGO AT APPLEBEE'S.
- LUCK CITY JAIL, MORGUE, AND WEDDING CHAPEL.

There was even a KFC, which smelled heavenly as we passed the front door.

"You guys stay right here," Mom said. She walked into a small ice-cream parlor and came out looking like she'd found renewed purpose. "I asked for directions to a safe hotel," she said.

She led us down a long series of staircases, taking a left, then a right, then another left, almost all the way to the bottom of the gorge, where we could hear rushing water from an unseen river below. We turned down a street called Widows' Walk and here we finally came upon a row of little inns. We walked past the first three inviting, polished doorways—with names like the Palace and the Sparkling Nugget—because it was obvious we couldn't afford them. Then past four more—less gleaming but still too gleaming for us. Finally we came upon a modest, crooked Victorian with a sign above it that said GULCH INN AND TAVERN.

Mom rang the little metal bell three times before we heard anyone moving inside, and then a woman ("Harriet," she said—we were relieved to learn she was human and that she accepted cash) showed up in curlers to let us in with barely a few words exchanged. She led us past a small dim parlor with a kiosk full of travel brochures, past old, sinking, dusty furniture and up the stairs to a crooked suite of rooms. The suite had gently sloping floors and mismatched but comfy-looking armchairs gathered in a central parlor, three bedrooms branching from the main room, a huge marble fireplace, and three tall windows looking down onto the street.

"This will do fine," Mom said, peeling some bills out of her envelope and handing them over. "Thank you very much."

Harriet gave her a tired but not unkind smile, laid the key on the table, and shuffled out into the hall.

"We have some time to get cleaned up," Dad said. "And then, your mom and I will talk about what to do next."

They gave Millie and me the room at the back of the suite, looking into the backyard of the house—a flat rocky space that lay between us and the canyon wall. I noticed that, next door, Harriet's neighbor had covered his or her own small lot with sod and grass, and in another moment I saw why. At one end of the lot was a cluster of three pegasusses, (Millie just looked over my shoulder and informed me that the proper word is "pegasi") glowing white!

I felt someone come up beside me, and turned to see Oliver. We both leaned our foreheads against the window.

The pegasi were gathered at an empty trough, as if waiting for something, and in another moment we saw what. A figure came ambling out toward them carrying a big bucket of water, and slowly she dumped it into the trough.

There was something strange about her hair, and then I realized, with a shudder, what it was. It was moving.

"Snakes," Oliver said.

The woman seemed to sense us staring down into her yard, and turned, but I had only a moment to see that her face was a deep, rich green before Oliver yanked me suddenly back behind the curtain.

"What?" I whispered breathlessly, my heart pounding against my ribs.

"That," Oliver said, daring to duck back to the window to see if the coast was clear, "was Medusa."

I gaped at him. I knew about Medusa from the *Immortals, Where Are They Now?* show. She's a goddess, and a well-known hoarder of pegasi. I figured she must have fallen on hard times if she'd ended up here, in Luck City, selling pegasus rides. And I was glad Oliver had pulled me back from the curtain. Wolf Blitzer from CNN said she could turn people to stone with her eyes.

"She must capture them out near the Sierra Madres," Oliver said, leaning back against the window now that she was gone. "That's illegal."

"Yeah, they're endangered," I said, trying to sound knowledgeable. "I donate some of my allowance to a unicorn rescue group, but I keep up on pegasus issues too."

"I guess the police aren't going to mess with Medusa," Oliver said. "I wonder if they even have police."

"Why don't the pegasi fly away?" I asked. But as soon as I said it, I noticed they were tied to a stake at the center of the property with long golden ropes. "Well, I'm surprised nobody steals them."

He gazed at the paltry lot disapprovingly. "It's not a big enough space for them. She's an irresponsible pet owner."

I thought about my poor dead dog, Poochie, and how I used to force her to sleep with me and paint her claws with nail polish. And once I made her wear doll clothes, and then piled my stuffed animals on top of her and put her in all these weird positions to take photos for a calendar I tried to sell to all my friends so I could get a new bike. I decided never to mention this to Oliver.

That afternoon, Mom ducked out for a few hours and bought us all some clothes from a thrift store Harriet helped direct her to. "I haggled with the clerk," she said. "I don't think your grandma would begrudge us buying just these few things; we're a little desperate." (Mom knows all our sizes; her brain is a catalog of facts about each one of us. She knows where and when we lost all our baby teeth. I wouldn't be surprised if she knew how many freckles there are on my nose.)

Bored, Sam and Oliver and I wandered the house, which had two decrepit, cobwebby back staircases and three separate parlors. Apparently, we were the only guests. We came upon Harriet in the kitchen, sitting on a stool and peeling apples for a pie. We hovered in the doorway uncertainly, but she nodded us toward the old linoleum table. "Have a seat," she offered. "Stay awhile."

We sat on the cracked vinyl chairs and watched her work, curious about where she'd gotten the apples. She noticed our stares.

"The cowboys bring in supplies. They pack them in on mules. These are pretty gamey and old, but still okay for baking. I always bake one for me and one to leave on Medusa's doorstep, next door. Kind of an offering. You want to be on good terms with a neighbor like her.

"I was wondering," I said. "Aren't her animals powerful enough to escape? Even though they're tied up?"

"They've been tamed with golden bridles," Harriet said, eyes still on the apple in her hand. "Nobody can even fly them without the bridles. Didn't you learn that in school?" As she peeled, the apple skins came off in long, thin lines. "I'm sure Medusa keeps those bridles well protected." She glanced up at us. There was a kind warmth in her eyes, but also a sadness. "Anyway, they can't fly very far before getting tired and having to land—they have a big wing span, but their bodies are so heavy. I guess it's not very practical to own a pegasus unless it's for something like selling rides."

"Why do you look so sad?" Sam asked. I shushed him, but Harriet smiled at him.

"Wouldn't you be sad if you were stuck in Luck City?" she asked.

"I'd be scared of all the monsters," Sam replied.

She put down her knife, wiped off her hands, and folded them on her lap. "I got stuck here, I guess. I grew up on an island off the coast of North Carolina, a beautiful place. But the mermaids started crawling in and stealing people. We had to adjust . . . most people left."

"And you came here?"

"I thought I could win enough money to resettle somewhere inland, back north, somewhere nice like upstate New York. I always thought I was good at cards. I'd always felt lucky. But once I got here, I only went into debt. And now I'm stuck. I run this inn for a ghost couple who own three other hotels." She turned her attention back to her work and began to clear away the apple skins, brushing them off the counter into a bin. "It's a rough place. It traps you in ways you don't expect.

And it's no place for children." She eyed Sam, then gave me a significant, questioning look. "People come here only because they have no other options." She spread the peeled apples on the counter to be chopped.

I was about to ask her if she thought she'd ever be able to leave the city, when we heard the front door jangle and creak and Mom's footsteps in the foyer.

Sam ran out to see what she'd bought for him, but Oliver and I only trailed behind slowly. I think the conversation had made us both uneasy.

That night, Mom and Dad said they were going out, just the two of them.

"Where are you going?" Millie asked, pointedly suspicious. It was the four of us, sitting in the upstairs parlor. I could hear Oliver and Sam laughing in the back bedroom; they'd been thumb wrestling for about half an hour, and I could only imagine how sore their thumbs must be.

"We have some things we need to do," Dad said, looking up at the ceiling, then at the decrepit fireplace, everywhere but at our faces.

"What kinds of things?" I asked. Every once in a while, Millie and I work as a team, usually when Mom and Dad try to keep something from us. We're surprisingly good at getting things out of them when we make a unified effort.

They looked at each other, then Mom said, "We're going to see the genie." We gaped at them.

"Grandma warned us about the genie," I said softly. I was thinking about what Harriet had said, about people getting trapped.

Mom looked tired and nervous (though still beautiful as always). "She warned us about Luck City, too," she said, "but here we are. And we think it's too good a chance to pass up." A silence settled over us as Millie and I took this in.

"Well, we're going with you," Millie said.

For obvious reasons, and also because he was still running a fever, Sam stayed home. Oliver volunteered to stay with him. Mom kissed them both on the forehead before we left. (With Oliver, she did it sneakily and quickly, before he could protest.) Though she'd tried to talk us girls out of coming, Millie was so adamant that she'd finally given in.

Once outside the hotel, we gathered on the front stoop.

"How are we going to find him?" Millie asked.

As soon as she said it, we noticed a pale green glow-ing footprint in the shape of Dad's foot on the ground in front of us, and then another and another, leading down the alley.

Dad studied it. "Supposedly, we just ask," Dad said, "and he finds us." He looked up at the three of us. "Looks like he already has." Millie and I looked at each other, nervous. When Dad followed the tracks, we all trailed along behind.

The trail took us along a crooked alley that sloped downward, even farther into the gulch. At the bottom we reached a wide boulevard bordered on one side by a narrow river of rushing water. Following the path along side it, we soon left the clusters of stone houses behind and found ourselves on a rocky trail that led deeper and deeper into the fold of the gorge—where, up ahead, its walls met in a point at a wide, deep hole that was surrounded by a thick stand of evergreens. Here, about twenty feet left of the hole, was where the river began—at the bottom of the waterfall we'd seen from above. Just as Dad had predicted, an enormous vertical wheel churned in the white water. "This is how Luck City runs," he said, putting his hands on his hips and taking a moment to study the engineering. Normally he would have stood there indefinitely, taking the thing apart with his eyes, but Mom tugged on his sleeve, insistent that we all keep going.

Up ahead, the green footsteps disappeared into the wide, gaping hole in the canyon wall, and we all stood staring into the shadows. From the darkness inside, just above the sound of the rushing water, we could hear distant moans.

"He's in *there*?" Millie asked nervously. It looked and sounded a lot like the cave in Grandma's backyard, like a cave to the Underworld.

Mom and Dad both looked nervous. "I suppose being related to angels, they have some connection between life and death," Dad said. He swallowed. "I suppose they don't mind living so close to the Underworld. Though they can never come out of their caves until they're set free."

"So he's trapped?"

Dad nodded. "Well, he's stuck to his bottle, which is in the cave. I read it in a brochure back at the inn. There's an ordinance about moving the bottle, all sorts of red tape involved. I think he can work his magic within a two-hundred-yard radius and that's it. Except, of course—the wishes he grants; those reach anywhere."

I wondered if I should feel sorry for the genie, but a few minutes later, I had my answer. He didn't deserve anyone's pity.

We entered in a group, clustered together and weaving through the trees. We walked into the wide mouth of the cave and let our eyes adjust to the dimness for a moment.

We were in a wide round cavern, its ceiling soaring above us and dripping with stalagmites and stalactites. A few small pines were gathered at the entrance behind us, straining toward the outdoors. Across the way, about twenty feet in front of us, was a kind of grotto—with candles tucked into the nooks of the cave wall and water gathered in a little pond that lay in a shaft of dim moonlight filtering in through a hole in the cave ceiling. The sources of all the moaning and rattling were out of sight, farther down the cave that continued on to the left of the grotto and curved into a deeper darkness.

Hovering in the shadows at one side of the pond was the genie. He was large and dim—at least eight feet tall—and green. He had a long flowing mane of dark hair and large bright green eyes that twinkled with intense cleverness, and he nibbled at his lips like he was dying to eat. A tendril of greenish smoke reached from the tips of his feet (which levitated in the air) to a golden bottle tucked snugly away under one of the trees.

Attached to the cave wall behind the bottle was a large white wheel, full of numbers and symbols and the words WIN A WISH, LOSE A BET dividing the circle in half.

We walked closer, and the genie watched us, waiting until we'd come within a few feet. His eyes gave me the chills.

"What are your wishes?" he asked. "I have a maximum of three."

He seemed eager, polite but with a thin thread of malice in his voice.

"We only have one," my Dad said. "I want to get rid of a Cloud. It's trying to take my son."

The genie surveyed us and smiled. "Yes, yes. I could do this for you." He smiled and turned his enormous green eyes toward Millie, then back to my Dad.

"And what will you pay for a chance to win this wish?"

Dad looked at me and Millie. "Kids, please wait outside. Your mom and I want to talk with the genie alone."

I knew what Dad was going to offer him. I knew it the moment he said that we should leave. And I hated it. But the truth is, I didn't need to be asked twice to leave the presence of the genie, and I guess neither did

Millie. There was something about him that made you feel prickly and terrified, like he was looking right into your soul and amused by what he saw.

We let out loud sighs as we emerged into the fresh air, as if we'd both been holding our breath the whole time, though Millie still looked pale and nervous. We stared up at the crescent moon, the few thin clouds in the sky, and our Cloud hovering just above the lip of the canyon.

A few minutes later Mom and Dad emerged, their faces expressionless.

"Well?" I asked.

"He'll let us play. Tomorrow at dusk."

My feelings were all mixed up at once. I felt relieved, even elated, about the chance to save Sam. But I'd also guessed the sacrifice we'd have to make if Dad lost.

"It's our house," I said, my voice catching. "You bet our house." Despite everything, despite how far we were from home and how far we might still go, I'd always held out hope we could get back home somehow.

Dad looked down at me, put his right arm around me, and readjusted his glasses with his left hand. "I did what I had to do," he said.

*   *   *

The one positive development was that on our way home we climbed the stairs up to KFC and got a big bucket of chicken and mashed potatoes to bring back to the Gulch Inn. Mom charmed the cashier into giving us the mashed potatoes for free, and that night in the parlor we feasted, though Mom was quiet and Dad's brow was furrowed like he was headed into one of his swamps. In bed afterward I thought about how I'll probably never be able to charm people into anything like my mom can, or be beautiful like her and Millie, so I'll have to be rich somehow. Then I won't need to sweet talk people into anything. When I brought this up to Millie, who was sitting on her bed looking out the window, she said, "You're less of a charmer, and more of a 'fury from the depths of hell' type of person."

Oliver and Sam came in a few minutes later, and we played cards on the bed until the boys went to their room to sleep. I went on playing solitaire next to Millie while she tried to read, and kept on thinking it was the perfect time to ask her about the Cloud. Still, I kept playing and playing like my life depended on it, procrastinating. I kept losing, and my tolerance for losing is very low, so finally I gave up.

"Millie," I ventured, pushing the cards back into their

box, "I saw something one night, back in the plains. With you . . . and . . ." I hesitated. "I thought I saw you outside, talking to the Cloud. When everyone was asleep."

Millie lay completely still, her eyes on her book, as if she hadn't heard me.

"I was wondering what you were doing?" I asked, picking at the bedspread and feeling my face heat up, as if I were asking her something deeply embarrassing, like if she secretly had a crush on someone. (Millie always has a crush on someone but is never all that secret about it.) "What were you saying to it?"

Millie sighed. "I was trying to see if I could trade something for Sam. Like my hair, or something like that." I felt triumphant for knowing her so well.

"Did the Cloud say anything back?" I asked.

Millie was silent for a few moments, then she shook her head.

"I guess we'll never see our house again," I said, "if Dad loses. I guess the genie will own it. What do you think a genie wants with a house, anyway, if he's trapped in a cave? Will he have someone sell it for him?" She didn't reply—she was gazing up at the ceiling now.

"I wish Dad hadn't gotten us lost," I went on. "Then

we wouldn't have gone over the edge of the Grand Canyon, and we could have bet the Trinidad. He's so absentminded. If he wasn't . . ."

Millie shook her head to stop me. "You're so dense," she said.

"If we do ever try to move back to Cliffden . . ." I continued, ignoring her.

Suddenly, Millie sat bolt upright, her eyes flashing and her cheeks pink. "How can you be so stupid! Haven't you figured it out? Do you think the genie would really settle for something as useless as our house, or *money* from our house?"

I stared, shocked into silence.

Millie sank back down against her pillows, as if she were exhausted. And suddenly a new and horrible truth settled down all around me. I knew what she was going to say before she said it.

"His *life*," Millie said flatly to the window. "Dad bet his soul."

My heart was suddenly flapping around wildly in my chest, and Millie turned to me, biting her lip, looking guilty.

"They told you that?" I breathed.

She shook her head. "I asked Mom," she admitted.

"She didn't deny it. She asked me not to tell you."

"Well," I sputtered, "he has to take it back."

"You *can't* take it back. Once you've bet on the genie's wheel, that's it. It's a binding contract."

Sometimes I'm afraid I've got a monster inside for a soul. If I drew my heart it might not look like a circus at all, but like a cavewoman with raw meat hanging out of her mouth and a club in each hand to hit people with.

I didn't sleep that night. I kept thinking how even though he isn't perfect, my dad has always taken care of me, and I haven't given him much in return. I thought about the night when he and Mom told us we were leaving Cliffden, how he'd called me one of his baby stars.

Since we'd lost the Winnebago, I had none of my good luck charms to wish on, but I still believed that if I *thought* how I wanted things to end, *enough* times, someone might hear me.

He wins. He stays with us. He wins. He stays with us. He wins. He stays with us, I kept saying inside my head. The wish needed to be extra powerful, so I didn't stop; I forced myself to stay awake as long as I possibly could. Dad wouldn't lose. He couldn't.

I repeated it over and over to myself until the darkness outside of the windows began to lighten, and the pegasi next door began to nicker good morning to each other, and I finally fell asleep.

December 4th

Even though it's been over a week since it happened, I remember the awful feeling of waking up that next morning perfectly. A shaft of sunlight was beaming down into the gulch, and, looking out the window and up, I could just make out the Cloud far, far above, keeping an eye on us. Down in the barn lot next door, the pegasi were still nickering back and forth to each other, and I could see Oliver leaning over the fence, feeding them carrots out of his hands. I walked out to join him, after first making sure Medusa was nowhere to be seen.

"Where'd you get carrots?" I asked.

"Harriet let me have them." He didn't look up at me, but slid a couple carrots into my hand, then gently pushed one of the pegasus's muzzles in my direction.

Her sandpapery tongue tickled my palms as she snuffled for the carrots, and I glanced up at the windows of the house nervously, looking for her owner.

"My dad bet his life on the wheel," I said, not looking at Oliver but instead focusing on the pegasi instead.

"I figured," Oliver said. The pegasi were vying for our attention, and Oliver gave away his last carrot.

I was buckling under the guilt, like I should have known better what my dad was walking into. I wondered how everyone had figured everything out but me. My mom says sometimes I ignore things I'd rather not know. She said that's why I always get Cs in classes like Cotillion and Life Skills.

Oliver leaned back from the fence and put his hands on his messy hair, leaving a bunch of hay stuck there, unwittingly. He looked up at Medusa's house, intent, like he was counting the windows or the numbers of shingles. I expected him to say something encouraging, which he's usually good at, but he appeared to be lost in his own thoughts. It wasn't like him, considering he's usually the most considerate person I know.

Dusk came too quickly. We spent the morning and most of the afternoon in the parlor (the chimney, it turned out, was blocked by an old poltergeist Harriet had been trying to have exorcised for years, so we couldn't light a fire in the fireplace), watching the clock and willing the moments to go slower. Oliver had offered to stay with Sam again while the rest of us went to see the genie. Mom and Dad hadn't even bothered to try to deter Millie and me from coming with them. I think, in a way, they were relieved to have us along. It would mean a little more time with the four of us together.

"How do I find you?" Oliver asked.

"Find us why?" I said.

"If you don't come back or something. I'd feel better if I knew where you were."

Relenting, I drew a little map on the back of a Western Gem tourist brochure of how we'd gotten to the cave.

Sam was actually feeling better for the first time in weeks, sitting in a blanket on the couch and smiling, blissfully unaware of the fear hovering over the rest of us. "Ask the genie for a new Winnebago," he kept insisting.

Finally, around five thirty, we got ready to go. Dad sat for a moment at Sam's feet on the couch and squeezed his toes, then leaned over and kissed him on the forehead, smiling as if we were going out to dinner, or like he and Mom used to do with each of us before they left us with a babysitter and went out on a date. It made me wonder how many other times my dad has put on a brave face for us without our noticing.

As night fell and we wound our way down into the gulch, I prayed; I wished on stars and my favorite constellations; I tried sending telepathy to the guardian angels in LA.

"What are you murmuring about?" Millie whispered, walking beside me.

I shrugged. "Just making wishes," I said.

"I'm going to wish too," she said. "Can you tell me how you do it?" She actually listened attentively as I pointed out which stars (well, at least the ones visible from the gulch) I thought were best for wishing on.

At the entrance to the cave, Dad tried to talk us into staying outside while he and Mom went in alone, but Millie shook her head furiously. "Absolutely not," she said, sounding very adult. "We know what we're facing. And we're coming with you." I marveled at her courage again. Finally Dad relented, and we followed them both into the darkness.

The genie was exactly the same as we'd found him the night before: hovering in the shadows at the edge of the grotto, calm but with a malicious eagerness simmering under his smile. The mournful sounds of the Underworld issued from the cave beyond him just as they had the night before.

"Spin the wheel . . . you made the deal . . . ," he said, and Dad swallowed nervously.

"Dad, please don't," I said, reaching for his arm. "There's got to be some way you can back out. Pay something else. Break your bet."

"I wouldn't do that, Gracie, even if I could. This is for Sam."

Dad turned to Mom and grabbed her hand tightly for a moment. She clutched his fingers and her lips trembled. I've never been very good at picturing my mom and dad as two people in love, instead of as just my mom and dad. But at that moment I could.

You'd think that something so important, so enormous in your life, would happen in slow motion, but that's not how it was at all. Things began to happen so quickly that it took my breath away.

Dad stepped forward, reached for the wheel, and gave it a hard spin. I held my breath as the arrow pointed alternately to the blurred words, then, as it slowed, WIN A WISH, LOSE A BET, WIN A WISH, LOSE A BET. Millie reached for my hand and squeezed it, digging her nails into my palm. I could feel myself growing woozy because I'd stopped breathing, but I couldn't get myself to take a breath. *He wins. He stays with us,* I kept saying in my head. *He wins, he stays, he wins, he stays. . . .*

Tick tick tick. The arrow clicked along the pins more and more slowly, lingering on WIN, then more slowly on LOSE, then, more slowly on WIN. Finally, it came to a complete stop. We stood in stunned silence.

"No," Mom said very quietly. "No. No. No."

Beside me Millie let out a choked sound. She let go of my hand. I felt adrift, like I was spinning away from the ground and sharply, horribly lonely. I felt like a howl, like a person wrapped in a moan.

LOSE A BET.

The genie smiled politely, but his tongue darted out to lick his lips like he was ready to eat. His fingers wiggled and twitched, as if he were holding himself back from just reaching out toward us. Was this how a genie took your life, I wondered—just by reaching out and grabbing it? The three of us clustered around my dad protectively.

"Say your good-byes," the genie said. "I'll wait."

Dad turned to us, his face ashen, his freckles bright. He walked us a few feet away, toward the trees clustered in the entranceway. I felt the genie's eyes on our backs, and Dad talked fast.

"Get to LA," he said. "Any way you can. You can hire a ship in Santa Monica. Don't linger too long before you set off."

"Dad," Millie said, shaking her head.

The world was spinning. Bright moonlight was filtering in from the hole above. Dad was feeling around in his pockets, handing Mom his wallet. He was counting on his shaking fingers, like he was running through his mind lists of all the practical things he needed to tell us so that we'd be okay.

"Dad," Millie repeated. "No."

"Girls, you'll have to take care of your mom. You'll . . ."

At that moment something hit me on the leg. I looked down to see it was a pebble. I glanced toward the cave entrance, and something—some tiny movement—drew my eyes into the trees clustered there.

The sight was so completely unexpected that at first I could only try to make sense of it. Hidden among the pines, panting and out of breath and practically invisible, was Oliver, staring at me with big, intent eyes. He held out his hands as if to show me something. There was a rope in his hands, glinting like gold.

Just beyond him, outside, I saw one small flash of white move past the cave entrance.

I made the connections crookedly but fast. I knew almost at once what that golden rope would be attached to.

I glanced back at the genie, who watched us, but from an angle where he wasn't looking toward the cave door. And I was already gauging the distance: How long would it take to run from where we stood to the stand of evergreens? Five seconds at most? How fast was a genie? How far would you have to fly to get beyond his reach, beyond the city limits? Oliver met my eyes again when I looked back, and waved me forward.

I hesitated and glanced at Millie, and then Mom and Dad, trying to communicate to them with my eyes—but they were too deep in conversation. In the corner of the cave the genie was watching us and rubbing his lips with one hand. Finally, Millie noticed my expression and managed to follow my gaze. She looked questioningly at me, and I shrugged almost imperceptibly. I tried to think of a plan.

But Oliver wasn't waiting for a plan. It turns out, he

already had one. He emerged from the trees, and just as the others noticed him, he launched a hail of stones from both hands in the direction of the genie. It was only a futile gesture—for a moment the genie floated backward, surprised, though the stones went right through him. Still, it gave me the moment to grab Mom's and Dad's arms, each with one hand, and pull them forward. "We're going," I said. "Run!"

By some miracle, they obeyed. We reached the trees just as the genie let out a screech and the ground beneath us coughed out a thick green mist that shaped itself into hundreds of filmy hands. They gathered toward my dad's feet and reached around his ankles.

It happened in seconds: We were running through the trees, we were outside with Oliver in the lead, and sure enough—there, in the little clearing of the gulch, were three pegasi, their muzzles fitted with golden bridles. Sam sat astride the tallest one, holding tight to its mane and waving us on with his other hand.

"Get on!" Oliver yelled. We hesitated for a moment, making sense of it. Then someone—either Mom or Dad—propelled me forward from behind.

There was a hungry scream from inside the darkness behind us as we flew into action, a sound I could never have dreamed could have come from the quiet, seething genie. I threw myself up behind Sam, and Millie scrabbled onto the pegasus next to us. It bucked under her weight as I tried to figure out where exactly to put my legs.

Mom was already awkwardly astride the third pegasus, though Dad was trying desperately to clamber on behind her and kept sliding down. Throwing a glance at the cave mouth, I could see the mist licking toward us along the ground, a pair of long, impossibly long, green arms stretching like taffy toward Dad's heels. Dad looked back in terror as he tried again, this time flinging himself over the pegasus's back, legs on one side and arms on the other. The animal backstepped, but he managed to hang on, and in another moment, with Mom pulling at his belt and Oliver jumping behind me with a "Haiyah!" our mounts all turned away from the trees and launched into a run at once, clattering down the gulch away from the cave. Braving another look back over my shoulder, I watched the genie's hundreds of hands, like puddles of green smoke, grasping for my dad's feet just as he was carried out of their reach.

It was an uneven and terrifying liftoff, the pegasus's legs pumping underneath us as they ran first on the ground and then on pure air. We burst up above the tree line and I dug my heels in to steady myself. I was only able to look down behind me one last time at the cave, its gaping hole glowing bright green and pulsating with rage.

We shot into the sky above Luck City in an upward spiral, bumpily at first. Within seconds we were high enough that the city lay beneath us in a patch of flickering light, getting smaller and farther away. By the time we leveled out, the city's light had fallen to our backs, only a shimmer peeking out of the canyon behind us, the Cloud a tiny dim shadow above it, being left far, far behind. The air grew cold quickly, the night dark. I could see, many yards away, the dim white glow of the other two pegasi and the figures astride them. Dad had finally righted himself so that he was properly astraddle behind Mom. I hugged tight to Sam and breathed deeply, my eyes throbbing, my throat aching with relief. "Thank you," I whispered to no one in particular. "Thank you, thank you, thank you."

Below, the flat dark earth stretched in all directions, no towns or lights in sight. I turned to look behind us; I thought I might be able to see the dark bowl of the Grand Canyon, or where the dark patches of the continent controlled by the monsters met the small pockets of light inhabited by humans, but there was nothing except Oliver, returning my gaze.

"Are you okay, Gracie?" he asked. "I'm trying not to hold you too tightly."

"We're flying," I said to him.

"Straight to LA," he said.

Beneath our legs, our pegasus flapped her wings in powerful gusts, her white fur catching the dim moonlight.

I wish I could record the moment better. What I need to say about it has already started to get fuzzy in my head. I think it's something about being so far above earth, but I'm not quite sure what. I think maybe what I want to remember is how it felt to picture what we must look like to a person on the ground. Far away, like a little dot of light. I think we must have seemed to disappear into the heavens like a shooting star.

December 5th

This morning I'm writing in the bath with a towel around my head, and big drops of water and steam are rising all around. And I guess now I'll finally tell you where we are and where I've been writing the last couple of entries from. We're in LA!

The lamps here all burn with whale oil, and we had to boil my water over a smelly oil stove. I've taken two baths so far this morning, just to pass the time. We're all on tenterhooks (I'm pretty sure that's the word) waiting for Dad to get home from his big errand.

Millie is sitting on the counter and plucking her split ends. Since we've been here, she never leaves me alone when I'm in the bath—she still thinks I'm a little kid even though I've told her I need my privacy. She always comes in to brush her hair in the mirror or clip her fingernails, but it's more like she just wants company. I've decided to ignore her and just keep writing until I'm finally caught up for real. Among other things, it's a good distraction.

The night we arrived here it was hard to believe that we were approaching a city at all—the valley was so dim and muted. The first whiffs of whale oil drifted up to us as we came in for a landing at the bottom of a place called Griffith Park, which Dad routed us to after spotting a strange domed building at the top of a big hill.

On the way Oliver had answered all my questions, explaining how on the morning he'd been feeding the pegasi carrots, he was actually spying on Medusa's house to figure out a way in to find the golden bridles . . . telling me how he knew things might go badly for us in the genie's cave, and he wanted to be prepared for it. I was shocked: He'd planned so much ahead, he'd risked his life for us, it was more than I ever could have hoped for, even from *him*. Not to mention how terrifying it would have been to be in Medusa's house. He said she was out grocery shopping when he did it, but even that sounds scary beyond words.

"I've already lost my parents," he said with his chin on my shoulder, so that I could hear him over the soft whooshing of the air around us. "I'm not going to lose yours."

The ground loomed up at us and we came in for a soft landing in a small clearing surrounded by thick trees. We all slid off our mounts and shook out our legs, regaining our footing as Oliver slipped the bridles off of the pegasi and rubbed their snouts. "You're free, guys," he said. "Go find your herd."

They snuffed and snorted and shook out their tangly manes, then turned away from us, launching into the sky the same way they had in Luck City—trotting a few steps on the ground before trotting on air and lifting up, up, and away.

"Where will the pegses go?" Sam asked, standing against Millie's legs.

"Probably to the Sierra Madres," Dad said, "where they're supposed to be."

Everyone gazed at Oliver then. Mom patted at her eyes with her fingertips, as if to push back tears. She kept clasping her hands together like she was trying not to reach out and grab him and hug him into oblivion. We all looked around at each other. I guess there were no words to thank him enough for what he'd done, so none were said.

Anyway, there we were, standing in a park in Los Angeles. We could hardly believe we'd come so far. The air smelled wet and salty and thick, and a heavy, vibrating buzz came from deep in the trees: the deafening sounds of crickets and cicadas and tree frogs. There had to be millions of them. The shadows of the trees loomed large all around us.

Then the clouds above parted and the moon suddenly flooded our surroundings with light. We were all breathless to realize there were huge, beautiful mansions rising out of the thick woods of the park. They all looked to be abandoned.

"Old LA," Dad said. It took us a few moments to take it all in.

"Now what?" Millie finally asked. "What was that building you saw at the top of the hill?"

Dad suddenly beamed. "Now, we climb," he said, mysteriously excited.

He started picking a path up the mountain. Vines reached across our path and had to be ducked under or climbed over, and the ground was covered in slippery moss, full of puddles and roots. Occasionally, when the breeze came in the right direction, I thought I could smell the ocean. I'd never gotten such a strong feeling of nature being *alive*. Even the leaves seemed to turn their faces up to the moonlight.

"When people were moving west," Dad said, "and LA was a growing city with all sorts of promise, the neighborhood around Griffith Park was one of the prime pieces of real estate, very popular with celebrities. Giants built the houses, charging steep prices. There used to be soccer games and hiking trails and picnics all over the area. But as the forest took over again, the beasts—sasquatches especially—would rob the houses, attack people, or force them out so they could use the mansions as dens to raise their young. People began to head back east in droves. Some of the braver types lingered, and there's still a fairly busy port for sailors to reload on food and supplies. But most people, if they aren't in the shipping business, are long gone—and the angels have taken advantage of the emptiness to move in. The angels, and also someone you've heard of, who hired the giants to help him build the observatory at the top of this mountain back in the eighties."

"Prospero," Mom breathed in wonder. I knew immediately who she was talking about—the famous astronomer, the one Dad went to college with. The one he'd made us all watch on *60 Minutes*.

Dad nodded. "I knew he'd built an observatory out here. I never dreamed we'd actually get to visit it. He's much smarter than I am, and knows just about everything. He'll have some ideas on getting to the edge of the earth."

The moon continued to illuminate our slow trek upward: woods, bungalows, and mansions strangled by thorns, all dark except for the occasional glow behind one of the windows, bright white, so luminous we couldn't make out the shape of whatever it was that was glowing. "What's in those houses?" Sam asked. He was holding my hand and had insisted on walking for a while.

"Those"—Dad grinned at us over his shoulder—"are the angels. Hiding out from the gods."

Millie and I gasped. Because of their brightness, angels can't be captured on film, though I *have* seen drawings of some. Though otherwise they look human, they are luminous and filmy . . . and often extremely attractive. I strained to catch a glimpse of one as we passed another cluster of houses, without any luck. Sam kept getting his shoes sucked off in the mud, so I finally lifted him up and piggybacked him.

"Ew." Millie pulled at a strand of moss that had just slapped across her face. Just then something blindingly bright crossed our path, speeding past us and disappearing back into the trees. Again, I'd missed my chance to get a closer look.

"I can't wait to meet ours!" Sam said. I couldn't agree more.

My thighs felt like they were on fire by the time we reached the top of the mountain and the building we'd seen from the air. We knew we'd arrived when we reached a rusted metal fence with a sign hanging from one of the fence posts that said WELCOME TO GRIFFITH PARK OBSERVATORY!

The sight of it knocked the wind right out of our sails. The gate had a lock, but it was rusted and flapping open in the breeze, and the sign was rotting away.

"It's deserted," Millie groaned.

Dad was clearly troubled. His bright look disappeared and his whole body deflated. He held the gate open for us and we walked up to the building itself—which was made of yellowing white stone, with a large, rusting metal door under a big central dome. Mom knocked loudly, and we waited. She knocked again.

We must have stood there for five minutes or more.

Mom tried the handle, but it didn't budge. We all just looked at each other.

Where would we eat? Would it be safe to sleep in one of the abandoned mansions? How far was it to the docks? All of that was running through my mind when there was a subtle shift in sound beyond the door, and then a moving of levers and locks and a twisting of gears, and suddenly the door was open.

At first glance Prospero looked to be a bit insane, his graying hair sticking up in all directions and his clothes mismatched and disheveled. Like I remembered from *60 Minutes*, he had dark skin the color of hazelnuts, and dark, intensely curious eyes, as if he was sizing us all up. Dad seemed starstruck. It was as if Britney Spears and the president and that guy from *Wheel of Fortune* were all rolled up into one person.

Prospero squinted at us, clearly trying to place my dad, teetering on the edge of recognition.

"Well," he said a moment later, "if it isn't Doofy Lockwood!" He reached out and pulled my dad in for a tight hug. Tears gathered at the corners of his eyes. "Doofy, as I live and breathe!"

Millie mouthed, *Doofy?* to me, and we let Prospero usher us inside.

*   *   *

"It's the best place to watch the sky," Prospero explained, after we'd all officially met, and all sorts of greetings and explanations of our arrival had been exchanged. Apparently elated by our presence, he led us into the dim, empty interior of the observatory, which smelled mildewy and gave us all chills. But I have to admit that it made me proud to see someone famous so happy to see my dad.

"You'll have to stay for a while," he went on. "It's so lonely here. No visitors for years, actually. No one has the stomach to make the trip west anymore. But I need to be here because"—he waved his hands skyward—"I need the darkness and the clear air blowing in from the sea to let me see the stars better. It's perfect for my needs."

It was obvious right off the bat that the observatory (an upper room of which I'm now bathing in) is a gloomy place. (I do wonder why someone with so much money, whose book is a gigantic best seller, wouldn't at least spring for some carpeting or some nice couches. If I had a best seller, I'd have all my furniture covered in silk, and I'd have a Jacuzzi in my room that I'd sometimes have the maid fill with Skittles.) But Prospero was proud as he led us on the tour, showing us to a large dwelling up above the laboratory, at the top of a wrought-iron spiral staircase.

That's where we're staying now, in a big spare loft with mattresses on the floor, full of old furniture with limp cushions, and photos on the walls of galaxies and super-novas. There are several bedrooms branching off to the sides, but they're all empty, so we're camped together. We have a view across the top of the park from which we can see some brick buildings covered in ivy (Prospero says they're old music studios) and the Cloud, which caught up to us yesterday and which is repeatedly being blown several yards east by the ocean breeze, only to drift back to its spot like a jellyfish floating on the ocean current. (I'm trying to use more similes in my writing. Mom says that's what Leo Tolstoy does, and supposedly he's really good.)

Anyway, back to first impressions. Prospero took us through the rest of the observatory—the parts he actu-ally uses to observe the sky—muttering about measure-ments and angles as he and my dad nodded to each other knowledgeably. They had, I noticed immediately, the same way of tilting their heads when they were talking about math, and the same way of getting lost in their own heads.

Millie smirked at me. "Dad found his twin," she whispered.

Eventually he led us upward along a winding staircase that clung to the walls of the dome. Climbing higher and higher, we eventually came to a small circular room with a giant telescope poking out of the roof. It was about twenty times the size of my dad's back home. Dad's mouth fell open, and Prospero smiled. "We'll have to take a look together later. All sorts of nebulas and clusters, easy to spot. I also have a cloud gallery with a glass ceiling, and an aviary where I keep all sorts of birds and ducks. I'm an astronomer first," Prospero explained, turning his attention to the rest of us, "but really I study morphology. It's the science of forms. I'm interested in the connectedness of all natural patterns. I'll be glad to show you what I mean but"—he looked around at all of us—"I'm guessing you might need some rest first? We can continue our tour tomorrow."

"Oh, Prospero," my mom took his hands in hers. "Thank you, for everything. And yes, the kids and I are exhausted."

"I'm looking forward to a long, long visit," Prospero said. Mom sent an uncertain look to my dad, who kissed her good night on the cheek. He and Prospero immediately launched into a discussion of something called apertures as the rest of us trailed quietly off to the loft.

I was just drifting off when Dad came into our shared room about an hour later. Mom was staring at the Cloud out the window.

"Don't worry," he said, low so he wouldn't wake us. "We won't stay long. I'll explain things to Prospero. Tomorrow I'll go get our guardian angel. We'll be on our way in no time." He didn't sound as elated as he had when we'd left him, though; he sounded more tired and worried. I wondered what had changed. He gave each of us a kiss good night before climbing onto the mattress with Mom. (The last time he gave me a kiss good night, I think I was seven.)

My wrist hurts from writing so much, and the bath has gone cold. I'll just finish by saying that it's still morning (as much as I was hoping to stretch this bath out into the afternoon), my dad has gone to get our angel (taking some of Grandma's sock money with him) and this diary is finally (!!!) caught up.

December 6th

It's only been a day, but everything has changed. Things are worse than I could have ever possibly imagined they would be! I don't know which terrible thing to start with. I wish I could go back to the last time I wrote, in my cold bath, when I still had so much faith in Dad and hope for the future!

Yesterday the waiting continued endlessly. Prospero had sent Dad, Grandma's sock of money in hand, to the Bright Market (where you can find angels for hire) clear across the city near Malibu, so we already knew it was going to take forever. . . . But it really, really took forever. I spent the morning trying to occupy myself and picturing who he was going to come back with.

Around ten, Mom, Millie, and Oliver went to the

aviary to pass the time, but Sam is allergic to feathers, so I stayed behind in the loft and entertained him. First I drew mustaches on our faces with one of Prospero's Sharpies, and we pretended to be the mayors of Los Angeles before the beasts chased them out. Then for about an hour we played office and I let him pretend to be my boss, saying "Yes, sir! Right away, sir!" and rushing out to get whatever he asked for. We measured ourselves with a tape measure and I realized I've gotten two inches taller, though Sam has stayed about the same. I pretended to be a magic carpet and kept piggybacking him to the window so we could look out at the overgrown park, the palm trees, and the blue, sunny LA sky.

When we heard a creaking on the stairs, we rushed to the doorway, sure it was Dad. But it was only Prospero calling us for lunch.

After tracking down the others, we all gathered to eat in his quarters—a disheveled and dusty set of rooms littered with star charts and binoculars, telescopes, mummified remains of butterflies and dragon claws, and anatomical diagrams of tigers, yetis, clouds. Oliver couldn't help touching things, studying them with his eyebrows furrowed in deep thought, but Prospero didn't seem to mind.

"I don't usually have lunch guests." He smiled, and cleared off a table in the corner of a massive pile of books and old newspapers. (The top one was ancient, announcing that Ronald Reagan and "famous fur trader Paula 'Plenty of Pelts' Ruskin" had just been elected president and vice president.)

"We're so grateful," said my Mom, sitting next to Millie who was already perched on a wobbly chair. Prospero served us bowls of soup from a small oil stove. "It's just Progresso. An angel brings it for me from Ohio."

We all nodded politely and dug in, and for a few minutes there was only the sound of scraping spoons and slurping.

"So how do you all plan to get back home, once your visit is over?" Prospero asked cheerfully. "Wagon? Horseback? I have some ideas. Though I want you to stay as long as possible."

"Oh, we're not going back home," Mom said, looking a little confused. "Didn't Teddy talk to you about that last night?"

Prospero laughed, his brown eyes twinkling, and shook his head. "Wow, you're an adventurous family! Where to next?"

We all blinked at each other, feeling suddenly awkward. "Well," my mom ventured, "Teddy has some questions to ask you about that."

Prospero laid his spoon down and folded his hands up under his chin, looking suddenly enlightened. "Oh! You mean about the Extraordinary World? He did ask me."

We all stared, practically leaning forward on our chairs, wondering what advice he'd give us. After all, this was the guy who'd written *The Atlas of the Cosmos*.

"Are you familiar with the concept of entropy?" he asked instead, smiling and leaning his chin on his hands. We nodded.

"Dad talks about enter-fee sometimes," Sam said. "I cover my ears, but I can still hear him."

Prospero smiled. "Well, then you know that things move from order to disorder over time, and that's called entropy. Some people say there's a lot of disorder going on in our world." He paused to let this sink in. "Our world is messy and wild and full of monsters (every-where we go, it seems we find more of them) and some people say that means it's 'high entropy.' Some scien-tists claimed to notice a sharp increase in entropy in the sixties, based on the weather and the number of beasts coming farther north."

I was a little confused, but enough of what my dad's always saying had sunk in that it did make a little sense. Prospero leaned back from the table. "Now, as you know, I study physics. And in physics, there are two major theories—one of them that deals with the very big things, like planets and space, and one that deals with the very small things, like tiny little particles— that's quantum mechanics."

Sam slapped his hand against his forehead with dread and whispered, "Count 'em mechanics, too," despondently, while Millie gave me a significant look of boredom. But somehow I found it more interesting coming from Prospero.

"Quantum mechanics tells us particles can jump all over the place," I offered.

"Yes," Prospero said cheerfully, impressed. "And people think it's completely up to chance where those particles go and what they become. They jump and jitter, and it makes them unpredictable. Which is kind of exciting."

"Dad says that's why in this world our Winnebago is a Winnebago, but in another world it could be an elephant."

Prospero nodded. "Exactly. Now, there's a theory that

links the two things together—the study of the really big things and the study of the small, jittery ones. It involves something called superstrings, and—if the theory's right—it means there are other dimensions out there, and other worlds. And maybe some of these other worlds are 'lower entropy' . . . more orderly . . . than ours."

"And you think the Extraordinary World is one of those places?" Mom asked. "One of those places that's less messy? You think we could be safe there?"

Prospero shook his head. "No, I don't." He picked up his spoon and then laid it down in the bowl again. "I don't, because it doesn't exist."

Sorry, I had to put down my pen for a minute because I was clutching it so hard I thought I might break it in half. But I've calmed myself a little now, so I'll keep going.

Prospero looked up at us from under his bushy brows. "I told Teddy as much last night. The theory I'm talking about, which says it *could* exist, is just a theory, and lots of scientists disagree with it. *I* disagree with it. We never trust a theory that's messy, and the theory of other dimensions is a messy one—at least for now." Prospero looked sympathetic. "Anyway, even if it turns out to be correct, you'd never be able to see another dimension like that. And there's certainly no way you'd be able to reach it."

Millie cleared her throat, and Oliver fidgeted in his seat. But I couldn't take being silent anymore, and blurted out, "We have proof!"

Prospero turned his eyes on me, surprised.

"We do! Back in our room. I'll get it!" I said.

I rushed up to the loft and came back with Mom's knapsack, carefully unloading the three items onto the table: the postcard, the encyclopedia page, the snack bag. I was so relieved Mom had rescued them from the Trinidad. (How stupid that relief seems now as I write this!)

Prospero picked each one up and studied it closely, looking intrigued and pleased. He smiled as he placed each item down on the table, then shook his head and chuckled.

"I remember these. They're great. The kind of thing people pay a lot of money for back north. Very nostalgic."

A tension settled around the table. Prospero seemed blissfully unaware of it. We all looked to my mom, who'd gone pale, her dark hair hanging around her face like it had gone limp, though I'm sure I'm just remembering it that way now.

"What do you mean . . . nostalgic?" she slowly asked, laying her hands down on either side of her soup bowl, rubbing her fingers against the surface of the table.

"Well, they're souvenirs," Prospero said, looking surprised. He stared around at us, more and more bewildered. "From that theme park that used to be in Florida. The World of the Extraordinary World. Didn't you ever go?"

Mom pressed her lips tightly together. "Theme park?" she asked.

"Sure. It was right near Disney. Closed down, of course. Doofy and I talked about it once—we think our parents might have taken us there the same week, when we were little. Right around our birthdays. He loved that place. Theodore's a fanciful guy, as I'm sure you know. I always liked that about him. Not so buttoned up, like so many of us hard scientists."

Finally, our distress must have sunken in, because Prospero frowned, his eyes widening in surprise. "He didn't tell you they were real, did he?" But he could already tell the answer to his question, and his frown deepened. He took the artifacts in hand, and pointed at the encyclopedia page apologetically.

"You just have to look closely. Look at the copyright."

Now I saw, in tiny type lining one side of the page, the sickening words: *Extraordinary World Studio Souvenirs.*™

"And the photo's been doctored, quite a lot," he went on, pointing to the fuzzy outlines of the images on the postcard.

"I see," Mom said flatly. "I didn't notice that before."

"The Extraordinary World doesn't exist?" Millie asked, her voice cracking. "You don't think we can find it?"

Prospero turned to look at her searchingly. "My young friend, I *know* you can't."

Just then, with the worst sense of timing ever, the front door opened and in came . . . not my dad, but possibly the world's shabbiest looking guardian angel. He appeared to be about nineteen, gawky and skinny, and was wearing a crumpled bowler hat. He was flickering dimly, and staring at all of us hopefully and a little shyly.

Dad appeared behind him, looking hopeful too. He peered around at us and smiled.

"Well, here he is!" he said, holding a hand toward the angel as if he were a rabbit he'd pulled out of a hat. We all stared back at him in stunned silence.

Dad took in the scene before him, and his smile began to fade. Still, he asked brightly, "What'd I miss?"

December 9th

It's been three days since I last wrote. To the west, a grayness is gathering—low clouds stretching across the sky. Prospero says a storm front's coming across the Pacific. Virgil, our guardian angel (even now it feels ridiculous to write that!—the idea of him being a guardian is like the idea of Dinky the farting dog being descended from wolves), is outside making curlicues in the air beyond the windows. He seems to be trying to get Millie's attention as she sits by the window staring out listlessly. It's unlikely he'll get it.

Here's what I know about Virgil so far. He has a flickering, transparent halo that floats above his ridiculous bowler hat, and like the hat, it's crumpled on one side. He's one of the lowest order of guardian angel—I don't know much about angels, but I know those are the angels who didn't rebel against the gods at all but just came along with the others to live on earth because they had nothing else going on.

Mom says he isn't "the sharpest needle in the sewing box." Last night he went out to get burritos at a place he knows—one of the few surviving burrito kitchens in all of LA, which caters to the shipping trade down by the docks—and when he came back he flew smack into the main loft window, which made me snort into my hand and Millie go into one of the empty bedrooms and slam the door.

He always straightens his posture whenever Millie sashays through the room. His devout admiration only increases her disgust. For one thing, he's translucent (angels are wisps of air, only barely touchable) and she's flesh and blood, so it could never work out between them anyway, but also he isn't nearly as good looking as Millie is. He's wiry and too tall and like I said, his halo is practically decrepit (maybe that's why he wears the bowler, to distract people), and instead of having a steady angelic glow, he blinks on and off like the lightbulbs in Luck City.

I do have to admit he seems to have a kind heart. He

calls us all "ma'am" and "sir"—even me and Oliver and Sam—and always tips his hat to us when we enter or leave a room. And he seems eager to help: He tried to make coffee for my mom this morning, but ended up setting a small oil fire in the kitchen, and then levitated around the room blushing and saying, "Wow, I'm sooooooo sorry. Wow, just, sorr-Y," as Mom put the fire out.

"I can't be around that buffoon a minute longer," Millie said, and disappeared up to the loft. She does that a lot.

Oliver, I can tell, feels sorry for him, but I think he's holding himself back from being nicer to him because of his loyalty to me. He knows that I don't want to have anything to do with him.

Only Mouse has been welcoming and kind. He likes to reach out his little hand and pat Virgil's wispy knee, as if to tell him everything will be all right. The sight makes me want to scream a little bit, because it was Sam that our angel was supposed to protect. I can barely look at Sam without wanting to scream, actually. I don't want to contemplate what we're going to do to protect him now. The truth is, I have no idea what we *can* do, and that's too scary to think about. It makes me so angry, it feels like I might burst into a million tiny pieces of rage, each one like a shard of glass. It feels like all the jagged glass pieces of me could float all over the world and stab everything.

My dad insists that Virgil is a good fit for us and that he wants to explain, but none of us are willing to hear it. I keep wondering why someone who can solve any equation and can easily quote the second law of thermodynamics has no common sense. Or, much more importantly, how he can be such a liar.

He's been sleeping alone on a mattress in the observatory. Mom hasn't said a word to him since that day at lunch.

At her request, Prospero has been helping us gather the things we need to get back home: giving us blankets, stocking up our food supplies with about a hundred cans of Progresso and Chef Boyardee, and fixing an old Land Rover he's had sitting out back behind the observatory for years, loading the back with drums of whale oil. It's big, with giant tires, and he says if any car can get us home, it's that one. He says he knows of some old roads and paths that could probably get us as far as eastern Arizona, and then from there we could wind our way back to the main road again.

All of us voted on this plan except for Dad—we've decided he no longer gets a vote. But there's no happiness in the thought of heading back the way we came. Sam keeps saying that, out the window, the smiling man hasn't been smiling at him recently, but only frowning a little, like he's sad. "Maybe we should just let him come in," he keeps suggesting. A couple of times Mom has disappeared into another room after he's said that.

How can you live with something that is impossible to live with? How can you accept something that's impossible to accept?

Prospero estimates we can leave in two days, and Mom agrees that's what we want to do. Dad hasn't said anything about it either way. Not that I care.

Last night I heard a beautiful sound down the hall and went to see what it was. I found Mom in the cloud gallery, playing a dusty violin she'd found among Prospero's treasure troves of old junk. With her head tilted up to the glass dome that lets Prospero observe the clouds, she played with her eyes closed, her head moving back and forth as if the music held her on a string. When she finished, she turned to see me standing there.

"That sounds really good," I said. "You're a good player, Mom."

She smiled sadly. "I'm good at lots of things I don't get to do much anymore," she said. "If your dad were more *present*, and could look after you guys more, I could—" She stopped herself short, looking like she regretted saying anything.

I walked up beside her and looked up at the dome with her—which gave a sweeping view of the clouds that had been gathering bigger and bigger throughout the day.

"It's an amazing sky," she said. "Even with all those clouds." Her lips quivered.

That's my mom. She sees the good in everything.

December 10th

I found my Dad outside the aviary this morning, gazing at the western horizon with a pair of binoculars. If you stand in that spot you can catch a glimpse of the Pacific Ocean through the trees.

He didn't look over at my approach, though I was sure he heard me.

"Dad," I said. He kept his eyes to his binoculars. "Dad," I said again. Enraged, I stepped in front of him and tilted the lenses at my face so that all he could see was my cheek, magnified a thousand times. He lowered his hands and looked at me.

"You need to come out to the dirt track and help pack the Land Rover."

He nodded. "Okay, Gracie." He rubbed meekly at

the stubble on his chin. There were lines on his forehead and around his eyes that I'd never noticed before,
and maybe even some new freckles. I realized that he
has been getting older on this trip. We all have, of
course. But my dad's always seemed exactly the same
to me, like he never changes. In the past few months,
he has.

I stood there wishing he'd say something annoying,
but he just looked down at his shoes. Still, I wanted to
yell out every bad thought I'd ever had about him.

"You're a liar," I finally said.

"I'm sorry."

Angry tears threatened to spill out, but I held them
in. "That's not good enough. I'll never forgive you.
Never."

A squawking arose from the aviary, and we both
peered inside through the big screen window. A turkey
was chasing a duck around in circles, and a few chick-
ens were flapping their way out of the fray. When they
settled down, we turned back to each other.

"Gracie, I'm so sorry I hurt you. I know what you must
think of me. But I don't think I was wrong."

I goggled at him. I couldn't believe my ears. I wondered if the pressure building inside me was the feeling

you get before you spontaneously combust. I wanted to turn into a weapon that could hurt him.

"I didn't have any other choice," he went on. "If we'd stayed at home or at Grandma's, we would have just been waiting there to give Sam up. I thought, even if we had the tiniest bit of hope, it was better than none at all. So I had to convince you, and Grandma agreed with me."

He leaned back against the white wall of the aviary, looking deeply tired. "When we were flying in and I spotted the observatory from the air, I was so elated. I thought this was my shot. I figured there was a chance Prospero might help us; I thought he might believe the same things I did. I knew it wasn't a sure thing by a long shot, but I hoped. He's been researching these kinds of things for years, and I've always admired him. I always thought if anyone could find the Extraordinary World, he could."

My anger was now congealing into a ball in my belly, like a lump of raw dough.

"But, Gracie," he said, looking up at me, "even if Prospero doesn't believe it exists, and even though I don't have proof, my gut still tells me it does. I believe it for no reason I can explain. It's not very mathematical or logical to say that, but I just do."

"You should have trusted us enough to tell us the truth," I said flatly.

Dad gazed into my eyes. "Would you have trusted me back?" he asked.

I tried to come up with an answer, but it got stuck in my throat. Dad didn't seem to be waiting for one. He wasn't trying to make me feel guilty. He was just standing there, clenching and unclenching his hands.

"I know you all don't think much of my theories and my way of doing things. But I can't give Sam up. I can't let him go. I wish I could make the Cloud take me instead of him, but I can't. So I think we have to keep trying . . . I mean, trying anything at all. And that"— he waved a hand out toward the ocean—"is the only thing I can come up with. We need to keep going."

I leaned back against the wall beside him. My anger was leaking out when I wanted so badly to hold it in.

The thing is, it's easy to be mad at Dad when I just think of him as someone who's in charge of me, and whose word always goes whether he's right or wrong. But at that moment he just seemed—not so much like a dad but like any person who didn't have things figured out. Maybe the world is a mystery to everyone, even the smartest people or the oldest people, even Prospero . . .

maybe even Michael Kowalski's old grandma down the street who I originally thought the Cloud was coming for. Maybe you get really old and things are still as mysterious as ever.

I guess it makes me think that the mistakes I make and the mistakes my dad or any other adult makes aren't all that different. Which feels like a grown-up realization, and which also makes me think I never want to have children, because they'll always be mad at me like I'm always mad at my dad.

Anyway, leaning there beside him, I felt the idea of going home slipping out of my grasp.

"Prospero could be wrong," I said. "He's only human."

Dad nodded. "I think so too."

"There's a chance it's out there," I said. "Despite everything."

"I really think there is," Dad said.

I thought about how maybe there are still some things left to be discovered. I have to believe that there are still mysteries left on our planet.

"I don't want to give up," I said, though I shivered a little as I said it, because I knew what it meant. It meant facing the sea, and whatever was beyond it.

*　*　*

And now I'm here on my mattress before dinner. I'm running over all the arguments in my mind. I'm going to do my best to convince the others, and I'm so nervous my stomach hurts. Wish me luck.

December 14th

If convincing the others was daunting (which it was, believe me—we argued for three hours nonstop, until I finally got Mom to admit that a sliver of hope is better than none at all no matter how angry she is at Dad), finding a ship and a captain was even worse. Yet somehow, we've done it.

It didn't really work in our favor that we want to be taken to a continent where few ships have ever been— and where the ones that have were met with disaster. But even beyond that, the cold in the Southern Sea is legendary, the Great Kraken lives in the waters around Cape Horn, and rumors run rampant that any sailor who's sailed much past the southern tip of Chile and lived to tell about it has come back speechless and insane.

Dad keeps pointing out that Ferdinand Magellan and his ship the Trinidad made it, conveniently ignoring that nobody knows what actually became of them, and that our own Trinidad went into the Grand Canyon, which isn't really a great omen.

We began our search at a dockside pub called the Squid's Arms. Prospero said it was the only place we might find a sailor drunk enough to say yes, and drew us a map to it. Mom said that she was the only one practical enough to hire the right captain, and insisted on going alone (coldly eyeing Dad as she said it). But when I tagged along behind her as she walked out of the observatory about an hour later, she didn't tell me no. I think she was actually glad for the company.

We found the pub on a narrow, overgrown alley near what Prospero said used to be Venice Boulevard. It was an old wooden building marked not with a sign, but with a cast-iron squid above the door lit from behind by a whale-oil lamp. The smell of liquor and smoke snaked its way out through the cracks in the door, along with the faint sound of a fiddle somewhere in the pub's depths.

Inside, the room was filled with *men*—men on stools, men behind the bar, men with big bellies in frayed polo shirts, men in wool caps. Most of them had beards and mugs of beer in their hands, and they all made a racket—laughter, yelling, loud conversations about the weather, and advice about where to sail next. A fiddler stood in an inner room near a fireplace, playing a jig while the firelight flickered on his beautiful reddish wooden instrument. Two men were saying to each other that if only they were back east, they could be watching the Ravens vs. Giants game on ESPN. But all this was only momentary, because as the men noticed us, a hush fell upon the room, until only the fiddler was left fiddling, and then even he stopped. They all stared at us expectantly.

My mom looked uncertain. And then she cleared her throat and tossed her ponytail back a little. "We're looking to hire a small ship and a captain to navigate us far south," she said loudly and stiffly. "We can pay ten thousand dollars." I gaped. I hadn't known Grandma had given us that kind of money (though maybe when you're a witch, coming by money isn't that hard). It still didn't seem like enough for anyone to risk their lives and their ship.

"Where do you want to be dropped?" came a voice from somewhere back in the second room.

I happened at that moment to lock eyes with a man near the archway that led to the back. He was tall and strongly built, about my parents' age, with intelligent blue eyes that kept darting from me to my mom, and a mouth—hidden under his dark beard—that was smiling a little.

"We need to get to the Southern Edge," Mom swallowed deeply, then went on reluctantly. "We're going to look for the Extraordinary World."

There was a moment of silence. And then, like a wave crashing over us, came the laughter. The men on the stools doubled over as if they'd been punched. No one could catch their breath. A few guys in the corner lifted their beer mugs and clinked them together, and one person shouted, "Let's all take a trip to the moon!" I looked up at my mom. Her face went from pink, to bright pink, to beet red. Another shout came from the back: "I'm on my way to go live on the North Star, who wants to come?"

I could feel my own face flushing with embarrassment, but what really made me angry was all those men laughing at my mom—my beautiful, book-reading, violin-playing, Sam-protecting mom who was better than all of them put together. I didn't mean to do what

I did, but something took over me that felt sort of like the time I hit Arin with the stick.

He was the only man not laughing, but still I grabbed a mug from the nearest table and splashed its contents into the face of the bearded man with the blue eyes. Then, for some reason I still can't fathom, I spit on the floor at his feet. I felt a hand on the back of my neck, and then my mom was dragging me out the front door of the Squid's Arms. The last thing I saw as it closed was the face of the man I'd assaulted—shocked, wet, his eyes glued not on me, but on my mother as she pulled me into the street.

Mom didn't say a word as we marched back down the alley in the direction of Venice Boulevard, which was really just a cracked, abandoned road with palm trees growing up through the cement. Just as we reached it and turned right, I felt a hand on my shoulder and whirled.

It was him. He was wiping his face with the collar of his T-shirt. Mom reached a protective arm between us, but he clasped his hands together and bowed, which made me blush with guilt! Why had I picked *him* to attack?

The man put an end to my misery by letting out a

peal of laughter, his voice crackling as warmly as our fireplace back home.

"I'm not here to make an arrest," he said. He patted my shoulder so hard I had to step back to absorb the impact, but it was clear he meant it to be friendly. "I'm here to make a proposal," he went on.

We stood staring at him, and Mom asked suspiciously, "What kind of proposal?"

The man tilted his head inquisitively, the way Oliver sometimes does. "I need a job. And you need a ship."

Mom went on eyeing him skeptically. "You'd be willing to take us?"

He nodded, just slightly.

"Why?" I wished her voice didn't sound quite so sharp. He seemed to be the only friendly sailor in LA.

He smiled. "That's my business," he said, but gently. "How about I come to discuss it tonight, once I get cleaned up. Where are you staying?"

Mom looked unsure whether she should give him the information, but then, what other option did we have?

"Griffith Park Observatory," she said.

"I'll see you there. Let's say around seven."

My mom looked startled, and then she nodded, giving in with relief.

Jodi Lynn Anderson

Back in Cliffden the only people who wink are crazy or sometimes old people. But this guy winked at us. And then he turned back in the direction of the Squid's Arms and tromped off, and Mom and I headed for home.

That night, at seven sharp, Captain Bill MacDonald arrived at the observatory like a burly whirlwind, introducing himself as he dumped an armful of rolled-up papers and leather-bound books onto the low table by the door of our upstairs quarters, which Prospero led him to (and then left us to it, saying he'd be at his telescope). Before we knew it, he had nautical maps and journals spread everywhere. Something about him was so commanding that it was impossible to do anything but gather around him eagerly and hang on his every word. I have to admit, I liked him immediately.

"Here's what I think," he began, running his fingers along a map of the Pacific. "We head down along the west coast of South America; there are islands there I know well where we can get supplies. Now, I've never been much beyond Cape Horn into the Southern Sea, but I do know my way around the cold—I've spent two winters up in the far north beyond Alaska importing oil, so I know a thing or two about handling the temperatures as we get that far

south. All the way to the cape is territory I'm pretty familiar with—down to the world's southernmost trading post
there just a few miles beyond Chile."

I looked around at the others. Captain Bill seemed like
a dream come true, and only my dad—of all people—
looked skeptical.

"Why are you willing to do this?" he asked. "There
are easier ways to make money."

The captain sat back in his parlor chair, which creaked
under his substantial weight. "My reasons are private.
Maybe I'll tell you sometime when we're sitting on the
deck with drinks in our hands, but right now I'd rather
keep it to myself."

Dad shook his head. "I can't accept that."

We all turned nervously to the captain. But he didn't
seem as annoyed by my dad's insistence as I feared. He
leaned forward and folded his hands together.

"No one wants to go to the edge of the earth unless
they have no other choice. No one wants to leave everything behind." The firelight flickered on his face and
danced in his eyes, and he held a hand against his chest
earnestly. I noticed his sweatshirt read, in faded letters,
Eat Bertha's Mussels.

"A nice lady like your wife, a young girl . . ." He

nodded to me. "There's only one reason why you'd all take such a risk. And I knew for sure when I came up the hill and saw it floating up there above the path." Captain Bill opened his hands now, as if he was offering us something. "It happens I have my own demons to face when it comes to Clouds."

The captain looked around at us, finally turning his keen eyes on our frail little Sam. Mom made a signal to Millie, but she looked so reluctant to go that it was Oliver who stood and took Sam off to bed. When they were safely out of earshot, the captain went on.

"I lost my wife to a Cloud, when we were just a young couple, newly married." Next to me, Millie reached out slowly and clutched my hand.

"The things is, she wanted to get away. She believed in the Extraordinary World, just like you do—she always had a lot of faith in those stories. I think she figured that since I was a sailor I could get us there. She had a lot of faith in me, too. But I didn't believe in those things back then. I thought I knew all the answers. I thought it was stupid to go searching for something that didn't exist."

Millie, who up to now had been silent, let out a long, pitying sigh.

"And now?" Mom asked.

"Now . . . I know there's a lot I don't know. I want to make up for my mistakes."

There was a long pause, and then Dad said, "Once we get to the Southern Edge, we'd need you to wait for us for a little while, to pick us up just in case . . ." He trailed off.

"In case it's not there after all. Of course."

"Two weeks, I think, would be more than enough," my dad said.

"Certainly."

Glancing over at Millie, I wondered if I looked as dazzled by the captain as she did at that moment. Her eyelashes were fluttering at about a thousand beats a minute. Virgil, who'd been keeping the fire stoked and trying to stay out of the way, had absolutely wilted. Oliver, who'd come back from the loft after putting Sam in bed, had his arm crossed over his chest—curious, but not convinced.

Finally, Captain Bill stood up. "You all can think on it tonight and get in touch with me through the bartender at the Squid's Arms. Leave a message with him with your answer. If it's a yes, we leave in two days. I'll need time to get the ship and crew all set."

I couldn't take my eyes off him as he stood to go, and neither could anyone else. We fluttered behind him to the front door. He patted me and then Oliver on the shoulder, bowed to Millie, and gave Dad a firm handshake.

I didn't notice, until he was already out in the hall, the friendly smile he gave to my mom, and the frown she returned to him. Sometimes her frowns look just like Millie's—they both have a way of frowning a smile.

Tonight the loft is silent as we all keep to our own thoughts before bed. I miss hearing the hum of Mom's and Dad's voices talking into the night, just thinking out loud to each other the way they've always done. But ever since Prospero told us the truth about Dad's lie, there's no hum of voices at all.

Outside the big window I can see the moon. Miraculously (since as usual I wasn't paying much attention the day we learned it) I remember a line from poem we read in fourth grade: "The moon was a ghostly galleon tossed upon cloudy seas." I just touched my fingers against the window to see if I can feel the warmth of its light on my hands, but of course I can't.

I'm still as scared of the ocean as ever. *More* scared than ever. But I love my little brother, and I know that out there may be the only way for him.

We're headed to the edge of the earth this time, for real.

December 15th

It's been ninety-nine days since I started this diary, and I'm just about to run out of pages. I'm surrounded by activity, but there's nothing I can do except sit here on the deck of our new ship and describe the scene in the space I have left. Luckily Oliver found an old blank notebook of Prospero's at the observatory, which he allowed him to have, just in the nick of time. I'll start with it the next time I write. Prospero also gave my mom his old violin as a parting gift. Not to mention that he's outfitted us with fur coveralls and coats and microfiber socks, extreme cold weather gloves and seal mittens to go over them, fur blankets, two tents, some instruments, and who knows what else for our trip—a mixture of old explorer gear and newfangled items he says he had flown in, via angel, from a store in New York a few years ago. (I guess we're not the first team of expeditioners he's sent into the wilderness on a mission of discovery—though probably we're the first going somewhere he doesn't believe in.) With his help (but not his blessing) we've also stocked up on crates and crates of food and water, tons of Slim Jims, canned soups, freeze-dried vegetables, and beans to stick in backpacks that are as big as I am.

It seems we're always packing and always leaving. And now everything's been carried on board. Eight men— each of whom is more muscular and smelly than the last—are lashing barrels and trunks to the back decks of our ship, which is called the *Weeping Alexa*. A skiff, which Oliver just explained is a smaller kind of boat, is attached to one side of the ship, just above the water line. Mom is vigorously discussing something with the captain, who seems to be doing several things at once: directing the men with strong thrusts of his arm in this or that direction, tying and untying things, and thoughtfully shoving obstructions out of my mom's way with his foot as they move down the decks.

The smell of fish is so strong I've had to cover my nose with one sleeve. The port is bustling with ships—

fishing vessels, steamers, and freighters on their way
north to Canada or south to Central America. There
are also cruise ships—emblazoned with names like
West Coast Wilderness Adventures or Far Flung
Global Expeditions—coming down from the northern
frontier city of Vancouver, making a day stop to show
people "Old LA."

Prospero said he couldn't bear to come see us off on
our "hopeless misadventure," so there's no one here at
the port to wave good-bye to us when we pull away, but
of course Millie is waving anyway from behind the railing to California at large. She probably imagines she's
waving to invisible admirers. Virgil is circling above
with the seagulls, and Oliver and Sam are sitting a few
feet away from me, making bets on how long they can
go without bathing. The Cloud is hovering just a little
bit farther down the shore, like a loyal dog on a leash,
waiting for its master to get moving.

I think I'm the only one who feels seasick already,
and the captain laughs every time he passes me, because
apparently my face looks green. "Hang in there, Gracie,
we haven't even left yet," he said a few minutes ago, clap-
ping me on the back. "Wait till our first storm." Then he
offered me some ginger root to suck on.

I've got that terrible *leaving* feeling, and it makes me sad that I forgot to pay attention to my last step on the solid earth before boarding the boat. It may have been my last footstep in my country ever. When I got on, I was stupidly thinking about how much I could go for some Twizzlers.

A FEW MINUTES LATER

Well, I'm already in trouble and we've only just let the final line loose from the wharf. Right after I wrote those last words as the shipmates were starting to pull up anchor and unleash us from land, I ran down the gang-way, leaped onto the docks, ran to the end, and touched the ground, said "Good-bye, America," and ran back. The captain shook his head in exasperation, and my mom went red with anger, but it was worth it. I'm back, but I keep putting down my pen to try to rub the lump out of my throat.

Now everyone is waving to no one on the shore, even Mom and Dad, so I'd better go because I want to wave too.

We're leaving our continent behind.

Diary Number
❧ Two ❧

December 25th
(Christmas Day)

I'll bet right now winter is tiptoeing through the hills around Cliffden, and Arin Roland's fireplace is lit and crackling orange and bright.

I remember that the year Sam was born, on Christmas morning Mom packed him on her back in a baby carrier, and we all hiked out to see the frozen reservoir and picked icicles off a big rock. Sam giggled for the first time when I touched my icicle just for a moment to his tiny hand. It's one of the few times I can recall Dad spending the whole day playing with us instead of focusing on the thin clouds over the reservoir or lecturing us about the scientific properties of snowflakes. It's funny, I can't really remember the winters at home before Sam came. I imagine they were similar, but with the feeling of something missing.

This morning, since we don't have a Christmas tree, we gathered around a potted plant Captain Bill has on the dining table of the galley, and Mom and Dad (who are speaking to each other, but only barely, because Mom will barely even look at him) presented us each with one gift: for Millie, a bottle of perfume. (Mom says she splurged on it in Luck City, remembering that her own mom gave her perfume for Christmas the year *she* was sixteen.) For me, a set of nice pens—which Mom said she found at Prospero's and took with his blessing. For Sam, a new teddy bear that she sewed together out of socks and buttons. And for Oliver, a signed copy of *The Atlas of the Cosmos.* The inside cover was inscribed in Mom's handwriting, *To our honorary sixth family member. Thank you for hopping into our Winnebago. We love you.* (I couldn't tell whether Oliver was pleased or just uncomfortable.)

"I know we can never take the place of your real family," Mom said uncertainly, "but we want you to know how much we care about you."

Oliver nodded shyly, and even though I felt sad for him, I also fought back a stab of envy. It's partly that there's never enough of my mom to go around, even for *me*. And it's partly that, when he first stumbled onto the

Trinidad, Oliver was *my* friend and *my* discovery, but these days he and my family belong to each other, too. I'm trying to learn how to be gracious about these sorts of things, but it's not always easy.

Now I'm sitting wrapped in a thin flannel blanket on the quarterdeck, with this diary leaned against my knees. You'd think I would have had endless amounts of time to write since we left port, but it's hard to explain—the sea is mesmerizing, and hours go by without me even noticing. The ship is so aflutter with activity that sometimes I forget to worry about the huge crossing we've embarked on, I'm so wrapped up in the sights and sounds around me. I've decided to believe that we're going to get where we're headed, and that it's all going to turn out exactly as Dad has hoped. I think it's the only option I want to imagine.

The crew keeps busy. There are eight of them, but I've only really talked to two: There's Troy, a balding guy from New Jersey, who says he used to work at a dart-and-balloon booth at the Jersey shore until the mermaids tore the boardwalk down. He wants to get back home just about as badly as I do, and every time I see him, he pumps a fist in the air and says, "Jersey forever." It's become our shared anthem for missing home, and even though I'm from Maine, I say it back to him. There's also a white-haired guy named Ronald who's lived in LA his whole life and has plenty of stories about giants. There are also a couple of young Canadians who apparently joined up when the ship last docked in Nova Scotia. At night just the captain and our family gather in the galley for dinner. The room is lit by glass lanterns with drippy white candles in them. The crew eats in a "mess," which I haven't seen.

Apparently it takes a lot of work just to keep the *Alexa* moving in a straight line, and the men are usually too busy to talk. Captain Bill seems to spend a lot of time paying attention to the winds and the stars, his face pressed to the breeze day and night, breathing in the air and always looking around him as if he's in perfect harmony with the ocean.

The breeze is fresh and cool today, and the water is such a deep blue, it's almost black. The farther south we get, the more alone we are. At first we passed other ships several times a day—on their way up to Canada with supplies, or slowly making their way south along the west coast of Mexico, full of passengers escaping the winter weather. Three or four days ago we saw two angels carrying a banner through the sky above the shore, and at first Millie and I thought it must be some sort of important announcement, but when we got closer we realized all it said was JOE'S VOTED #1 MARGARITAS ON THE COAST. I'm guessing that Joe's may have the only margaritas on the coast, as Mexico has an infamous sea snake problem that keeps the beaches empty.

I've asked Captain Bill if he'd like to own a shiny new steam-powered ship like the ones we've seen, wishing that we were on one of them. (Oliver says the *Alexa* is about a hundred years old.) But he only shook his head. "They're so hard to produce, so expensive, I couldn't afford one even if I wanted one. Still, I *wouldn't* want one anyway. This girl," he said, patting the rails of the *Alexa*, "she's solid. She's reliable. I'd rather have her than a hundred new ships."

Now we've peeled away from the Mexican coast, and we're lucky if we spot one or two ships a day.

Yesterday morning we did run into some excitement. I was in the galley, doing a sock puppet show for Sam, when a shout of "all hands on deck" startled us. Upstairs the men were trimming the mainsails and steering us away from what—at first—looked like a bubbling, churning hole in the ocean, about fifty yards away and large enough to swallow ten ships our size. I hugged Sam against me and held my breath as the others—Oliver, Mom, Millie, and Dad (coming from another direction) surfaced from below. The size of the swirling hole, the sheer force of the water, made my heart pound.

"Whirlpool," the captain said lightly, taking my mom's arm and leading her toward the center of the deck. "Don't want you to lose your footing near the sides, it can get bumpy." His jaw was set with concentration, but his smile was reassuring. "The sea's full of 'em. Don't worry. We're too far away to get caught in it"

Under his orders the ship listed left, then right, and soon we were skirting the danger. It didn't look like we had much room to spare, but none of the deckhands seemed worried. Only when the whirlpool was shrinking in the distance did I remember to breathe.

"Deadly whirlpools are the least of our concerns," Captain Bill said, trying to console me but only making me more nervous. He must have read it on my face, though, because he quickly added, "I'm sorry, Gracie. I forget what it's like encountering it all for the first time; I've been on the sea so long. The ocean is a wild place, but we'll make it." He smiled at me gently.

Millie says she thinks he's "wildly romantic" (I think she got that from a movie): He's so strong and full of life when he's throwing barrels around the ship, or giving orders, or helping his men to hoist the sails, but then when he's not busy, he turns very melancholy and thoughtful. He likes to watch the sunset and read books of poetry from a tiny library he keeps in the galley. (There are some paperback romance novels in there too, which he says are Ronald's.) Millie and I have gotten into the habit of spying on him there through the windows. (There's something about him that makes us feel giggly.) Virgil, who spends most of his time hovering at the top of the mainmast being a lookout, is depressed by this, but resigned.

Captain Bill knows everything there is to know about the ocean—he knows the exact moments the tides turn, he can gaze at a clear blue sky and predict a storm, or glance up at an ominous patch of clouds and declare carelessly that it will blow over. He's given us several enthusiastic tours of the ship, his dark beard glistening in the sun and his blue eyes bright with excitement. (The ship, as I wrote before, is ancient, but he's added some modern conveniences: a few battery-operated radios here and there, a nice compass from

REI duct-taped beside the ship's wheel, a renovated bathroom.) He's taught us all the difference between a quarterdeck and a poop deck, a keel and a rudder, and all kinds of sails, from the mizzen topgallant to the spanker. Oliver memorizes it all easily, and I'm not bad at picking things up either. Millie mostly just says, "Oh, that's so interesting!" But really I can tell she's not interested much except in just being polite to the captain. Mom says one day Millie will "find what her real interests are" and then "she'll be unstoppable." But I haven't seen any evidence of that yet.

This morning, getting up just as the sun was rising, I found Oliver and Captain Bill standing at the keel, silhouetted in the early light, the breeze ruffling their hair as they watched something in the water. At first I couldn't make out what it was that kept breaking the ocean's surface and then disappearing, but then . . .

"Mermaids?" I asked, clutching the rail, giddy. I'd never seen one in real life.

A cry came across the water, and a few distant shapes surfaced in the ship's wake and went under again.

The captain nodded. "We're crossing over a well-established mermaid city," he said. "They're just waking up, like we are. They follow the ship because we churn up fish they like to eat." Seagulls did the same, swooping down to stab the water with their beaks and then sailing upward again.

I sucked in my breath as a handful of mermaids surfaced again: smelly, slimy things with pale white faces and hair stuck to the sides of their cheeks, their eyes glittery and flat. I'd seen them on TV, but I'd never realized they were quite so nasty looking.

"Are they ever friendly?" I asked as one by one they dove again, their tails rising into the air before disappearing.

"A few've gotten used to humans and become more tame," the captain said. "But mostly, they're hungry creatures. They'd drown me as soon as look at me if I fell overboard, and then happily eat me. Or you. Still, they're civilized. They've built beautiful things under the sea, which a few hardy scuba divers have lived to tell about. Stone houses, towers, sculptures . . . maybe you've seen documentaries." He surveyed the wake of the ship. "We'll leave them behind once we get to the really cold sea. The arctic waters have gotten too frigid even for them."

It was such a sublime, fluttery, but also peaceful moment, with just the three of us awake (besides the crew, who were up near the front of the ship busy with their morning chores) and the mermaids dipping and rising in our wake, that I wished it could last all day. The crisp air felt nice as it gently blew through my hair, and the sun warmed my face.

"Captain," Oliver said quietly, "why do you keep sailing, when the sea's so dangerous?" I'd actually been wondering the same thing.

Captain Bill looked thoughtful and rubbed his dark beard. "I can't imagine life without it. The ocean's always a mystery. There are fish deep down in the dark, so delicate that if you brought them into the light they'd disintegrate. There are depths we'll never reach, hidden valleys and mountain ranges right beneath us that we'll never see. To me, the ocean is a never-ending surprise. I only feel alive when I'm drifting along with her."

He glanced in the direction we'd come. The Cloud was in the distance behind us, keeping a steady pace.

"It's the sea ghosts that scare me. They're mostly victims of krakens—poor drowned sailors who never had a chance. They're the most vicious ghosts on earth, I'd wager, intent on dragging sailors into the Underworld with them. I had an encounter with them on my first voyage that I'll never forget. It nearly turned me off to the sea forever." He stared into the distance, his focus growing hazy.

"What happened?" I asked.

The captain looked at me, smiled, and rubbed my head as if I were still a little girl. "Let's just say, I was lucky to make it home, Gracie." Seeing our faces, he looked like he regretted bringing it up. "The ocean is a big place," he rushed on, "and the chances of running across a phantom ship are very small. Anyway, I know what to do should we ever come across one. I'm prepared for anything." He smiled confidently. He was just taking in a big, happy lungful of air when my dad emerged from a door behind us. His glasses glinted in the sun, and he tripped over a rope as he walked in our direction, gazing up at the thin layer of clouds. He was clutching an anemometer in his hands—one of the instruments Prospero gave him for the trip. (It's a small metal post with three twirling cups on top that are supposed to measure the wind.)

"G-good morning," he stuttered, trying to get his sea legs. (I've finally adjusted, but Dad hasn't taken to the ocean very well, and spends a fair amount of each day looking like he might be sick.) I said a distant "good morning" back, Oliver gave a sheepish wave, and the captain nodded politely. Sometimes my dad looks so small and lost and befuddled by ship life, and the burly men around us, that I want to forgive him (just because I agreed to this voyage doesn't mean I've forgotten what he did), but this morning wasn't one of those times.

"I wonder if you could tell me which is the poop deck?" he asked Captain Bill, squinting up at the clouds. "I'd like to set this up and do some calculations . . . figure out how fast we're traveling and start getting used to the instrument. It might come in handy when we're in the Southern Sea."

Captain Bill looked skeptical, but nodded, giving us a sideways wink that seemed to hint at my dad's silliness. "Yes, sir. I'll take you up." And the two disappeared up the deck, the captain striding ahead while my dad tripped along behind him. Oliver turned to me. "Ghosts ships," he said, and gave a jokey frown, like could anything be scarier?

"Yeah. I know."

We looked out at the water. The sun had risen high enough that the glow of dawn was gone.

"When do you think you'll forgive your dad?" he asked.

"Your guess is as good as mine," I replied.

"I'd forgive him really soon, if I were you," he said. "If he were my dad."

I looked down at the rail, feeling guilty. I knew what he meant; I know that if he could have his parents back, he'd forgive them for *anything*. But how can you *make* yourself forgive someone? It's like making yourself like ravioli—it's not something you can really force.

"I wish he were more like Captain Bill," I said. "Captain Bill is really *aware* . . . or *alive*, or something."

Oliver shrugged and looked away. "I bet he has his faults too. He seems a little dramatic to me."

"Well, he does seem passionate," I offered. But I'm not sure that's exactly what Oliver meant.

I've just put down this diary to have an interesting conversation with Virgil. He came out on the quarterdeck with some sort of glowing ball of light in his hand, walked to the rail without me noticing it, and let it go. It fluttered out of his hands like a dove and flew off north. As he turned, he saw me, floated back a little in surprise, and adjusted his bowler hat. "Hi, Gracie," he said.

"Hi." I'm trying to be nicer to him these days, since we're stuck with him and he's stuck with us. "What was that?"

Virgil looked in the direction of the little ball of light, getting farther and farther away. "Oh, not much. Just a letter to my supervisor. We have to check in and report our progress when we're on a job."

"Who's your supervisor?" I asked.

"Oh." Virgil floated up beside me and then settled in to sit a couple feet away. "I have tons of them. There's a lot of hierarchy in the angel word. Everybody has a boss."

I waited, curious, hoping he'd explain. Virgil seemed pleased that I was interested.

"There are three spheres. In the top sphere are heavenly counselors. Those are the cherubim, the seraphs, the elders. The bigwigs. Very high up, old, and powerful. Then there's the second sphere. There are the dominions, who are kind of like middle managers. They're in charge of us third-sphere angels. They're all very beautiful. I think if Millie ever met a dominion, she'd . . ." His voice trailed off, and I felt a sudden pity for him. "Then come the virtues. They control the motions of the stars and the cosmos. They keep things moving." He looked at me. "Is this boring?" I shook my head.

"There are the powers after that, they're like the

angel warriors. And then, you get to angels like me, down on the third sphere. We're the ones who interact with people the most. I guess you could say we're, like, the front line. We're the messengers, the protectors." He blushed.

"And we all love to sing. That's the big thing about angels. We're all in the choir—every last one of us. We used to gather so high above the clouds to do that, nobody on earth could hear us. But since the rebellion, we just kind of sing among ourselves, quietly."

"Have you ever been anyone else's guardian angel, besides ours?"

Virgil looked down at the fish netting near his feet. "This is my first job," he said. "I'm afraid I'm not doing all that great. I'm not"—he hesitated—"all that coura- geous, to be honest."

"You're doing fine, Virgil," I said. "I'm sure if we were really in danger, you'd do a great job saving us." I was just saying it to be nice, though. Still, it seemed to cheer Virgil up.

I know I'm always bringing up my dead dog, but I have to say that Virgil reminds me a bit of her. She used to sit at the window to guard the house, but then run and cower when she saw a squirrel out the window. I don't want to think about what would happen if our lives were ever really in Virgil's hands. I'm pretty sure we wouldn't make it out alive.

"Thanks, Gracie," Virgil said, adjusting his bowler. "It means a lot that you believe in me."

"Of course I do, Virgil," I lied.

December 31st
(New Year's Eve)

*In my bed a little after midnight, under the covers, rock-*ing along with the sea, which is especially choppy tonight. Mom has been playing the violin. It's an eerie sound—the notes drifting back to us from the foredeck, where she's been standing for over an hour.

This evening we came within view of the first land we've seen since we peeled away from Mexico: a group of islands called the Galapagos. It's one of the places where drag-ons spend the winter. I've never seen so many of them in one place, circling above the rocky islands and clustering together like crows on every surface! We were probably a mile away, but it was easy to make out their dark silhou-ettes. We all gathered to watch the scene go past, even Dad.

"Oh, isn't it beautiful?" Mom said, coming to stand

next to Captain Bill, her long red skirt and her dark hair fluttering in the wind like ribbons behind her. The captain nodded agreement.

"It's one of my favorite sights coming and going," he said. "Seeing those islands always means either I'm off for an adventure, or I'm almost home. Both are nice in their own way."

Mom turned to look at him. "The voyages must feel long." She rubbed her bare arms in the cool breeze.

"Long and lonely," the captain agreed, but still he was smiling faintly as he watched the dragons swoop and pirouette. He took a long, deep breath. "And not much to come home to. But back in Nova Scotia, where I'm from, I've got a warm house that looks at the ocean. I get there maybe once every year or two. It's got all my favorite things: most of my books, an old piano I can barely play . . . Halifax is a beautiful seaside town, remote but lively. Ships in the harbor and pubs where you can hear live Irish music all night, mountains and beaches to explore nearby. You'd like it there."

He rubbed his hands together vigorously. "We can't stop in these islands for supplies this time of year, for obvious reasons. But San Cristobal, a couple of days up ahead, is dragon-free. They've been really successful with an antidragon initiative they started back in the seventies—all sorts of reflective surfaces posted in the water around them to keep dragons away. We'll lay over there for a couple of nights and load up." With that, he disappeared belowdecks. We thought he'd gone for good, when he returned carrying a rough wool blanket, which he handed to Mom. She looked at him gratefully and pulled it around her shoulders.

Dad was standing just to her left with a manometer, another one of the many instruments he'd brought aboard, this one a palm-size gauge to measure the air pressure, or something like that. Mom's eyes went to him for a moment, almost as if she wished *he'd* handed her a warm blanket (even though she ignores him at meals and goes to bed to read when the sun sets, while he stays out and examines the stars from the ship's telescope and takes notes). I wonder if he's even picked up on the fact that it's chilly out. Dad is much better at measuring life than at noticing it.

"It seems," Dad said, glancing down at his manometer, "as if a storm may be blowing up from the east."

The captain peered into the eastern sky, then glanced toward our Cloud following behind to the north and shook his head. "Nope. It's going to be a fine evening."

Dad followed his gaze, squinted, then looked back at

his instrument. "But it says here that . . ." He trailed off a little.

The captain interrupted him. "Well," he said, stretching into a big yawn. "It's getting dark, and I have a little something set up for you all in the galley. How about we head indoors?"

We entered the galley to a surprising and cheerful sight—a table full of noisemakers and paper hats and bottles of champagne in rusty buckets. The radio sat on a shelf, blaring staticky oldies. (It's recently been picking up an English-language station from Ecuador, though we've noticed that sometimes it's mixed with a station playing salsa music.)

Anyway, it's been such a wonderful night! We gathered around the table and played cards, and danced (me with Captain Bill and Millie with Oliver, and then Captain Bill with Mom while Millie and Oliver and I danced with Sam), and talked and laughed, and forgot about the hours flying by. Mom even let Millie have a full glass of champagne (and me half a glass!). She beat all of us at cards, and Dad disappeared sometime during a game of spades that went on forever.

At some point Ronald and Troy (the friendliest shipmates) came in to join us. They said they'd invited Virgil but that he wouldn't leave his post (he's appointed himself lookout from the topmast), and that he wanted us to know he'd spotted a whale about an hour ago. He did fly down a little before midnight to visit, and at twelve on the dot (Captain Bill has a Timex watch he's had since the eighties, which he says is indestructible and keeps perfect time) we all cheered and kissed each other. Virgil got to kiss Millie on her hand (though an angel kiss is like brushing air), and Mom kissed Captain Bill on both cheeks and blushed, and I kissed everyone except for Oliver—who very awkwardly planted a kiss on my chin that maybe he was aiming for my cheek. We all showered Sam with dozens of kisses, waking him up, since he'd fallen asleep on one of the benches. Captain Bill turned the music up after that, and we all danced in a circle to "The Twist," and "Boogie Shoes," and "The Locomotion."

I think it's been the happiest time we've had since we left Cliffden. I even said to Mom, out of breath, that it almost felt like being at home instead of in the middle of a vast and mostly empty ocean. "I think we carry home on our backs," she said. (I'm still trying to figure out exactly what she meant.)

Anyway, we both looked at Sam, who'd fallen asleep

again, and Mom smiled. "I better tuck this one in," she said, and wished everyone a quick good night.

Now here I am in bed, a little dizzy from the champagne and still wide awake. It's a new year, and Mom's violin playing has finally stopped. I suppose she's gone to sleep, and I guess I will too.

PS: It's turned out to be a fine, clear night, just like the captain promised.

January 7th

I'm back in my favorite corner of the poop deck, sitting on some fish netting. We're making our way down the coast of Chile after two full days off-ship. All afternoon South America's been winking at us, green and sparkling, arching up out of the water or tapering down into pristine beaches. Massive giants guard the shores against modern day pirates who sometimes invade the beaches, and every once in a while I think I can just make out a distant, enormous figure waving a club in the air and warning us to keep away.

Our stopover at San Cristobal was, as Millie puts it, *divine*. The morning we arrived, we woke to find we were already docked and that the captain and most of the shipmates had already departed for the other side of the island in the skiff to do some trading. Before us was a thin sliver of turquoise water leading up to a pristine white beach, and some gleaming white rooftops in the distance beyond the trees (probably hotels, Mom said). It was all we could do to be patient enough for Troy to get the rowboat loaded and lowered and row us to shore.

Sam and I spent most of our time on the island building and knocking down sand castles. (I'm a little bit ingenious with sand sculpting and made some very nice creations, but Sam tore down everything I built while pretending to be a giant. I didn't mind at all because he's been feeling so good recently.) Virgil must have picked a hundred tropical flowers for Millie, flying all over the island to find the ones that were hardest to get, his wiry body shooting through the sky like a rubber band. No sooner would he hand a batch to her than she'd lay them down in the sand and forget them, or drop them into the waves while she waded. Finally she noticed the effect it was all having on Virgil's halo and general flicker, and the next flower he delivered (a Venus flytrap—poor Virgil thought it was a lily), she tucked between two buttons in her dress and gave him a faint, almost friendly smile.

I thought that was especially nice of her. She's been quiet lately, and going to bed early every night (Mom thinks she's not getting enough vitamin C), but she's also been in a strangely good mood. She spent most of our time on the beach wading and looking for shells, just smiling at nothing. She said at one point that the island made her feel like we were on a "luxurious vacation," and she didn't even beg to go spend the night at one of the hotels we could see in the distance. (We slept on the ship both nights.) I agree that the whole place did kind of feel like resorts we've seen advertised on TV. It was sort of nice hanging around the deserted beach and having it all to ourselves. Even the Cloud hovering far offshore didn't dampen our pleasure. I could almost imagine it with a pair of sunglasses on (though I still can't picture how Millie and Sam both see it as a face of some sort) just lounging up in the sky, being mellow.

Our second day on the island—yesterday—happened to be Oliver's birthday.

I've decided Oliver may be fishlike after all, because we could barely entice him out of the water the whole time we were docked. Troy dug out some snorkels and flippers the captain had stored away, explaining that the water was too shallow for mermaids or sharks, and that was pretty much the last we saw of Oliver for the entire two days. Occasionally he'd stand up in the water to wave at us and yell something like, "I just saw a starfish!" then disappear again, and only trudge up the beach—soaking wet—in time to eat, or in search of more sunscreen (also provided by Troy).

I took advantage of his absence to make him a present—collecting the best shells I could find on the beach and putting them all in a brown paper grocery bag from the ship (the best wrapping I could find). "Can we say it's from me, too?" Sam asked, crouched beside me with his hands on his cheeks and his elbows on his knees, watching me place the shells in the bag.

"Of course," I said. "You hand me some shells. That would be a big help." As I worked, I watched my dad, standing in a big hat to shield his face from the sun, picking his way along the palm trees edging the beach with a balloon he planned to launch high into the air on a string, then pull down and make some recordings from a small meter at its base. He was, of course, the only one of us who didn't relax at all.

Mom cobbled together a cake-ish construction out of

a box of graham crackers, some melted chocolate chips, and marshmallow fluff she'd rounded up on board. Even Millie had something for Oliver, which she'd beautifully wrapped in netting and a blue twine bow. (Her favorite color is blue, and she'd dyed the twine with some dark berries she'd found among the bushes.)

We set everything up on a blanket under some trees, and when Oliver came back from his latest snorkeling excursion, it was all waiting for him. He smiled, surprised. His cheeks were sunburned, and he still had his dive mask up around his forehead.

Millie's gift was much better than mine, it turned out: a drawing of Tweep, which she'd made herself. "You remembered Tweep," Oliver said, his voice soft. He was touched. "I didn't even know you could draw."

"I fiddle around," she said. I watched Oliver admire her work, and I jealously admired it too. Millie does have Mom's artistic gene, but she rarely uses it.

"That one's from me and Millie," Sam fibbed, scooting away from me and distancing himself from my rolled-up, wrinkly grocery bag, which I picked up and handed over only with reluctance. Oliver unrolled the top and looked inside.

"Wow, shells?"

"I didn't really have anything else," I explained. "And I can't draw."

"I love them, Gracie. Thank you." He rolled up the bag and held it tight. "I'll never lose them."

A while later, after we'd all eaten the cake (which was pretty much a blob of sugar, and which sent Sam racing in circles around the palm trees), Oliver walked back down the beach. He took my bag of shells with him, like he didn't want to leave them behind. Millie's drawing—though it was the far superior gift—lay on the blanket, and Millie looked slightly amused, her lips turned up at one corner in a subtle smile. For some reason it embarrassed me.

Millie had also remembered to bring one of the radios from the ship, and now she turned it on and pulled me up to dance. It was a weird Hawaiian song, which was perfect for the setting, and Millie tugged at my hand as she did a hybrid-hula. I tried to follow her, and soon we were shimmying and shaking in unison, halfway between hula-ing and club dancing like we'd seen on TV. Millie threw back her head and so did I, like we were just too carried away by dancing to think straight, and Mom and Sam applauded us, trying to catch their breath from laughing at our crazy moves. Looking at us from far away, you might have thought we were two sisters who got along and even enjoyed being together.

Captain Bill and the others came back early this morning with big crates full of fruits, vegetables, and even some items from home that had been imported, like boxes of cereal (including five boxes of Fruit Loops! Joy joy joy!!!), cans of evaporated milk, and about a million boxes of macaroni and cheese.

It was a great haul, but when the time came to get back aboard the ship and take up anchor, I think we were all a little heartbroken. Oliver, especially, kept staring out at the place where he'd done most of his snorkeling, looking wistful.

But in the end—and to my surprise—it was Millie who was the most reluctant to leave the beach. I've never known her to be sentimental, but she filled her pockets with sand as we crossed to the water, and even brought a couple of Virgil's wilted bouquets with her. Before we all climbed into the rowboat, she was the one who stood on the shore the longest, staring back at the trees where we'd picnicked, the breeze blowing her hair back. Finally, reluctantly, she climbed in with the rest of us.

*   *   *

Now here we are, with the mainland far in the distance and San Cristobal behind us. Captain Bill says we'll be sailing along Chile's shores for at least two weeks.

He's been giving us a colorful history of our route: South America, he says, is the wealthiest continent in the world, partly thanks to the giants that guard its shores and treasures. It's got cities made entirely of gold, the Fountain of Youth that keeps its inhabitants young for years (though not forever), a big technology hub in Argentina, and it's completely impenetrable from the outside except through a very strict customs process. Tourists are allowed to visit, but visas are very expensive, and sometimes even though the voyage is long, people from Chile, say, or Brazil, go to New York to shop because it's so much cheaper, and because they love the Gap and Levi's.

In other news, I've grown three inches since we left Cliffden (another inch since Sam and I checked)! Mom measured me on a whim after lunch.

"You're stretching like a string bean," she said, wrapped in a wooly blanket on the quarterdeck. She's been sketching a ball of twine and a fishing pole. She says she used to draw a lot more. When she's drawing, her face softens, like she forgets everything she has ever worried about.

If I haven't made it clear already, Captain Bill and she have become great friends. She likes to stand at the ship's wheel in the morning, listening to his stories about everything from how he got his scars (a tsunami left him stranded on a rock, mermaid attack, etc.) to his descriptions of the beauties of the Sea of Cortez. And he's always asking after her comfort: Is she getting enough to eat? Does she like the meals? Is she cold? They even laugh together over dinner, while my dad is usually puzzling out the wind speed and direction in his notebook.

Millie's strange good mood has continued. Sometimes I find her just smiling to herself about nothing, and when I ask her why (usually I expect her to tell me to get lost), she says something like, "the ocean is so pretty," or that she's just "enjoying the feeling of the sun on my face." The thought has crossed my mind that she's fallen in love with Virgil, but then I look at Virgil again and I know that can't possibly be.

ABOUT AN HOUR LATER

Okay, I've moved indoors and borrowed Captain Bill's radio (which is fuzzier than ever, though every few seconds I get enough salsa music to make it worth it). A fog has rolled in, so thick that we can barely see the bow of our own ship. We've all tucked ourselves into our warm and dry cabins for the evening. Outside my portal, I can see a sliver of moonlight cutting a thin slice through the mist.

Being out here on the ocean makes me miss the busy, bustling world sometimes—even the parts I didn't like. It never occurred to me before, but there could have easily been a world with no buses, no horns honking, no red lights, no shopping carts, no gum stuck to the bottom of benches downtown. For that matter I guess there also could have been no sun, no trees, and no ocean. None of those things had to exist, I guess. It makes me feel lucky that they do.

Something's just happened and I don't know what to make of it.

I just got up to go for a walk to see if the fog had thinned at all. Walking along the quarter galleries, I was picturing myself as a ghost and imagining how spooky I must look in the thick mist, and I'd just decided to walk to Millie's porthole window to scare her, when I caught sight of her silhouette headed toward the back of the ship. She was moving in a stealthy way, walking softly on the pads of her feet, so I followed her as silently as possible. Once she reached the stern, she leaned over the railing into the fog and stood there for a while, as if she was whispering into it. I froze for a while, watching her, and then tried to creep forward to see if I could hear better, but a plank beneath me creaked, and she turned and saw me. I don't think it was just the fog that made her face look as white as an eggshell.

She stared at for me a moment, startled. She looked afraid—but maybe not of me.

I could just make out the shape of something floating away in the thick air, away from the ship.

"What are you doing?" I asked.

Millie looked over her shoulder at the departing shape, then turned back to me. Her face became distant and careless, like a curtain had been closed. She smoothed her curls back over one shoulder. "I was just looking at the waves behind the ship." She brushed past me.

But I knew what the shape had been. Because I'd seen her do the same thing before, of course, that night in the desert.

January 13th

It's been almost a week since I wrote last. There hasn't been much to tell until tonight. Over the past several days Captain Bill has easily navigated us around two more whirlpools, a nest of sea serpents (I didn't see any actual serpents—just a big patch of bubbling, churning water the captain pointed out), and a giant squid that Virgil spotted from miles away. We've almost gotten used to those kinds of hazards.

But now, in two or three days, we'll round the lowest tip of South America—Cape Horn. Captain Bill says that just past it, about twenty miles southwest, is the Land's End Trading Post—the southernmost trading post on earth. (Apparently, hundreds of ships converge there to link up to each other and trade and sell, since it's the farthest any of them are willing to sail.) And then, beyond that . . .

"It's the end of the world as most people know it. Beyond it, there's just about nothing." The captain said this to me as he turned his face to the wind. "The Trading Post will be crowded this time of year. We won't linger. . . . We'll trade for a few supplies and keep going. Also, afterward I think it'll be better to depart in the dark. If they find out we're headed south, they may just *laugh* us to the edge of the earth."

Since we left San Cristobal, the weather's gotten much colder and grayer, and the days blend into each other: fog in the morning, fog in the afternoon. We Lockwoods (and Oliver) have run out of things to do with ourselves. There's only so much war and spit a person can play, and Oliver's attempts to teach me and Millie bridge have come to nothing. Jersey Troy took pity on us and dug out his old Sega Game Player, but it ran out of batteries after only a few games, and there are no AAs left on the ship. One big drawback of all the downtime is that Mom's decided it's time to get back to our school work. She's been painstakingly creating lesson plans for us the last two nights, working patiently on them at the galley table, her hair in a graceful bun and a cup of coffee in her hand. I wonder if she's partly doing it to avoid Dad, who—when he's not reading his instruments—has started following her around like a lost puppy. It's clear that he's getting more and more desperate to be forgiven as the weeks stretch on.

Millie's strange kindness has continued to grow. She's been saving me the crusts of all her sandwiches because she knows that's my favorite part. She's lent me two of her shirts, which I'm almost big enough to fit into. (She's managed to keep her things from Luck City pristine and perfect, while all my shirts and jeans and sweaters are already full of holes.)

Tonight we crossed paths on the poop deck. I was just walking along daydreaming, and she was running her hand along the rail, looking lost in her own thoughts too, when she stopped, studied me seriously, and said, "You need a makeover." I thought she was just saying it to be rude, and was half relieved to have her back to her normal self, until she grabbed me by the wrist and led me into her room.

Once inside, she sat me on her bed and started combing my dishwater rat's nest into something like a style. I winced when she ran the hard bristles through the tangles, but didn't complain; it felt too nice to be getting so much attention.

"I'm just about fed up with Captain Bill," she said out of nowhere.

"I thought you liked him," I said, shocked. "You said he was wildly romantic!"

Millie shook her head. "I don't like how he acts with Mom."

She turned me to face her and studied my features, then pulled her makeup bag onto her lap and dug out a tube of mascara. She brushed my eyelashes, first one side, then the other, going very slowly, and leaning back to study me after every stroke. "And he's rude to Dad. He doesn't take him seriously."

"None of us take Dad seriously," I said.

Millie pulled out her eye shadow and began on my lids, applying three shades of brown so delicately it would have put me to sleep if I wasn't so interested in the conversation. "Yeah, but we're allowed to be that way," she said. "*He's* not."

We were silent for a while, and Millie tucked away her eye shadow compact and pulled out her blush. She made me suck in my cheeks and swept the brush gently along my cheekbones, and then finishing with that, she unpacked a tiny tube of clear lip gloss and coated my lips. I was beginning to daydream, when her next words jarred me back to the moment. "Do you think Mom would ever leave Dad for someone like that?" she asked.

I couldn't say a word. The question didn't completely surprise me. I'd wondered it a few times myself, though I've never wanted to admit it on paper.

Someone like that, I thought. Mentally I cataloged what kind of someone Captain Bill is. Attentive. Brave. Cultured. Loves poetry. *Wildly romantic.* Then I thought about my dad, and how I couldn't really say he's any of those things.

"Mom would never leave Dad," I said, but it sounded unconvincing. I wanted to say just the right thing to Millie that would make me sound wise and worth confiding in. I also wanted my words to be true.

"They laugh together a lot," Millie said despondently, zipping up her makeup bag. "Mom and Dad never talk anymore, much less laugh together. Dad's really hurt her. Those kinds of things matter."

"Maybe, but . . ." I tried to protest, but found I didn't have one good argument in Dad's favor, and it gave me a sudden stomachache. Then I remembered one. "He tried to give his life for Sam's," I said hopefully.

Millie took this in silently. She stared down at her hands. "But he lost," she said.

"Were you trying to trade *your* life for Sam's, when you were talking to the Cloud the other night?" I asked.

She laid her makeup bag aside and brushed her hands together, looking at her fingers. "No. I promise you I wasn't. I was just . . . trying to negotiate." She didn't meet my eyes. "It's useless, apparently."

She picked at the bedspread for a moment, and then looked up and smiled at me. (I can't remember the last time Millie smiled at me like that! What is the world coming to?) "You're done," she said, scrutinizing her work. She handed me the small mirror, and I looked at my reflection.

Someone stared back at me, but I barely recognized her. She was older than I was, and prettyish. Not as pretty as Millie, but not as uglyish as the usual Gracie either.

Millie made a big deal of presenting me at the dinner table about an hour later, making me wait outside the galley until she announced me, which was embarrassing.

As I stepped inside, Mouse's mouth dropped open in surprise. Mom's eyes widened. Captain Bill laughed with pleasure, and Oliver blushed and looked at his feet under the table as if *he* were the one showing up to dinner in mascara. Even Dad was taken aback.

"Gracie Bee, you're growing up under our noses," he finally said.

"You look like a girl," Mouse said.

I could feel my face going red. Millie smiled encouragement at me again, like this was all good feedback.

We ate our dinner by lantern light. (Macaroni and cheese—yes! And mashed potatoes! My dream meal.) The sky outside the windows was getting blacker by the minute and squeezing the stars out—*pop pop pop*. Soon I forgot what I looked like and started making a mashed potato sculpture for Sam, and Millie tried to stand a hardboiled egg on its bottom, while Mom and Dad got engrossed in a discussion with the captain about what mermaids eat. "Mostly sea cucumbers and large fish, like tuna and swordfish," the captain said. "Sometimes people, but they don't prefer it." I watched his face for special wildly romantic attention to my mom, but I couldn't tell if there was any. Though I'm not much of a romance expert. I noticed that Dad, also, looked especially attentive: He was watching the captain and Mom interact, and I could tell he didn't like what he saw. Had he been noticing them all along? Or was I only just noticing him notice?

After dinner Millie piggybacked Sam away for a game of go fish, and Mom and Dad went on talking with the captain. Oliver and I found ourselves with nothing to do, so we left the galley and walked along the leeward deck, far away from everyone else.

"Do I look weird?" I asked suddenly. I wanted him to say something nice, because I did feel I deserved a compliment of some sort.

Oliver shook his head. "You look very pretty, Gracie. You know that, I think."

"Thanks," I said. "I guess I just wanted to hear it."

Above, to the west, two dragons were flying toward each other—one from shore and one from over the sea— leaving trails of smoke scarring the dark sky. They met each other in the air and circled, parted, came together and circled again, their claws almost touching—like a dance. Up above in the topmast, Virgil was following their movements with his hands—like he was doing a hand ballet. It was kind of sweet and weird at the same time.

"Oliver," I said slowly, "I've been wondering . . . has it helped?" I asked. "We're far across the earth. Are your memories of your family fading?"

Oliver looked down at the ocean, frowned, and shook

his head. "No. But . . ." His shoulders lifted and fell, like he was pushing at some weight and then accepting that it wouldn't leave. "I'm not so sure I want to forget them anymore."

I nodded. "I don't think I'd want to forget either," I said. I was thinking maybe the more Oliver tells me about the things he remembers about his mom and dad, the more I can help. I wonder, if a person cares about you enough, if they can help you carry all your difficult memories. I wanted to say that to Oliver, but the moment was so quiet and perfect that I decided to save it for another time. For now, it felt right to say nothing at all. I never really knew before this year that sometimes silence is best.

The whole world felt peaceful for the moment. The Cloud was nowhere in sight—maybe temporarily snagged on a piece of beach somewhere along the coast, or obscured by the fog. I wished I could freeze the moment, keep us all happy and together forever, never get to the Southern Edge, never find out whether we are wrong or right.

A few moments later the captain appeared at our side, followed by my parents. "You'll all want to get a look at this," he said, summoning us to the opposite railing.

Soon Millie was beside us, then Mouse. We strained to see what there was to see.

To the southeast, a shadow loomed up from the Chilean shore, getting bigger as we got closer, looking impossibly tall but also, somehow, fragile. It dwarfed the shore itself—rose and spread its limbs like enormous arms sheltering the ground beneath it. It was a tree (the biggest tree in the world, I know now), thick and wide. It seemed to call us closer, though the ship listed leeward and held steady.

"The World Tree," Captain Bill said. "Legend goes that as long as it lives and thrives, all is right with the world." I tried to gauge how "thriving" it looked, but I couldn't really tell. The captain rubbed his beard, gazing at the shore. "This is where we turn seaward to try to get around the Horn. We'll be at the Trading Post when you all wake tomorrow morning."

We watched the World Tree slip by us, lonely and defiant. We watched until it was small in the distance, until the shore of Chile began to shrink away in the darkness. We kept our eyes on the land as long as we could, each understanding the reason why, without saying it.

And then we turned to face the open sea.

January 16th

I can barely keep my hand from shaking as I write this. We aren't safe. Something is very, very wrong.

We've arrived at the Land's End Trading Post. The coordinates are right, the captain is sure of it, but the whole area is completely empty. No ships anywhere on the horizon, not even seagulls, or fish jumping, or mermaids playing in the wake of the ship. Not a sound.

The captain, for the first time since I've known him, looks frightened—his eyes scanning the horizon intently and his jaw tense. Virgil said a while ago that he was going off a little ways to see what's going on, and he hasn't come back yet. I'm pretty sure he's gotten spooked and flown away. Millie keeps saying she's worried about him (my guess is he's halfway up the coast of Chile right now) and she's been asking me how I can sit here writing at a time like this. She's on the bench kneeling beside me right now (we're in the galley) with her face pressed against the window, watchful. I know she's right, that I should be looking out the window with her, or at least just sitting and chewing my nails like a normal person. But writing is the only way I can get myself to feel even a little bit calmer. I—

Wait, we think we see a ship. It's coming fast toward us across the water, and there's something odd about it, but I can't tell what from this far away. We're going above deck to check.

ABOUT AN HOUR LATER

We're all (except the captain and the shipmates) now hiding in the galley together. I'm writing in case this is my last chance to write anything before we disappear. I'm taking deep breaths between sentences to make my hand steady.

Arriving above deck right after I last wrote and joining the others at the rail, I could see that the ship that was approaching appeared blacker than most—like a smudge on the horizon. As it got closer, it became clear that it was burned and blackened, that the mast listed to one side, and that its sails were torn to shreds.

The captain knew long before we did, of course, what was coming for us, and started shouting orders to the men. It was only then that I noticed the strange shimmer to the ship's form—the way I could see through the filmy hull right into its wooden interior.

"Phantom ship," Dad said, his voice tight, putting an arm around Sam protectively.

Captain Bill nodded, his eyes glued to the dark vessel, unblinking, his face grim. "Most likely a trading ship dragged under by the Great Kraken. Now it's sailing again, only it's not what it was."

As the ship grew closer, we could see its inhabitants moving quickly around the deck—ghostly figures in shipmates' clothing: slickers, cargo pants, some vests, one in an "I ♥ Hawaii" T-shirt, drifting hurriedly to lower the shredded sails while others hailed us from the bow.

"Just keep going past them," Millie breathed, terrified. "Please don't stop."

Captain Bill glanced at her. "It's too late for that. Now we just wait for them to board."

Mom let out a small moan, and the captain looked over at her.

"It's all right. We just have to give them what they

want, and they'll most likely let us pass." He looked down at Sam, who was clinging to my dad's leg, staring over the rails with huge eyes. "You might want to take the little one below."

As Mom hurried Sam downstairs, the captain gave a signal and several of the deckhands rushed downstairs, returning with several crates, lids sealed tight.

"I keep these in the hold for just this possibility," he explained. "Try not to worry. We have a good chance here. I've stockpiled these items especially for this kind of situation."

The phantom ship pulled up beside us, and its crew— luminous, gaunt, glowing—busied themselves tying up to the *Alexa*. Oliver stepped closer to me, protectively, but it crossed my mind that, as the far more fiery and bloodthirsty one, I should protect *him*. I scanned the horizon for Virgil again, but of course, he was nowhere to be seen. This, I thought bitterly, would have been the ideal time for him to step in and really *guard* us.

The ghost crew numbered in the thirties or forties— some just glowing bones and gaping eye sockets, and some more human-looking. They floated over from their ship onto ours in a wave of dim light and gentle moans as my family and Oliver and I clustered together.

They eyed us excitedly, their jaws curving at the hinges in chilling smiles.

One woman in khakis—maybe the only woman on the ghost ship—reached out to touch Millie's long gray skirt, and the captain rapped his cane down on the decks between them, cutting her off.

The ghost frowned, her eyes turning deadly angry, but the captain put on his most charming expression. "Now let me direct you to some items that I think you'll like even better," he said. She, and many of the others, trailed behind him dubiously to the collection of crates on the forecastle. With a flourish, the deckhands opened them all at the same time. There was a collective gasp. The crates were full of shiny objects—silver bars, pewter, and brass bowls and cups. I remembered Grandma, with her box of shiny objects for the ghosts in her yard.

There was a flurry of excitement and grim smiles and a rubbing together of filmy hands, and all phantom eyes turned to the one who seemed to be their captain—a tall man in a rain slicker, with piercing hazel eyes that flickered as he gazed around the decks, and a dark slash down his bluish nose. He nodded, and his crew began to transfer the crates to their own ship. It was all so simple and quick, we were dumbfounded.

When all was loaded, the ghost captain stared around at us for a moment more, sniffing, as if trying to smell out whether there was anything else on board that he particularly wanted. And then he nodded to Captain Bill, who nodded back. He drifted backward, keeping his eyes on us as he floated over the rail and onto his own ship.

Watching them drift away a few minutes later, we could see the phantom crew squabbling over the contents of the crates. Their ship got smaller and smaller in the distance, and it wasn't until I looked back at Captain Bill that I saw he'd been sweating, and that his fingers were trembling as much as mine were.

Maybe he knew, at that moment, what I hadn't even guessed. That we'd only just had a taste of what was coming.

I'll start again at about ten minutes ago.

I was down in my berth trying to quiet my nerves with a game of solitaire, when Oliver appeared in my doorway, looking shaken.

"What's wrong?" I asked.

"We have a problem," he said, swallowing.

"Another ship?"

He seemed not to know how to answer. "A bigger problem," he finally said. He stood back and nodded for me to head up the stairs. Sensing his urgency, I climbed them two by two.

Millie and Dad were already on deck, looking over the railings. I walked up beside them.

At first, I couldn't comprehend what I was seeing. It was too much to be believed.

Not one, but *hundreds* of shadows were moving toward us the same way the ghost ship had, as if gliding on air.

"It's a fleet," Dad said, his voice empty of hope. I could see on Millie's face too, only despair. Mom and Sam had come up behind us and were just taking it in.

There had to be hundreds of ships—some burned and charred, some missing their sides, some barely holding together. They were still far enough away that their crews looked tiny and indistinct, but there was no doubt they'd spotted the *Alexa* and were shifting sail toward us. I could hear the sound of their moans even from here.

"The Kraken has drowned them *all*," Captain Bill said from his post at the ship's wheel a few feet away, his eyes hard and flinty, his lips colorless. "Every last ship that's come here. This isn't a trading post anymore, it's a graveyard."

"What do we do?" Mom asked frantically. We were fast approaching the edge of the enormous fleet. Soon we'd be in the thick of it.

"We can't fight them," Captain Bill said. "We have nothing to offer them." He rubbed his hands against the railing in front of him in agitation, thinking. After about thirty seconds, he finally spoke again. "The only thing we can do is hide below. Hope they think the ship's deserted—that maybe the Kraken's taken us already."

"I suggest . . ." Dad glanced up toward the sky and around, opening his mouth to speak, stopping, and then going on, "When I picked Virgil, he said he was an excellent . . ."

"We'd better all get belowdecks before we're spotted," Captain Bill said, impatient.

"Well, I don't know much about ships, but I think . . . ," Dad ventured apologetically. We all turned to go without hearing what he went on to say.

So here we are. Hiding isn't a good plan, but it's the only plan we have. I can hear the crew banging around above—tossing barrels and nets all over the top decks so that it'll look like maybe we were attacked and that the *Alexa* is deserted. They'll come below too, in a minute.

I've been glancing out the window from time to time, but otherwise we're all sitting here like statues, Sam on Mom's lap, Dad with his arm around Millie, Oliver and me side by side.

Oh! I just heard the crew coming down the stairs! They've retreated to the galleries behind us, and I can feel the ship turning with the tide because it's no longer being steered.

I guess I'll stop now. I can't steady my hand enough to keep going.

SAME DAY, 3:15 P.M.
ACCORDING TO CAPTAIN BILL'S WATCH

I can hardly believe I'm alive to write this down. I just kissed this page because the last time I closed this diary, I thought I might never open it again. Millie and Oliver and Sam are dancing around in circles, and the strangest thing of all is that we owe our lives to . . . Virgil!!!

I must be getting very disciplined, because I'm not even tempted to jump ahead. I'm going to write down exactly how it happened and not leave out one detail.

After I put down my diary last, we all just sat in the

galley, waiting and watching out the windows. For a few minutes nothing but ocean floated past us. None of us even whispered to each other. The *entire Alexa* had gone silent; the only sounds were the creaks and groans of her floorboards and walls.

When the bow of the first ship drifted into view, I felt like my heart might break out of my ribs and make an escape without me. And then came another ship, and another, their hulls gliding past us and blocking out views of anything else. Most of them were old like the *Alexa*, but some of them were newer steam ships and ocean liners. We were drifting right into the middle of them, surrounded on all sides. Still, none of them moved closer to tie up against us or try to attack us. I had to keep reminding myself to breathe.

"This could work," Dad whispered. We slid our way along, or rather the phantom fleet slid along around us, parting to make room for us but otherwise keeping a steady course. This went on for what seemed like forever.

The moment things changed, I think we all knew it. I know now they must have been just lulling us all along. Because right when it seemed that we were in the very middle of the fleet, the ships suddenly began to drop anchor all around us, turning toward us from all directions. Somewhere ahead of us we heard the captain yell, "Hands on deck!" Then (the thought of it makes me break out in goose bumps) we saw one ghost floating down the side of his ship, holding a rope. He turned to look toward us, made eye contact with me, and smiled.

"Sam," my mom said, gazing at the ghost. "Get under the bench. And don't come upstairs, no matter what."

The captain and the shipmates were already above deck when we emerged, and everything was in chaos.

"Starboard port!" Captain Bill yelled, throwing himself at the ship's wheel and trying to steer away from the closest ship, which was bearing down on us so fast it was nearly on us. A cluster of ghosts stood at the other ship's bow, jumping up and down and getting ready to come aboard.

Even *I* could see the captain's efforts were useless. Steering away from one ship only moved us into the path of another, and we wouldn't be fast enough to maneuver through whatever space was left within the fleet. Still, Millie threw herself onto the wheel beside him to help. The rest of us scattered across the deck, looking for weapons; Mom grabbed a loose plank and held it back over her shoulder like a baseball bat, Oliver grabbed two empty champagne bottles from a barrel the captain used for trash, and I grabbed a rusty barrel lid.

Suddenly Sam was on the deck beside me, and even though I hissed at him to go back belowdecks, he too went looking for a weapon and ended up with a grubby old fishing net. He came to stand right beside me, and I reached for his hand. Oliver moved to his other side.

"Are you going to net them to death, Sam?" Oliver asked, giving Sam a smile that—looking back on it now—seems so brave, since we knew at that moment we were facing certain doom.

"I might have to," Sam said solemnly.

"Can ghosts even be hit with *anything*?" I asked softly over Sam's head, and Oliver mouthed back, *I don't know*.

That's where we were, standing with our useless weapons waiting to be boarded, when there was a deafening sound above us. I can only describe it by saying that in Cliffden, when I was little, the man at the shoe store used to give me a free balloon whenever Mom took me to get new shoes. He'd blow it up right there in front of me with a big metal helium tank. The sound was like that—a whooshing and whistling of air—only times a thousand.

We all looked up at the same moment—even the ghosts on the other ships.

Virgil was hovering high above us. But he didn't look like Virgil. His head and feet and arms and legs were all normal and Virgil-size . . . but his usually skinny chest was now enormous and expanding outward—like he was sucking in gallons-full of air.

Actually, it turns out he *was* sucking in gallons-full of air. Because in the next moment he began to blow.

A wind came out of Virgil's mouth that was stronger than any winds we'd encountered on the entire voyage. He blew right into the backs of our sails, and suddenly we began to move—so fast that I, and even a few of the crew, went tumbling onto the deck.

We were cruising, and now Captain Bill and Millie threw themselves against the ship's wheel with renewed strength—their arms and backs trembling from the effort. The captain kept shouting orders over his shoulder and the crew obeyed. Suddenly everyone had a job, easing the sails, adjusting the jib. The *Alexa* slid narrowly between the two ships on either side of us, which had been just about to board—missing each of them by a few yards—and then veered right. We immediately pivoted left and slipped between another two.

The ghost ships, without Virgil's wind working right behind them, moved too slowly to adapt.

Carving a crooked and chaotic path, with barely any idea of what we were doing or what we'd do next and at breakneck speed, we made our way through the ships coming at us in all directions. Any wrong move would have sent us crashing into another boat's hull, but Captain Bill made no wrong moves. Every once in a while the wind would stop for a moment as Virgil took in more air, but he did this marvelously fast, and his lungs seemed like they could blow forever. He never faltered once.

Finally, the fleet began to thin, so that soon we were passing through the stragglers, which were more and more spread out. The deluge had slowed to a rush, and then to a trickle, until finally we left the last of the ships behind us, its vaporous crew gazing after us and trying to turn about in mute rage.

It wasn't for another few minutes that Virgil let up on the blowing, and we finally all began to relax. Captain Bill let out a long, ragged sigh and beamed at us. He put his arm around Millie, who stepped away with her head held up, looking at my dad. Dad stepped up and laid a hand on the captain's shoulder.

"Thank you, Captain," he said. I wonder if I was the

only one who remembered that Dad had tried to tell us about Virgil before, and the captain had cut him off.

"Who knew Virgil could breathe like that!" Mom said, gazing into the sky and beaming.

"Of course he's got good lungs," Dad said, looking befuddled. "Why did you think I hired him?" He looked around at all of us as if it was the first time it had ever occurred to him that we'd thought he'd hired a useless angel.

Above us, now back to normal size and hovering above the topmast, catching his breath and with a hopeful smile on his face as he looked down at us, Virgil didn't flicker. He blazed.

January 30th

We're far into the Southern Sea, and the world has gone white. The water is pearly, almost colorless, and still as glass. White slabs of ice float along the ocean, butting against the ship in little thuds as we move south. There's hardly any land, and the land that we do see is covered deep in snow. The Cloud, up high and directly above us, is the darkest thing in sight.

Right now I'm bundled in the thick winter clothes supplied by Prospero, and perched dizzyingly high in the basket of the topmast. It's so cold that my breath is puffing out in clouds around my head. But I needed some space, and Virgil told me I could borrow this spot for a while.

Technically, now that he's saved our lives, he should

be headed back to his angel boss at the Bright Market in LA, but he says he's staying on the technicality that he won't have officially saved us until he gets us to the frozen continent in one piece. He says his boss has ways of knowing when his job is done, but also that he won't mind if Virgil fudges things to linger a little longer, and that it happens all the time when guardian angels like the people they're working for.

It's a good thing: It's taken his lungs to keep the ship moving in this windless place. Dad's anemometer has actually turned out to be pretty useless here, since there's zero wind to speak of. Our sails are forlorn from all the wear and tear, and we haven't been able to stop anywhere to patch them properly, but they're still holding up well enough.

Anyway, right now Virgil's taking a little break. The last time I saw him he was in the galley with Millie: She was wrapped up in a blanket watching the fire, and Virgil was in a corner pretending to read but occasionally stealing glances at her. He admitted, one night about a week ago when I asked him, that he did fly off in fear when the first phantom ship approached us. He told me that he *was* headed up the Chilean coast, just as I'd imagined (though I didn't tell *him* that), when he changed his mind. But I promised him I wouldn't ever reveal that to Millie.

The captain says we'll be arriving at the shore of the Southern Edge in a matter of days. I can hardly believe we're almost there! Ever since the day of the ghost ships, everything—us, the crew, Captain Bill, and the world around us—has gotten quieter, whiter, more subdued and more still. Last night was the one exception—and it was something I'll never forget.

Millie and I were in my berth conspiring when it happened. We'd been discussing Mom and the captain again, and the fact that they seem to pal around even more since the day we escaped the ghost fleet. We had decided, after about half an hour of going over all the evidence, that if anyone is going to stop what's happening between them, it will have to be us. (We just haven't figured out how yet.)

Suddenly the door opened and Oliver appeared, his green eyes wide and full of excitement.

"What is it?" I asked.

"You have to see." He turned and hurried up the stairs. We followed, wearing only our fleece long johns and hats and thick wool socks.

On the decks it was snowing—a soft steady stream of white puffy flakes that drifted down slowly, blowing gently back and forth in the cold breeze. The sun was setting behind a thick gray blanket of clouds on the horizon, and a large indistinct lump sat on the water. It took another moment to realize it was an island. And then I noticed, with amazement, that it appeared to be inhabited. Warm yellow lights glowed from its snowy shore. And moving in front of those lights, dark shapes on four legs . . . hundreds of them.

The captain tilted the wheel to the right, and we drifted closer. The shapes soon sorted themselves into creatures with enormous antlers, so plentiful they were like a walking forest.

"Reindeer!" Mom gasped. I didn't know she and Sam had come up behind me.

The lights grew brighter as we got closer, illuminating the thick-furred creatures moving across the snowy pasture, sniffing and puffing in the cold air. Beyond them was something even more astonishing: a great dark lodge—tall and wide and rambling, with spires at the roofline and log walls that went on and on in all directions, topped with pale green and dark red curlicues. It reminded me of pictures my mom had shown me once in our encyclopedia, of Viking chapels from hundreds of years ago, only bigger, and more rambling and crooked.

"What is it?" Mom asked.

"That's the home of the wild frontiersman, Santa Klaus," Captain Bill said. Sam let out a chirp of excitement, straining on his tiptoes at the railing, his wool hat all askew.

"This is where all the presents get made?"

Captain Bill nodded.

"What are those little huts?" Mom asked, pointing to the sprawl of pointed houses scattered around the main lodge.

"Those belong to the elves, a cold-weather people who've lived here for centuries. And this is the only island on earth where reindeer have evolved to fly. Klaus is the only Northerner who's figured out how to exist down here among them all. He came, I suppose, hundreds of years ago by ship—from Finland, rumor has it. And the Cloud has never come for him. Who knows, maybe he's not from Finland, maybe he's from the Extraordinary World. Maybe that's why." The captain widened his eyes at Sam, who grinned.

"Anyway, once he discovered the secret of the reindeer, he made the choice about using them to deliver gifts . . . or at least that's what I've read. I think it's the way he deals with the isolation, all that cabin fever."

Now even the crew was gathered with us at the rails, watching the shore. I knew they all must be thinking the same thing I was: I wanted so badly to be in that warm, cozy lodge, sitting by a fire, maybe even talking to Santa Klaus, safe from harm and the cold.

"Can we stop?" Sam the Mouse asked. "Please please can we stop?"

The captain rubbed Sam's head, but Sam pulled away, rubbing his hair with his mitten as if trying to wipe away the captain's touch. The captain didn't seem to notice.

"I wish we could, Sam. But he's a private man. He doesn't allow visitors. And anyway, we need to get to where we're going. I'll bet he knows the secrets of the edge of the earth," Captain Bill went on. "But I suppose he'll never tell."

We all stayed and watched as the lodge grew farther and farther away and more and more obscured by the dusk. The lights grew smaller, until they were so far away that we couldn't see them anymore, and Santa's island was swallowed by the dark.

I'm getting too cold to stay up here, but I wanted to write one more thing: that Oliver and I were standing on the deck about an hour ago, watching for more islands (with no luck), when a floating slab of ice drifted past. On it was a single polar bear, her dark eyes peering at us through the mist while the rest of her body was barely visible against the gray horizon.

"I wonder where she's going," Oliver said.

As she floated past, it seemed I was looking right into her eyes and she was looking right into mine. I imagined maybe she was wishing us good luck, and I wished her good luck too.

It looked like she was floating into oblivion. Will she ever make it where she wants to go? Will we?

February 2nd

In my bunk, late late at night, and the smell of ice is in the air. I'm trying to keep my hands warm by writing under the covers. I can't sleep; it's been an eventful night.

It was the three of us, Millie and Virgil and me, who saw what happened. We were perched in the topmast basket together, taking in the view of nothing much and chatting (also about nothing much!). I was bundled to the gills, but shivering and ready to go inside. Still, Millie had insisted we stay and keep Virgil company. I don't know why she wants me around her so much these days, but there we were in any case, with a bird's eye view of the sea below us and the icebergs ahead of us that mark the outer boundaries of the Southern Edge. Our breaths were fogging around us, and I huddled closer to Millie for warmth. She handed me the thermos she'd lugged up for Virgil (she'd forgotten that angels don't get cold or drink or eat) and I took a sip.

As I did, I glanced over at Millie and noticed she was moving her lips without saying anything, staring at the icebergs ahead of us.

"What are you doing?" I asked her.

"Oh," Millie looked slightly embarrassed. "Just making wishes, like you do. About the Extraordinary World. I keep saying to myself . . . *It's there, it's there, it's there.*"

I looked ahead silently, and Millie stopped her wishing after a while and gazed at her mittened hands.

"I've been really hard on Dad," she said quietly. "I regret that."

"I'm sure he knows you love him," Vigil consoled her.

We went on staring at the dim silhouettes of icebergs ahead until a noise below distracted us. It was Mom and Captain Bill, Mom holding the Captain's arm to steady herself as they came out on the poop deck and sat on a bench, both bundled tightly in their coats. The captain had a bottle of wine tucked under one armpit. He set it down, then lit the lantern with a matchbook from his pocket, the glow of the flame lighting up his face.

"I always bring a special bottle to celebrate arriving at

the end of a voyage," he said. "It helps to have a pretty lady present." Millie met my eyes and rolled her own in disgust.

He moved a coil of rope aside so that Mom could get more comfortable.

"I'd love to know more about your late wife," Mom said, "if you'd be willing to talk about her."

The captain took a sip of wine and examined the glass, then he smiled. "She loved plants. She grew one in every pot, sometimes in tea kettles . . . everywhere. She was a ball of fire, always excited about something new—a new song or a new type of flower she'd found out about. You wouldn't think a Cloud would take someone with so much life in her. There's a lot we don't know about Clouds, I guess."

"You don't have to talk about it if . . ."

"No, I like talking about her. She loved to go down to the ocean and look for shells. We were down there one day searching, when we saw the Cloud for the first time, way down the beach, just hovering along the sand. I didn't think much of it, but she knew. Somehow she knew right away it was her it had come for."

My mom reached for the captain's hand and stroked it, and he took hold of her fingers. "I'm so sorry," she said. Millie reached for *my* hand and dug her fingernails into my palm.

The captain looked up at my mom. And then he leaned forward, almost touching his lips to hers.

Mom shot up off the bench in surprise, making us all flinch, especially Captain Bill.

"What was that?!" she asked.

The captain tried to recover himself; he leaned forward pleadingly, looking tortured, like the romantic hero of an old poem. "Mrs. Lockwood, *Rebecca*, you're headed into this frigid wilderness, on this futile search. You've been led from one danger to another and lost everything you ever had. And you, well, I wonder if maybe you don't deserve better. I think we could be there for each other."

My mother gazed at him intently; it was impossible to tell her thoughts. My heart was in my throat, and I could feel Millie's pulse through her hand.

"From the minute I set eyes on you at the Squid's Arms, I knew you were something special. You're the reason I'm here; you're the reason I followed you and Gracie onto Venice Boulevard and the reason I've been here ever since. When we arrive at the continent and the others get off," Captain Bill said, "I'd like you to stay behind, with me. Come to Nova Scotia." He swallowed deeply. Mom appeared to be transfixed, in shock. He took this as an encouraging sign, and reached up to touch her face, trying to raise his lips to hers. She stepped back so abruptly that he lost his balance, almost falling off the bench.

"I'm a married woman!" Mom stuttered. "You're . . . supposed to be helping us keep our family *together*! You're supposed to be our friend." She looked down at her hands, as if she'd just discovered she had them. "I haven't lost *everything*! Do you think I'd ever leave my family?" she asked. She turned on her heel, then said firmly over her shoulder, "*They're* my everything." She hesitated for a moment, as if she couldn't believe what had just happened, and then she glided down the deck, where she disappeared from view.

Up in the crow's nest, two happy crows and one angel watched it all, and hugged each other tight in utter relief.

Tonight—after we celebrated in Millie's room by drinking hot chocolates together, and after I'd gone into my room to turn in for the night—I changed my mind, bundled myself up again, and tiptoed up to the poop deck to look at the icebergs in the distance one more time before sleeping. *It's there*, I said under my breath. *It's there*.

The clouds had thinned enough so that the moon was

shining down brightly. Doesn't the moon sometimes make you want to find a way to attach yourself to it so that you can always have that light around you? I don't know what made me glance back behind me before I walked inside, but when I did, I saw Millie climbing up to where Virgil sat in the topmast, keeping watch.

Virgil was saying something quietly and gesturing toward the icebergs in the distance. Millie raised a hand in the air. And then she leaned up toward him and gave him a small kiss on the lips. A kiss that must have felt like a brush of air, but a kiss all the same.

She started to shimmy back down the ladder without a word, and I hurried ahead into the darkness, unseen. Tiptoeing back toward my berth, I peered for a moment into the porthole of my parents' room, and saw them both asleep, my mom curled against my dad and holding him tight.

I wonder if the captain is still awake, and what he's thinking about all of us now that my mom has rejected him. It worries me, but then, worry is something I've gotten used to. Because if there's one thing I've learned on this trip, it's that I never know what's around the corner.

And who knows what we'll find when we reach the southern shore?

Diary Number
❧ Three ❧

February 5th

I've had to start a new diary in the back of my mom's lesson plan book, because my other one had a small disaster that involved Sam, a sumo wrestling match, and an open barrel of water. It's still legible, thank goodness, but the pages have gone so wrinkly that they're hard to write on, so Mom took pity on my and gave me this book instead.

It's morning, our first morning on the Southern Edge. I'm sitting by our camp-stove fire, wrapped in a blanket. The cold is hard to escape, even this bundled up and close to the flames. Everyone is asleep, but there's so much to do that I know as soon as they wake we'll have to start packing up, so these may be my last quiet moments for a while.

* * *

Yesterday around midday I was lying in my berth counting the cracks in the ceiling, when there was a thud so jarring that I fell out of bed. I rushed out on deck along with everyone else, thinking we'd hit an iceberg.

The clouds had given way to a bright day—I shielded my eyes and looked out, trying to adjust to the glare, and saw only ice before us.

"How are we going to get through the ice?" I asked Dad, who happened to be standing right next to me.

"It's not ice," he said, smiling, and reached out to pull me close to him. "It's *land*. We're here, Gracie. We're really here."

I could hardly believe it. Sunlight reflected off the snow-covered shore so intensely it was blinding. We were surrounded by white as far as the eye could see, and Virgil was executing triumphant circles in the air. My breath puffed around me, and Millie and Oliver were trembling with cold. (Mom had Sam bundled in her arms in a microfiber hat and under a fur blanket with his socks-and-buttons bear peeping out the top, so they looked toasty.)

It took me a moment to notice the flurry of activity up at the front of the poop deck. Captain Bill was hard at work, heaving from here to there at a breakneck pace, throwing things over the side of the boat. It took another moment for me to realize *what* he was throwing: our belongings. Peering over the rail, I could see our backpacks, piles of our clothes, Prospero's instruments (including the anemometer, with one of the cups broken off and lying beside it like a severed hand), strewn across the ice. The captain's face was bright red with exertion; he was swearing under his breath with each toss. Finally he walked over to us briskly.

"I know you'll all be prompt about disembarking. I'm on a schedule," he said.

Mom and Dad looked at each other in alarm. Dad approached him. "What do you mean a schedule? You're supposed to stay here and wait, in case we don't find anything!"

"I'm due back in LA," Captain Bill said coldly. "The trip took longer than I expected, and I need to get back. This is where I leave you and wish you good luck."

We all stood, flabbergasted. Sam was clutching his bear as if he were frightened it would be the next thing to be thrown over the rails. Meanwhile I stared out into the emptiness of the world around us, trying to imagine being left here alone, with no way to get back if we needed to.

"But, you said you'd wait." Dad swallowed. "You promised us." Next to Captain Bill's hulking frame, Dad looked small and fragile, but he was getting angry, his body coiled up as if he might be about to throw a punch.

"You must have misunderstood me," the captain said, picking up Mom's violin case and dropping it over the side. We heard it land in B-flat, and Mom held Sam closer, wincing. "Anyway, aren't you a genius? Aren't you sure your calculations are correct?"

"Now, look . . . ," my father said, his face red with rage.

I was hoping maybe he *would* punch the captain, so that I could jump into the fray, and Dad was leaning in and looking like he might do just that, when Mom shifted Sam into her left arm and took Dad's hand into hers.

"Let's get the rest of our things," she said, looking only at him and ignoring the captain completely. "You said we'll find the Extraordinary World, and we will. We won't need a rescue."

I would have begged to differ, but the look she turned on all of us made me keep my mouth shut.

The captain stared down at the planks beneath his feet, and I thought for a moment—hopefully!—that he

might be on the verge of changing his mind, when he
picked up another backpack and threw it over the edge.

Less than an hour later we were standing on the snow,
fully bundled in our coats and fleece leggings and fur
hoods and seal mittens and scarves, and trying to get
our land legs back, watching the last of our food supplies
being carried down the planks by the shipmates. They
looked apologetic, but they also wouldn't look any of us
in the eye.

Once they were all back on board and the planks had
been lifted, the anchor began to wind upward. It was a
sickening sight. We stood paralyzed beside our belongings, watching helplessly as the *Weeping Alexa* prepared
to leave us behind. Sam the Mouse nestled against my
legs, and Virgil circled up and down, throwing snow-
balls at Captain Bill, but missing.

I've decided that the sound of an anchor being lifted is
one of the loneliest sounds on earth. I wanted to turn
away, I think we all did—to show the captain we didn't
care—but I couldn't help it, I was transfixed—watching
the last link we had with the rest of the world drift back
and away from us, turn slowly in the icy water, and set a

course north. Only Troy stood at the keel, looking back at us sorrowfully. He held up a hand in the air, staring directly at me. I held up a hand in reply.

"Jersey forever!" he yelled.

None of us spoke after that as we watched the *Alexa* get farther and farther away. It shrank toward the horizon, and still we kept watching it. We stood there for what must have been an hour—until it was a tiny speck in the distance, and then gone completely.

It left a wide expanse of cold, bright, clear sky behind it. And there, about half a mile away and no surprise to any of us, was our Cloud. Our Cloud, unfortunately, hadn't abandoned us.

Dad began rummaging through our things for supplies to set up camp. He circled his arms a few times, warming them up, and pulled some goggles down around his eyes. Mom dug the rest of the goggles out of the piles on the ice and told us to do the same. Then they slowly started assembling one of our two tents. Millie and Oliver found another bundle and began to unroll it, and I set to helping Dad.

"Your instruments," she said, staring down at the broken anemometer. Dad looked at it and shrugged. "It's not important."

"This one's still working." She crouched and dug the manometer out of the snow, clasping it in the palm of her mitten and holding it out toward him.

Dad looked at it. He reached for her hand, pulled the manometer out of her grasp and dropped it on the ground, then reached back for her fingers and held them to his cheek. Millie and I looked at each other, uncomfortable and pleased at the same time.

"Am I big enough to help?" Sam asked me.

I turned to him. "Of course you are, Mouse." I handed him a corner to hold that would prop up to be the zippered front door.

And together, we set about making our shelter for the night.

I'm back. I've just managed to shiver from my long johns into my full gear. Mouse has woken up, and now he's looking around wide-eyed at the white and wide-open world. He's in my lap, so I'm trying to write around him.

We slept piled together like puppies, our arms wrapped around each other for warmth—Oliver, then Sam, then Millie, then me. Mom and Dad have their own tent, and the rest of us are sharing one. (None of us minds being cramped together though, because it creates more heat.)

I thought we might have to keep watch for polar bears or abominable snowmen (even bigger versions of yetis). But our surroundings appear to be deserted, at least so far, and Dad says we probably won't have to worry about running into any beasts or creatures of any sort, because they've all moved north to warmer regions.

It makes me want to cry as I write this: Virgil left us last night, after we'd finished setting up camp. He said that he couldn't stretch the rules any further and he had to get home.

We all said our good-byes and gave him our thanks. It was hard not to hug him after all he'd done for us, but it was also hard to hug someone so wispy. We all did our best.

After we'd said good-bye, Millie walked him off somewhere we couldn't see. She came back a while later pretending like she hadn't been crying, but her eyes were all red behind her goggles, and she kept wiping her nose with her scarf.

"Is the smiling man still following us?" Mouse asked just a moment ago. He's decided he doesn't like looking at the sky and has started asking us to look *for* him instead.

"Yes," I said.

"Do you think we can go to Santa's house on the way home?"

"We can try," I said. He stood and scrambled off my lap, hearing Mom stirring in her tent.

This is how I'm spending my first morning on the continent. Lying to Mouse about the future.

I'll have to finish this entry later—it's time to start taking down camp.

February 10th

We've been hiking for five days, always setting up camp before dusk, which comes early here.

I'm writing this from our tent, by the light of my headlamp, which I'm not supposed to use except "when completely necessary." I have to keep shaking the pen and warming it in my mittens, because the ink keeps freezing. Millie is beside me up to her chin in her sleeping bag, just staring at me while I write; she looks like a gopher peeping out of its hole. She just asked me, if we were attacked by an abominable snowman, if I would sit here writing it down until I got eaten, and I said probably. But she didn't say anything rude back. . . . It's like she ran out of rude things to say weeks ago. Actually, she even gave me a compliment, in a way. She said she wishes she had a hobby she liked as much as I like writing. I think she was trying to sound like Mom, but still, it makes me feel good.

We've also been discussing how the land here isn't flat like we expected, but rolling—all the way up to a mountain range in the distance Dad said we'll have to cross. He says it's there because the earth is pushing against its edges and wrinkling.

For the rest of the day he went on directing us with the compass Prospero gave us, stopping occasionally to check it as we trudged in the direction of the mountains (or the wrinkles, if you want to be accurate), and then taking Mom's hand and walking on. He says the edge of the earth will lie on the other side of it. He says that much he knows for sure.

The cold is biting, even though we're all bundled so thickly that we're shaped more like balloons than people. We wear our goggles most of the time, but I swear sometimes my eyelashes have frozen to each other, and yesterday my eyebrows got so frigid that I thought they might fall off my face. The temperature is beyond breathtaking—it's one of those many things I can't capture in words. We're carrying only blankets, clothing, our camp stove, and we've divided food into our packs depending on our size and strength.

To our surprise it's Sam who suffers the least. He's like a miniature furnace, and even though it's hard to piggyback him, I always look forward to when it's my turn, because it's like being strapped to a heater. (We're taking shifts; Oliver's and mine are the shortest. I can't carry the load for more than half an hour without feeling like I'm going to keel over.)

This is an utterly quiet world. No rocking of the sea, no cry of seagulls, no sound of a breeze. The air is muffled and blank. But as dead and empty as it may seem, there's actually a lot to see. I never get tired of looking at the glaciers in the distance. We can actually see them growing in place, rising out of the rolling snowy earth, and if the wind is right we can even hear them creaking.

"As the cold grows, new ice gets born," Dad says.

From time to time our trek has taken us along the coast. We must be slowly climbing, because we keep getting higher above the ocean, and yesterday, peering down from a sheer rise, I could see the vaguest hints of rooftops just under the surface of the ice-frosted sea. There were curling spires that looked to be made of shells and stones, and domes white as marble shimmering just under the frozen film.

"The old mermaid cities," Dad said, noticing my gaze. "They're abandoned now."

Studying the view, I imagined empty mermaid streets and abandoned mermaid theaters. I can't explain why it made me sad. Dad kept walking, but I lingered, and a moment later I felt Millie beside me.

The others had moved on, though Mom kept glancing back to make sure we'd follow, her pigtails hanging out of her bright red hat. Oliver, beside her, kept glancing back too.

"Do you think we're actually headed somewhere, Gracie?" Millie asked, nodding toward the mountain range where Dad's taking us. "Do you think anything's waiting for us on the other side?"

I looked at her. "I don't know."

Millie nodded, looking out at the ocean and the ice-shrouded rooftops. She took in a deep lungful of breath and let it out. "You know what?" she said. "Even if there isn't, I won't regret coming."

I followed her gaze down to the ice.

"I guess I won't regret it either," I said.

We smiled at each other, a bit goofily, like two

strangers just meeting. Then Millie reached for my hand and tugged me along, and we walked to catch up with the others.

Tonight before we crawled in here to sleep, we all sat by the camp stove for a while (Mom was boiling water for tea), bundled in our supposedly "best money can buy" sleeping bags that Prospero said would keep us warm, but that actually just manage to keep us from being really, really cold. Sam was sitting on my lap again, and while everyone else was lost in their own thoughts and just looking at the flame of the stove, he asked me to tell him the old story about the night he was born.

"I'm not really in the mood, Mouse," I said.

"Tell me," he said plaintively.

I sighed.

"On the night you were born," I began, "Dad called from the hospital to say you were a boy, and I cried my eyes out."

Sam settled against my belly, warming me up, pushing his little bundled face to my chest so that I wondered if he was going to fall asleep.

"I'd always wanted a sister." I took a breath, then went on, feeling his little heart beating against me.

"I didn't want to hold you, but Dad tricked me."

"He said can you hold these potato chips," Sam murmured into my coat.

I nodded. "Then he put you in my arms. And when I looked at you . . . and you looked at me . . . I felt . . ."

I paused, trying to remember back to that day. Maybe for once, after all my practice writing in here, I could actually put it into the right words.

"I felt a mystery all around me," I said. "That's all."

I thought about the last time I'd told Sam the story, in the Winnebago what seems like a thousand years ago. Being here at the Southern Edge of the earth, all together and alone, almost feels like the only real life there ever was.

"Is the Cloud up there right now?" he asked, not willing to look.

I gazed up at the sky—full of stars, too big for us. And the Cloud, drifting just off a ways, along the shore.

I shook my head. "It's not there tonight," I said. "Maybe it forgot about us."

"Maybe it won't take me after all," Mouse whispered. He hugged me tighter and drifted off to sleep before it sank in, what he'd said.

My tears froze on my cheeks. I waited to pluck them

off, because I didn't want to wake him up. How long had he known?

My family is like a mermaid city.

If nothing's waiting for us on the other side of the mountains, we'll go extinct.

February 12th

We've finally come to the valley at the foot of the ridge. Beyond our camp, the mountains rise up in huge spikes and crooked blue-white points. Millie says they look like rows of shark's teeth.

Usually we hike until just before dusk, but today we've stopped early to rest. Tomorrow we'll climb, and we'll have to start early.

Mom is boiling water again, and Dad is staring up at the mountains with his binoculars. "I think we can make it over in a day, maybe two," he said a moment ago. Oliver and Sam are snug in our tent, playing cards; Millie is taking a nap in Mom and Dad's.

I keep finding myself staring up at the mountains too. Just looking at them sends shivers through me, and I keep inching closer to the fire, though it hardly gives off heat at all. If we're lucky, and nothing terrible happens to us on the way, in a day or two we'll get to see what's on the other side.

February 16th

Today I, Gracie Lockwood, sit at the edge of the earth, and I'm going to try to record what I see. I'm writing this down for whoever may read it one day. I hope it doesn't show up buried in the ice.

Four days ago, when we left camp, Dad made us leave everything we didn't absolutely need in a pile, saying we could come back to it if things didn't go the way we hoped. And then he and Mom dug in their packs and attached special metal spikes to all our shoes, and put us all in special belts with metal loops. They examined a bag full of ropes and ran along each rope carefully with their hands, checking the little pulleys and levers and clips attached to the ends. All this preparation got our hearts racing, and Millie and Oliver and I kept looking at each other with a combination of fear and excitement (whatever amount of fear and excitement you can communicate through goggles).

Mom went through our packs one by one to make sure we weren't carrying any extra weight ("You'll regret anything even slightly heavy when we're halfway up the mountain," she said), and when she came across my diaries, she looked at me uncertainly.

I didn't know how to explain that if she made me leave them, it would be like asking me to leave an arm behind. But maybe Mom understood without my saying it, because she nodded at me slightly, then closed my pack as if she hadn't seen anything.

Finally, it was time to go. We all wrapped our scarves tighter around our hoods, readjusted our goggles and our mittens, and began the slow trek upward.

The snow began to blow against us within an hour of our climb. We went up the first mountain tied in a long single-file line, Dad at the front with Sam on his back, and Mom behind the rest of us. Our progress was shockingly slow. "At this rate, we'll be over the mountains by next year," Millie said during a quick rest. My legs burned, and I know it must have been hardest of all on my Dad, carrying Sam, but we all pressed on.

Reaching the pass between two ridges before night-fall, we felt like we'd accomplished something special—until we saw all the mountaintops ahead.

"Shark's teeth," Millie repeated, holding her hands on her knees to catch her breath.

Still, that first night, as exhausted as we were, we were proud that we'd come so far, and a little more animated than we had been the night before as we settled into our tents to eat our cold dinners (beef jerky and freeze-dried peas). Millie even dabbed a tiny patch of freeze-dried peas under her nose to look like boogers, which made Sam laugh so hard we thought he might pass out.

The second day was harder. There was less snow and more ice. We had to navigate through crevices—ice tunnels as big as cathedrals, slick and glossy on all sides—Dad going first to see if he could find a way through. The tunnels made me feel like I was in the belly of the earth, like the earth was a big animal swallowing me up. We turned back several times from dead ends, and at one point Oliver lost his footing and slid down the slope behind us for about a hundred feet. But with all of us tied together, he merely came to a stop like a puppet on a string, then started to climb back up.

By halfway through the day, my muscles felt like jelly. When the sun started going down, we camped in one of the tunnels, again without even lighting the stove. We were all very quiet. I think we must have all been thinking the same thing. What if it wasn't there, waiting for us? What would we do? As much as I wanted to reach the end of this slog through the mountains, I feared it too.

Yesterday morning the snow blew on us so hard we could barely see in front of us. I got so tired, just before we stopped for lunch, that I cried into my goggles a little bit and my tears froze to my face. In front of me Millie trudged ahead, and I think the only thing that kept me going was thinking that if she could do it, I could too.

Just as it seemed we'd never reach the end of the up-and-down climb, the land began to slope and taper downward, toward the flatlands. We couldn't see very far because of the snow, but we knew without a doubt we'd finally reached the end of the range.

I could have cried again, in relief. The snow began to let up, and within a couple of hours we reached a wide flat valley and came to a stop, untying ourselves, but not saying anything. Looking ahead, it was hard to tell where the ground ended and the gray sky began. The dim, shrouded sun was low but not yet setting. It had taken us three days to cross the mountains, but we'd done it.

"Let's set up camp here," Millie said. "I can't move another foot." She began to slip out of her backpack. I did the same. Looking up, I couldn't see the Cloud, and wondered if it was hanging back on the other side of the ridge.

"It can't be much longer," Dad said, his hands on his hips. Sam had slid off his back and now moved to hold Mom's hand. "I think we can reach it before dark," he went on, gesturing forward, his eyes bright behind his goggles.

We all looked at each other, unsure we had it in us. And then Mom nodded. "Let's try it. Another hour."

I don't know how we found the strength to start again. I think it was that the thought of being so close to the end spread among us all like wildfire. We gathered our packs, caught our breath, and spurred ourselves forward. The snow continued to let up, and soon stopped altogether.

I'm not sure how long we were walking—the light stayed the same dim gray, and our steps were so rhythmic it was hypnotizing. Up ahead, a solitary mountain tumbled down onto the horizon, where it met what looked like the southernmost corner of the frozen Southern Sea.

Dad stopped for a moment, staring.

"That's it," he breathed. "That's the edge, right where that mountain meets the water." I don't know how he knew. He started jogging, unable to hold himself back. We all followed.

At the foot of the mountain, coming around the bend that blocked the view beyond it, he came to a sudden stop, his arms shooting out to the sides just as we caught up with him to stop us from running past him.

He gestured for us to stay still. We stared ahead of us, gaping.

We were perched just on the edge of a thin sliver of frozen ocean. And beyond it . . .

Nothing.

Well, not nothing.

There was space. Endless, open space. A black sky full of stars as deep as forever, clusters of galaxies, exploding stars far in the distance.

From where we stood, we could see that our frozen ocean was pouring right off the earth—hanging from the edge of the planet like an enormous icicle. There was no telling how far down the frozen waterfall went.

Beyond it the stars stretched on endlessly. I clutched Mouse's hand, stricken silent with shock and wonder. Because amid all the emptiness and vastness, there was one thing that commanded all our attention. And we all knew what it was without having to ask or wonder.

There were two things I knew about it right away, just by sight.

The Extraordinary World existed.

And we were not going to reach it.

February 17th

I had to take a break from writing for the night, because I didn't know quite what to write or how. I'll try to pick up where I left off, now that I've gathered my thoughts.

We could see it was an enormous planet—blue and lush and surrounded by white clouds just like ours, but round instead of flat—floating out in space and revolving around its own fiery sun that was also just like ours.

It wasn't just a different planet. I could see it was *our* planet, but a different version of it. The shapes of its continents were identical to ours. Its sky was the same shade of blue. It seemed so close that I felt as if I could reach out and touch it—I even stretched my arm toward it. But it was, in reality, far far away.

Again, tears were freezing to my face beneath my goggles. I saw the others were crying too. But I don't think it was just because of sadness. I think in that moment, we were heartbroken and overjoyed at the same time.

"We can't get there," Millie said, as if she was accepting something she'd suspected all along. But she blinked in amazement at the sight. We all did.

After all the endless lectures and mutterings, we knew what it meant. It meant that Dad had been right, and that we were looking at one version of our world and that there might be a million or a billion more. Just like he had said all along. It meant everything was different than what we'd thought. It meant quantum jitters and alternative universes and endless possible Millies and Gracies and Sams. It meant endless possibilities.

We stared at the round planet, so seemingly peaceful and safe, so far away. I wrapped my arms around Mouse and held him close to me. And we all gathered together in a knot, wrapping our arms around each other.

Do the people who live in the Extraordinary World realize how lucky they are? Do they feel constantly surprised by the wonders that surround them? Do they ever get used to it?

*　　*　　*

There was one more thing, another surprise waiting for us right there at the edge of the frozen sea. Something stuck out of the ice in front of us that didn't belong to the natural shapes around us. Dad noticed it first, walked over to it, and squatted down beside it. We all followed. It was an ice pick, dug into the ice and holding a colorful piece of cloth in place—archaic looking, like an antique, but perfectly preserved. The colors were red and green, and Dad ran a hand along it carefully before saying, "It's a very old Portuguese flag." He looked up at all of us. "The kind of flag Ferdinand Magellan would have flown."

Does the flag prove that hundreds of years ago, Ferdinand Magellan was here? Did he hike off the edge of the earth? Did he find a way to journey across the galaxy to the place he'd come to find?

All I know is that the most eye opening, amazing thing that has ever happened to the Lockwood family is right here in front of us. And it's wonderful. And I'm so glad I saw it. And it can't save my brother.

February 19th

I woke this morning with a feeling of such heaviness, as if the black holes in outer space had crawled into my chest, making me empty inside. Before I'd even remembered where I was, or the reason for the way I felt, the feeling was there.

We've crossed back through the mountains and are resting before we make the long, rolling hike back toward the sea. With no ship to get back to, and nothing really to look forward to, we're taking our time. We're making our way back to where we left the *Alexa*, for no reason any of us can really say. What else can we do but go back to where we started from? Where else do we have to go?

* * *

Millie was sitting on her pack, looking up at the clouds when I climbed out of the tent early this morning. (Our Cloud is still strangely absent, and I wonder where it's gone and what it means.) I shivered into my boots and walked over and sat down beside her. Mom was stirring breakfast over a pot, hiding her face in her hood. I knew she couldn't have slept.

Millie, too, looked exhausted. She was dry-eyed and pale. I sat down right next to her and she linked her arm through mine, and we stared at the fire for a while.

I was trying to get the courage to ask something, but I didn't know if I could say it, because saying it made it real, like I'd given up. And I didn't want to give up. But I was thinking that, deep down, we all knew the truth—that at last, we had run out of places to run.

Finally, I turned to look at her. "Millie, what do you think it will be like? When the Cloud takes Mouse?"

She turned to me with a look that reminded me of something, but it's hard to describe. She looked the way I feel whenever I try to explain to Mouse about the day he was born—the bigness and fullness and worry all at once.

She opened her mouth, closed it again. And then she picked at a spot on her boots, looked at me, rubbed her lips, and said, "It's not Mouse that the Cloud came for."

And I don't think I can write any more today.

A page taped into the middle of Mrs. Lockwood's lesson plan book

Captain's log, March 5th

Today at approximately fifteen hundred hours, five people were found drifting in a small vessel just northeast of Cape Horn, two adults and three minors. All were brought aboard safely and in good health. They will disembark in New York when we make port in May.

April 2nd

When I was little, and something made me sad, my family could always fix it. Mom would come in and make a funny face or tell me she was going to take me to the hospital. "You need your feelings amputated!" she'd yell with pretend urgency. Or my dad would rub my face with his whiskers until I'd squirm and laugh. Or Millie would annoy me into forgetting what I was sad about.

I never knew what it was like to feel something unfixable, or to have something hurt that will never stop hurting. It feels like entering a different world. It's not that it's not a happy world, or just as beautiful of a world as the one it was before. But there's a piece of me now that feels like it's chipped off and floating around somewhere else, and I don't think I'll ever be able to reattach it. The good thing is that it hasn't disappeared. I know that floating piece is out there somewhere, even if I don't get to keep it.

It's been over a month since we left the Southern Edge, and I've finally decided I'm willing to write again, just for a little bit.

The SS *Labrador* picked us up off the eastern coast of the Crozet Islands after we'd spent almost eight days sailing our way north. (I'll get to *how* we were sailing in a moment.) The *Labrador* was such a shocking sight, it nearly blew us over, and even as we were being hauled aboard, it was hard to believe it was actually happening. (I suppose we only made it as far as we did without being bothered by sea monsters because our boat was so small and flimsy we just weren't noticed.)

They've treated us like royalty ever since. The ship is by far the most luxurious thing we've experienced since leaving home. It's taken weeks to feel comfortable sitting at the fancy captain's table and dining off his fine china. But try as they might to get us to talk, to tell them about what's happened to us, we've been a limp, lost crew.

*   *   *

I think now that some time has passed I can write a little bit about Millie. I'll try at least, and see where I end up, even if it's just not being able to write anything much at all.

I think I'd suspected longer than I'd admitted to myself what Millie's middle of the night talks with the Cloud had meant. I even imagine I knew why, that night, she kissed Virgil up in the topmast, and why she'd started changing toward all of us. That morning, after I last wrote, she told the others. Mom kept insisting that *nothing* was going to happen to *anyone*. The boys walked off together and huddled a ways away in the snow, their heads down. Dad had taken off his glasses and was staring out at the ocean.

A few days later, arriving at the shore where we'd originally disembarked, I don't think any of us were surprised to see that there was nothing but empty horizon where the *Alexa* had once been.

What did surprise us was that when we got right up close to the water, we discovered something we hadn't seen from farther back. Butting up against the land's edge, anchored by a metal hook in the ice, was the skiff—the small boat that had always been attached to the *Alexa*'s side—filled with provisions, and a note nailed to the bow.

I apologize for my dramatic exit, and for behaving in a way so unfit for a ship's captain. I believe that maybe I thought life owed me something for what I'd lost. I've come back to my senses, and remembered things don't work that way. I'm sorry it didn't happen sooner.

We returned the day after we left you, and waited here for the agreed upon amount of time. But you haven't come back, and I can only assume this means you've made it to the other side. For that, I'm so thankful.

In case you haven't, I'm leaving this skiff here for you. She's not fancy or big, but she's all I have, and better than nothing.

I hope you won't need her. You all deserve for your dreams to come true. You are a beautiful family, and I wish you the best.

Sincerely,

Captain Bill MacDonald

I think we all felt a momentary surge of hope. But it didn't last for very long. Because along with the boat, there was also the Cloud, hovering low about a hundred feet away.

It was just starting to snow—not driving, windy, sideways snow, but gentle, with drifty big flakes. Everyone had gone silent, but finally Mom spoke. "We'll keep going," she said. "We'll get on this boat and sail northeast and see where we end up. Surely we can get somewhere worth getting to."

Everyone turned to look at Millie, who was shaking her head softly. "No," she said. "No, Mom, it's time. I'm sorry, but I don't want to run anymore." She had her determined face on, the one no one can ever talk her out of.

I was standing closest to her, and I slipped my hand into hers. I thought she might push it away, but she held it tight and smiled at me gratefully.

"I can't let you go," I said.

She smiled at me sadly. "You have to, Gracie."

I felt my face fill up with pulsing blood. The feelings inside me were too big and wanted to burst out, needed to explode. "Then I'll go with you," I said, my voice cracking. But she shook her head again.

"No." She squeezed my hand tight. She stared up at the Cloud. "I *am* scared though, Gracie," she said. The Cloud was moving now, drifting lower toward us, so that it was now at our height and about fifteen feet behind Millie. I stared into the black hole in the center of it that Millie and Sam said was a mouth, and shook my head.

"We let you down," I whispered.

"Gracie," she put her hands on both my shoulders, "remember what I said, when we were looking down at the mermaid city. I'm so glad we came. Remember that."

She pulled away, and then hugged each one of us. My mom held on tightest and longest, unwilling to let go, and finally Millie had to unpry her arms and kissed her cheek. Dad stood beside them looking like he might disintegrate. Millie gazed at him and said, like she was reading his mind, "You've never failed me, Dad. Never. Don't ever think you did."

She hugged me last.

"There are endless possibilities," she said. "That makes me hopeful. It really does."

Ever since it had first shown up on our horizon, I'd always thought the Cloud was cruel: something that wanted to hurt us, waiting for the time to be right to break us apart. But that's not what it looked like when the Cloud took Millie away.

Once she'd said her good-byes, it beckoned for her to come closer with a little tendril of white vapor, gently, like a friend. It reached toward her, and she reached back—her hand disappearing into the mist.

"You know," she said, looking back at us, "Sam is right. It doesn't look much like a clown. It looks like someone smiling at me."

Tentatively she stepped farther into the Cloud, and it wrapped itself gently and softly around her shoulders. It looked like it was giving her a hug.

She turned to wave at us as the mist spread around her. She didn't look scared anymore, but curious, like she was thinking about what came next. Her waving hand was the last thing to disappear into the white puff of air, and then the Cloud began to rise.

As it did, for some reason I can't explain (except that I couldn't make myself watch Millie float away), I reached a hand out to catch the falling snow. I kept looking at the snowflakes, trying to see each one individually, tiny one by tiny one. You can't tell each snowflake is different just by looking—they all appear the same to the naked eye. But science tells us they are, and we can *imagine* how different they must be. We can't see it, but we know it.

I don't think I'll write in here again. In fact, I'm probably giving up my writing career forever—it doesn't seem very interesting now. So these will probably be the last words you read from me. The thing is, my hand feels too heavy, and nothing feels magic anymore.

October 31st

It's October in Cliffden—Halloween, in fact. The leaves are falling like they do every year. From my window I can see the trick-or-treaters getting an early start—it's not dusk yet, but already I can see a gaggle that includes a witch, a pumpkin, and a rock star running up our neighbor's steep driveway as if their lives depended on it. I don't even feel tempted to dress up this year. I think I've outgrown it for good.

Mom is making apple crisp downstairs. Mouse is out jogging. Yes, jogging. It's his new thing. He says he's training for the Olympics. Dad keeps telling him he's too miniature-size for the Olympics, but Mouse doesn't seem deterred. He's grown two inches in the last two months. His doctor says that his medication has been effective, and that in another few months he might even be able to come off it. All signs point to Sam having a healthy life. He doesn't even hide under furniture anymore.

I always wonder, before I think things through, what's Millie doing. I forget sometimes that she isn't here. One minute I'll be missing her so terribly, and the next minute I'll say to myself, "I wonder if Millie will let me borrow her mirror." And then I realize my mistake and miss her worse. Having a sister is a hard habit to shake yourself out of.

Tonight, a few minutes ago, I sat down on my bed in my room and looked around. And I decided it was time to dig this diary out of the closet, where I threw it as we were unpacking the day we arrived home. I want to see if my hand isn't so heavy anymore.

So here it goes.

I'll tell you about the last few days of the voyage home. They were uneventful, so don't get your hopes up.

It's easy to feel, the longer you're at sea and the waves rock you and the quiet stretches on, that the world is a beautiful place, and an endless one, and that you're a small speck on the planet, and not as big as you used to think.

I've never felt so small as I did on the trip home, but

it didn't bother me anymore like it used to. It actually made me feel a little better. For the first time I think I began to understand what Oliver said that night at Grandma's, about how he likes being small.

We sailed for weeks before the weather started getting warm. One day it was finally so nice out that the captain had the dining table carried onto the deck so we could eat "alfresco." The clouds were threatening rain, but the captain was determined, and the fine linen tablecloth, and the cutlery, the shiny china plates were all laid out.

We sat eating in silence, as usual, and the captain looked disappointed that even this special treat hadn't pulled us out of our shells. And then it got worse. The first huge drop of rain fell with a smack right in the center of the table where we could all see the wet spot it left. I felt another on my head, and another thwapped against a glass.

"It's just a drizzle," the captain said, though it was clear our alfresco dinner was about to end in a soggy mess. We were all silent and awkward, not wanting to hurt the man's feelings by going in, but not wanting to stay outdoors, either.

And then it started to fall more steadily, and Dad was just about to take a sip of his iced tea, when a drop landed in it and splashed some of the tea against his glasses.

He looked up at the sky, at the dark clouds, and then he said in a hopeful voice, "Maybe a tiny drop of Millie just fell into my cup."

There was a moment of silence, and everyone looked at Mom tensely. She was going to say it was a horribly inappropriate thing to say—I was sure of it.

She seemed to be thinking for a minute, about to cry, when instead she let out a deep breath and turned her face up to the sky. She opened up her arms and the rain fell harder, and soon we all had our faces up to the sky. The captain laughed, turning his face up too, not getting the joke, or what it meant to us.

That was when I knew that even though we'd never get over Millie, we'd still be us. We'd still be a family. She was still with us.

Dad said one night, before we landed in New York, that it's very possible, according to the laws of physics, that things happen endlessly, over and over again even if we don't know it. I wonder if I like that idea. It would mean losing Millie all over again, and the Cloud chasing us across the earth—all the fear and uncertainty happening over and over again. But then it would also mean fighting with Millie over her hairbrush and laughing with her, and the night she kissed Virgil, and our time together in the Winnebago as a family being endless too.

I'm not even sure it matters what physics says. In *this* time and place, there are Clouds and monsters, and in *this* time and place, we don't have Millie anymore. That's what we've been given, and we can only do our best with what we've got.

Still, life is full of surprises. I saw something on the news the other day—just a tiny two-minute segment buried between a story on a local policeman and an interview with the mayor of New York. An obscure circus in New Mexico, by the name of Big Tex's, was faced with an unusual problem on Tuesday when all of its animals—every single one, including the pygmy unicorn, somehow escaped from their locked pens. Big Tex is offering a big reward to anyone who knows their whereabouts, because apparently not one of the animals has been found. It's as if someone loaded them into a truck and drove them away to freer pastures.

Oliver has been on vacation in Georgia with his new foster parents, who happen to be hippies, and who only live in the next neighborhood over from us. (My mom wanted to adopt him in the worst way and tried to convince him. But he said it would be weird to be related to us, instead of just our really good friend. And I have to agree with him.)

Anyway, it's suspicious, of course, and I'll have to see what he says about it all when he gets back. But it makes me think. . . . Maybe in the case of Big Tex's zoo, Oliver just wasn't willing to accept the world we've been given. Maybe he was trying to turn it into what he wants it to be, instead.

Anyway, back to our journey. The rest of the voyage is probably easy to guess. Soon New York was looming out at us through a fog. And soon we were on a bus home.

The last miles leading into Cliffden were some of the most exciting of my life. Every turn, every tree, every corner became more and more familiar. It might have been the best day of my life if Millie had been there too, but of course without her, it couldn't be. Still, it was a dream coming true, and I strained for the first glimpse of our house on the hill, and when I saw it up there perched like a familiar old face, I thought I might explode.

But to be honest, coming home wasn't what I expected at all.

Here is what I didn't expect. The stairs seemed to have

grown smaller. The yard was just a little square of grass, and the valley below didn't seem as deep as it used to. The house itself looked like a doll's house. Everything felt like it had shrunk.

It took me a moment to realize that it wasn't the house that was different, but me.

I'm running out of ink and will have to go find a pen. I'm not sure how much more I'm going to write. Arin Roland is coming over later, believe it or not. She still gets on my nerves, but I think we're both getting a little nicer.

What's changed the most, maybe, is that ever since we've been back, I've been spending more time with my dad. He doesn't spend nearly as many hours upstairs with his telescope like he used to, or writing calculations in his notebook. He pays more attention to real things now: the trees, the house, my mom, and me and Sam. Sometimes he even sits beside me near my church stone and watches the town and the sky with me—just enjoying the view. Sometimes we lie on our backs and look up at the sky and daydream. The other day he quoted to me from a book he's been reading recently: "'Not only is the universe stranger than we think. It's stranger than we *can* think.'" And that makes me look at things this way: We don't know where Millie went, and we don't know if we'll see her again, but there's no reason not to hope. We just don't know the answers, and maybe that's a nice thing. Strangely enough, it's made me pay more attention to science, even the weather. All of it seems to mean more than I used to think it did. I guess Dad and I have rubbed off on each other. I think we both feel that the world is messy and getting messier, but that it's still our world, and we love being in it.

Okay, last thing. I've finally decided on the epigraph I'm going to put at the front of my first diary. It's from *Hamlet*, which Mom made us all read on our trip. I think it's fitting.

Who knows. Maybe out there someone somewhere will read this, maybe even in some other world; maybe someone's reading it right now. Anything is possible, I think. So if you're reading this in some other place: Hello. I was here. I spent time on this planet. And it was extraordinary.

And I love and miss Millie. Now that's really all.

For real.

Forever.

Bye.

Acknowledgments

Without my editor, Liesa Abrams, whose passion and patience for this project has been beyond measure, this story wouldn't exist. I'm very thankful to my agent, Rosemary Stimola, and deeply indebted to "Ukulele" Ben Katsuo Johnson for teaching me everything I know about clouds and lovable scientists. Many thanks go to Adam Smith for his keen eye.

Finally, this book wouldn't be what it is without the feedback, generosity, and unwavering support of my husband, Mark, who makes all of my days extraordinary.

Quiet, quirky May Bird discovers a ghostly
dimension in this otherworldly series
from Jodi Lynn Anderson!

Read on for a glimpse at Book One: *The Ever After* . . .

May Ellen Bird, age ten, occasionally glanced at the brochure her mom had taped to her door that afternoon, and scowled. SAINT AGATHA'S BOARDING SCHOOL FOR GIRLS WITH HIGH SOCKS. A few minutes ago May had taken her black marker and written the word "socks" over what had originally been the last word of the headline. Judging by the photos of girls in stiff plaid uniforms plastering the brochure, girls with "high prospects" was not nearly as accurate.

The woods watched silently through the farthest east window of White Moss Manor as May tried to concentrate on her work. And sometimes, looking up from the curious project strewn across her desk, chewing on a pencil, May watched them back.

Skinny and straight, with short black bobbed hair and big brown eyes, May ran her fingers over the objects before her—a clump of black fur, a lightbulb, a jar, a book titled *Secrets of the Egyptian Mummies*, and some wire. Occasionally May swiveled to gaze at Somber Kitty, who laid across her bed like a discarded piece of laundry. His belly faced the ceiling and he eyed her lazily.

Neither May nor Somber Kitty knew it, but passing squirrels and chipmunks thought the cat was decidedly ugly. He had huge pointy ears and a skinny tail, and he was mostly bald, with just a little bit of fuzz covering his soft skin. His mouth was turned down in a thoughtful frown—an expression he had been wearing ever since May had gotten him three years before, on her seventh birthday.

May had disliked him immediately.

"He's bald," she'd said.

"He's a hairless Rex," her mom had replied. "He's interesting."

"He looks depressed."

"He's *somber*."

May's mom had then explained that "somber" meant "sad," which also meant "melancholy." So that was the one thing they both agreed on. The cat was most definitely sad. It was almost as if, from the moment he had set his tilty green eyes on May, he had sensed her disappointment in him, and sympathized.

May had not wanted him, of course. Her first cat, Legume, had died when May was six, and she had resigned herself to a life of grief. She knew there could never be another Legume, which, by the way, is another word for "peanut." She'd insisted on wearing black ever since.

But her mom had insisted on another pet. "You spend too much time alone," she had said with big, brown, worried eyes, even bigger and browner than May's. Mrs. Bird had long ago given up trying to get May to bring home friends from school.

"Why don't you invite Maribeth over?"

"She has the chicken pox."

"Claire?"

"She's only allowed out on Presidents' Day."

"Mariruth?"

"Leprosy. It's so sad."

Finally one afternoon May had stood in her mom's doorway, crossed her arms, and announced that she would accept a cat as long as it was a black tiger.

She got stuck with Somber Kitty.

Noticing her watching him now, Somber Kitty opened his mouth and asked, "Mew? Meow? Meay?"

"That's my name, don't wear it out," May replied.

Knock knock knock.

May's mom poked her head into the room.

"So what do you think?" she asked hopefully, smiling. "It looks like a great school, doesn't it?"

May crossed her arms over her waist and looked toward her bed. "Maybe if you're a nun," she offered thoughtfully.

The smile on Mrs. Bird's face dropped, and May felt her heart drop too.

"Maybe it's okay," May added. She looked at Somber Kitty, who looked at her. Their traded glance said Somber Kitty understood, even if Mrs. Bird didn't: May could never be happy at a school like Saint Agatha's, wearing high socks and stuck in New York City without the woods.

"Well, it's something to think about," Mrs. Bird said hopefully, biting her lip. "I think the structure would be good for you. I'd live right nearby. And we could tour the city on the weekends."

Mrs. Bird ducked into the room, stooped down, and made her way to May's desk. From the ceiling hung a number of objects: a dragonfly wind chime, a clothes hanger strung with old sumac leaves, old dry strands of ivy. At the window sat a pair of binoculars to watch for insects and critters, and a telescope aimed at the sky for looking at the stars.

The walls were so covered in pictures that you couldn't see the old calico wallpaper. They were drawings of Legume, of Mrs. Bird, of the woods, and of imaginary places and friends and creatures: some with wings and purple hair, black capes and horns, and one particularly spooky one with a lopsided head. There were none of Somber Kitty, who often followed Mrs. Bird's eyes to the wall with hurt curiosity, searching for a likeness of himself.

Studying the spookier, darker pictures, Mrs. Bird's eyes sometimes got big and worried again. "You don't want people to think you're eccentric," she'd say, looking more somber than a certain cat.

"You ready for the picnic?" Mrs. Bird asked, walking up behind May and hugging her tight.

May nodded, tugging at the tassels of the sari she'd wrapped around her body like a dress. Because Briery Swamp was too small and empty to have a Day, May and Mrs. Bird always attended the annual Hog Wallow Day Extravaganza and Picnic. It was two towns away, but it involved a parade and games and seeing all the kids from school. "Yep," she replied, trying to sound bright.

Mrs. Bird kissed the top of May's head, her jasmine perfume sinking into May's sari.

"Your classmates will be happy to see you."

May blushed. She doubted it.

May didn't mention that since school let out, she had made improvements—*in secret*—getting ready for this exact day. She had gained two pounds, eating sesame-and-peanut-butter balls two at a time, so she wasn't *quite* so skinny. Her knees didn't look as knobby as they had. And she had worked on her smile in the mirror. Usually May's smile looked like a grimace. But she'd gotten it to look halfway normal, she thought. Girls with nice smiles made friends. Mrs. Bird liked to remind May of this when she came to volunteer on hot-dog days and saw how May sat at the end of the fifth-grade table, curled over her carrots.

"I don't know how to make friends," May would say, embarrassed.

"Well, actually, you don't really *make* friends," Mrs. Bird always replied. "You just have to let them happen."

May didn't think that was very helpful.

"What are you making now?" Mrs. Bird asked.

May surveyed the pieces in front of her. "A materializer. It makes things you imagine real. Like if you imagine a pair of emerald earrings, it makes the earrings appear."

Mrs. Bird crouched, moved back toward the door, then turned a thoughtful gaze on May. "Maybe you should be a lawyer someday—then you can make enough money to get me those earrings *for real*." May glanced at the materializer. It was *supposed* to be for real.

"You'd better get a quick bath. I'll run the water."

May lounged on her bed, picturing what it would be like if she went to the picnic today and her classmates couldn't recognize her with the extra two pounds and the big, real-looking smile pasted on her face.

Who's that girl? one of the boys, Finny Elway, would say. *She reminds me of May.*

"They'd see the best me," May said aloud to Somber Kitty.

"Meow," the cat replied with interest.

A few minutes later Mrs. Bird's footsteps sounded on the stairs again, then came the squeak of the spigot being turned off, and the footsteps retreating. May stripped off her sari and walked out into the hall for her bath. Just outside the bathroom door, she paused. Inside she could hear the splash splash of the water being swirled around the tub.

May grasped the ceramic door handle and twisted it, opening on an empty room. In the middle sat a white tub with claw feet, with water gently waving back and forth. Leaning over, she inspected it, then climbed in. May was used to strange things like this. Her mom had always said all sorts of quirks came with a house as old as theirs. May used to insist it was ghosts. But Mrs. Bird had long ago given her one too many stern looks on the topic. So May simply sank beneath the water and let bubbles drift out of her of nose.

When she stepped out of the bathroom in a towel a half an hour later, the steam poured out behind her, engulfing the tiny figure of Somber Kitty, who waited in the doorway, licking his paws one by one. With the cat at her heels, May walked into her room and pulled on the turquoise tank top and shorts her mom had laid out instead of the usual black clothes.

Last summer May had built a tiny shelf that snaked its way around the whole room, way up high. Along the sill was the collection of quartz rocks she'd carefully picked from the woods. Her mom swore they were worthless, but they seemed as dazzling and precious as diamonds to May. There was also a complete zoo of lopsided animals she'd made out of paper clips, a perfect heart-shaped pinecone she and Somber Kitty had found together in town, and an onyx brooch left behind by the lady who'd once lived here before them—a lady by the name of Bertha.

The quartz rocks stared at her, as if they, too, wanted to go wherever she was headed. Once she was dressed she pulled the smallest one off the shelf and let it hitch a ride in her pocket, for luck.

The picnic was a disaster.

Sweaty and red-faced, May Bird spent much of the afternoon pedaling around the lawn of Hog Wallow Town Hall on a bike with tassels flapping from the handlebars and a stowaway Rex cat who'd insisted on coming tucked into her backpack. She'd spotted a gaggle of classmates across the grass, talking and laughing.

May kept herself busy, scaring crickets out of the grass, then sat against a tree near the picnic table where mothers had gathered, working on her smile.

She overheard the parents talking. "Thank you, we love the house. We're always getting offers," Mrs. Bird was saying, adjusting her hat in a familiar way. She had always said the sun on her face gave her wrinkles. "But I think May needs to be somewhere more . . . average." May's mom looked down at her hands while she said this.

Unseen, May blushed. She knew that the reason her mom wanted to move was because she thought *May* needed to be more average. At that moment, Mrs. Bird's eyes drifted toward May's direction and widened, embarrassed.

May pretended she hadn't noticed, plucked grass between her fingers, and then stood up. Without looking up she made her way toward the other kids.

Pollen blew across the grass, and Somber Kitty nipped at her heels. She lifted him up, frowning at him. "I'm going to hang out with the humans," she said. "Go play." He kissed her, his tiny pink tongue darting out to tickle her chin, making her wince before she placed him on the grass and gave him a pat on the butt to shoo him away. She nervously straightened out her clothes and made her way against the breeze to where the children had huddled into a tight group. There she tacked herself to the circle awkwardly, like a losing try at pin the tail on the donkey.

Claire Arneson stood at the center of the group of kids. Instead of being pulled into the usual pigtails, her hair was down and combed across her back, shimmery as mountain water. Two bright, pink-ribboned barrettes held back her bangs. May had always wondered why she couldn't be more like Claire, when Claire made being herself seem so easy. She always had something funny to say. She never looked big-eyed and serious. And she had a million friends, none of whom were bald cats.

"I'm only allowed to have eight people," Claire was saying, "Maribeth's coming, and Colleen. . . . Finny, can you come?"

May smiled big as Claire singled out the kids that would attend her annual Kites and Katydids birthday party. Maybe they hadn't even recognized her yet. Maybe Claire would invite her to the party, thinking she was inviting a mysterious stranger.

"Hey, May . . ."

May brightened and nodded as Claire turned to her, her heart doing a jig in her chest. "Isn't that your dancing cat?" Claire pointed one perfect finger across the lawn and all eyes followed.

Oh. Disappointment. "Yes." May tried her nongrimace smile again. It felt like the old one—grimacelike.

The whole class remembered Somber Kitty because May had brought him in for her "How To" report in February. Everyone else had done their reports on things like "How to Make a Bologna Sandwich" and "How to Sew a Pillow." May had done hers on "How to Teach Your Cat to Dance." It was one of the few times May's classmates had actually noticed she was alive in a good way. (They'd noticed her in a bad way many times.) It had also sort of been cheating, because Somber Kitty, despite his general sadness, loved to dance and had known how since he was a kitten.

"That was so cool!" Finny Elway said.

May cleared her throat, her disappointment fading. They thought she had a cool cat.

"Yeah," Elmore Smith said. "But the best was when May tried to fly off the roof of her mom's car with that bunch of balloons, remember?" Everyone burst into giggles. May's heart sank. She tried to smile, as if she was in on the joke. She rubbed at the scar on her knee from that incident, which had happened at last year's picnic. Ever since then she'd been afraid of heights.

"Hey, remember May Bird, Warrior Princess?" Maribeth asked. Now the laughter exploded, and May began to really and truly blush, remembering the day the photo had fallen out of her social studies textbook and onto the floor. It had been a shot of her and Somber Kitty pretending to be Amazon warriors hiding in the trees. In it, May had on her black sparkly bathing suit that made her feel like she was wearing the night sky, and a belt wrapped around her shoulder with long sticks tucked beneath the strap for arrows. Mrs. Bird had said May shouldn't dress like a half-naked wild thing, but she had stuck the photo into one of May's notebooks to surprise her and make her smile. It *had* surprised her by falling out. It *hadn't* made her smile. It had made her want to sink into the gold and green tiles of the school floor.

"Remember when May forgot to lock the bathroom door on the bus trip, and it swung open?"

May shifted from foot to foot, looking at the ground to hide her flaming face. She gazed toward the adults' table helplessly, wanting to make sure her mom couldn't see. Luckily Mrs. Bird was still busy talking with the other grown-ups.

It was the three-legged race that saved her. The mayor of Hog Wallow announced that everyone was to line up across the lawn by the pink flag.

No sooner had he said it than, shouting and laughing, the children went tearing across the grass. Dazed, May dragged herself after them, her long skinny legs straggling. Races were her favorite. She was deadly fast.

But you needed a partner for a three-legged race. And everyone paired up without her.

"Mew? Meow? Meay?" Somber Kitty asked, appearing out of nowhere and rubbing against her shins.

"Cats can't race," May said with a sigh. They watched the racers line up, and then the starting bell went off, and Claire and Maribeth pulled out in front. They were way slower than May would have been. But May would have traded her speed for a partner to race with.

She turned around and walked back to her bike, far away from the crowd, and plopped down next to it in the grass.

"I think if I could go somewhere else, I could be someone else," she whispered to her cat. She picked a puffy white dandelion out of the grass between her sandals and blew at the seeds.

Somber Kitty, who always seemed to know May had no one else to tell her feelings to, mewed in agreement, though he had no idea what she was saying.

"But that doesn't mean I want to move to New York," she quickly added.

Then she slumped. She felt as heavy as a sack of beans. But then, a sack of beans never got embarrassed or did stupid balloon tricks in front of other sacks of beans or forgot to lock the bathroom door. Come to think of it, life was probably easy for all the beans of the world. Being a sack of them wouldn't be so bad.

May picked another dandelion and blew on it. "Maybe

I'd rather be a sack of beans," she told the fuzzy white floaters. Somber Kitty meowed disapprovingly.

"Don't worry, Kitty. I'm not going anywhere."

Somber Kitty rolled himself into a ball and continued to stare at her. He didn't look so sure.

"Unless you know something I don't."

At the edge of the grass, the trees watched her.

They knew better.

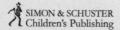